Spell Ya Later

The Pruitt Witches Book One

Zoe Shae

This book is a work of fiction. While some places or people are real—Chagrin Falls, OH being an example—most names, characters, places, and incidents either are products of the author's imagination or used fictitiously.

SPELL YA LATER

ZOE SHAE

Cover design: Luisa Sipia, @luy_co

Editing: Jax McQueen at Starry-Eyed Scribbles, and Dewi Hargreaves

For information of subsidiary rights, please contact the author at authorzoeshae@gmail.com

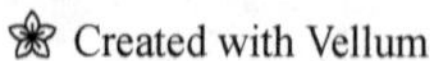 Created with Vellum

Also by Zoe Shae

Standalones:

Sugar

The Pruitt Witches Series:

Spell Ya Later

Witchy Woman

Coming Soon!

Once again, you're subjected to a story that makes me apologize if you identify with it. I see you, and my DMs are open if you'd like to yell at me.

To my beta readers, alpha readers, editors, and those who gave me glowing praise and constructive criticism. I wouldn't be the writer I am today without you. Writing a second book is harder than the first in a lot of ways, and my community is everything.

I'm going to dedicate every book to my father. He would be so proud of me, and I miss him every single day.

Thank you to my partner. You are Noah, and I can't believe how unbelievably lucky I am to have found you.

To Paisley's Tea Room. You're at least 50% of the reason this book is even done.

And to my daughter. I love you, don't read romance books until you're 18. But if you do read them beforehand, just don't tell me about it.

Thank you for picking up Spell Ya Later. If you don't want any spoilers and are okay with the possibility of being triggered, please skip this page. If, however, you would like to avoid certain triggering topics, here is a list of the ones that appear in this book. Please protect your own mental health.

- Parental Neglect
    - Mother/daughter unhealthy dynamics
    - Unhealthy family dynamics in general
    - Death of a parent
    - Murder
    - Referenced suicide of a family member (past event, off page)
    - Explicit language
    - Explicit sexual content
    - Violence and blood

CHAPTER 1
FOUR WITCHES WALK INTO A DINNER

My lungs scream as I fight the overwhelming urge to take a breath. My little sister's eyes are like saucers as she stares at me, cutting off the circulation in my hands with her death grip. We have our orders.

Don't breathe.

Don't move.

Don't make a sound.

Or you will die. We will all die.

The edges of my vision are dark; a gray veil lies over everything else.

My mother's back is to us, shielding us, so I can't see her face. I can only make out the tension in her shoulders as she holds herself still. Still as a tree in the dead of night. My unanswered question rings in my head . . .

Where is Daddy?

She didn't answer me—just told me to protect Laura and stay quiet.

Shuffling draws my attention, the slow drag of an injured leg along a wooden floor. The echo reverberates against the walls. I don't even know where we are.

"Where are they?" a scratchy voice asks from only a few feet away.

"They must have escaped while you were . . . preoccupied." That's a voice I haven't heard before. Has this man been here the whole time?

"You're blaming me?"

"There's no one else here to blame, is there? Come. They can't hide forever."

Are they gone? There is no sound, but the heaviness in the air has somehow lightened. I open my mouth to speak, to question, but my mother's hand lands on my forehead.

"Forget."

My eyes close.

~

"IT'S ALMOST FIVE AT NIGHT, HAZEL. ARE YOU SERIOUSLY napping?"

My eyes blink open to find my sister, Laura, staring at me. If the hardness of her gaze is any indication, waking me up was a chore.

I've had the same nightmare almost every night for the past thirteen years. Ever since my dad died, I've been plagued by a memory that doesn't exist. A memory that never happened. My sister and I were at home the night my father died. I can still smell the buttery popcorn Grandma made for us as we watched some silly cartoon. I can feel the slip of the freshly washed sheets that Laura and I shared because she didn't want to sleep alone after such a fun night.

But tell all that to my subconscious.

That part of my brain apparently hasn't gotten the message.

"How can I help you?"

Laura opens her mouth and closes it as her eyes snap to the open sketchbook I fell asleep next to. I hastily close the book on a pair of eyes that have captivated my attention for the past few weeks. I can draw them despite not knowing their owner. Eyes of the darkest brown, almost black. With a little fleck of green in the corner of the right one in the shape of a star.

"Homework from class?" she asks, a half grin lifting the side of her mouth.

I narrow my eyes. "No. I'm the instructor, I don't have homework." Granted, I'm an unpaid volunteer, but the access to decent supplies and fresh inspiration is too good to pass up on. Plus, it's pretty much the only time Mom lets me out of the house. It's also the only time she leaves the house. Sunday morning brunch with the few friends she has left.

She scoffs, allowing me to move on from the subject for now. "I've come to brainstorm ideas on how to get out of dinner tonight. I don't know about you, but I really don't feel like dealing with Mom and Grandma." She flops on my bed beside me. The vintage wooden frame groans under the added weight. The only thing holding it together is magic and my mother's determination.

"Good luck with that. You don't show up and Grandma will hex your hair puke green. Again."

Laura cringes, running her hand through her hair as if to check it's still blonde. "We could go out after?"

"When have I ever, and I mean *ever*, wanted to go out?"

"Please?"

Oh no. Not the puppy dog eyes. Why am I never able to say no to the puppy dog eyes?

"Maybe."

"You'll have so much fun, Hazel, I promise!"

Yes, Laura, being your designated driver while men fall over themselves just to be noticed by you is my idea of a fun time. Sign me up!

The best part is the constant reminder that I'm practically a spinster at the ripe old age of twenty-five. But it's pretty hard to find a boyfriend when you're simultaneously parenting your sister and being smothered by your mother.

"GIRLS!" Mom calls from downstairs. "Come down and help me finish setting up!"

Laura practically dances out of my room like a little wood nymph or some shit. Standing up, I collect my colored pencils and put them away in the antique desk in the corner. It's not my style in the least, but mom insists I keep it since it matches the bed and dresser. And whatever she wants, she gets. Was I allowed to go to college? No, Hazel, you're not ready. You can't leave Laura. Was I allowed to get a job? No, Hazel, what if someone finds out you're a witch? Was I allowed to move out? Well, at that point I didn't have anywhere to go and no money to my name. My mother weaponized the hell out of my father's death and she did a damn good job of it. I'm lucky she lets me volunteer for the art class.

I turn off the light and walk down the worn wooden staircase. The old Victorian house groans and creaks beneath my feet. Not even carpets muffle the noises of the home. At this point, I swear it's sentient.

"Set the table, please." Mom pushes the silver into my hands. We only bring out the fancy stuff once a month when Grandma comes for dinner. Not that Grandma is impressed by that sort of thing. She's not impressed by bullshit, and for that I am thankful.

Despite knowing it's bullshit, I follow orders like the obedient daughter I am. The obedient soldier. I place the silverware on the delicate lace place settings and light the candles in the middle of the dark wood table. According to Grandma, this table has been in our family for generations. I swear I saw a furniture store sticker underneath it.

The family portrait stares at me from above the fireplace. It's an imposing beast of a painting, commissioned by some old friend of my grandmother's when I was a child. My grandmother sits in a regal high-backed armchair of royal purple, reveling in her place as matriarch of the family. My mother and I stand behind her on opposite sides . . . symbolic in its own way. Laura, only six or seven at the time, sits on the floor. Despite it being a painting, Laura's eyes almost dance as if she's begging to be allowed to go play.

My father insisted the portrait should feature the women of the family when my mother tried to include him. Looking at it now, I wish she'd fought harder.

I wish she'd done a lot of things differently.

"Where are my girls?" Grandma's voice travels through the home as if magically amplified. Knowing her, it is.

I double-check the table before making my way to the kitchen. It's a partially renovated chef's dream. Admittedly one of the largest rooms in the old house, the cabinets and island are a rich mahogany wood. The countertops are a smooth complementary marble that my father personally installed right before . . .

. . . before.

With my first step, I'm immediately smacked in the nose by the scent of butternut squash, garlic, and rosemary. And bread. Delicious, flaky, made-from-scratch bread. My mother is a lot of things —not all good—but an excellent cook is top of that list.

"Grandma!" Laura is wrapped immediately in a belly-crushing hug. Laura's always been Grandma's favorite, probably because Laura is everyone's favorite. She's bubbly, sweet, just a smidge sarcastically spicy, and gorgeous—who wouldn't love her?

Mom's standing at the stove, stirring the soup. I note her silence and her tense shoulders. If it were up to her, we'd never speak to Grandma again. I have no idea what happened between them, but it was around the same time my father died. The same time my mother stopped using magic.

The same time my sister and I were forbidden from using our powers.

"Where are your thoughts, dear?" Grandma lays a hand on my shoulder, dragging me back to reality. I turn to her, her bright blue eyes pulling me in first as they always do. They're like two liquid pools, bright and unblinking as she stares into each and every thought I've ever had.

"Hi, Grandma," I reply, avoiding her question. I hug her, her curly silver hair brushing against my face with her familiar scent. I always think of her when I smell lavender and smoke.

As we pull away, her gaze roams me with a sympathetic touch.

She knows something is wrong. Joke's on her though, something has been wrong for years.

"Mother," Mom says from where she remains at the stove. Not a muscle has moved.

"Sarah," Grandma replies.

Lovely, so the icy one-word conversations are starting early tonight. Maybe going out with Laura is a good idea. If anything, it gives us an excuse to leave early.

"Dinner is almost ready," Mom says.

Laura dutifully grabs the plates and bowls, and I follow her back into the dining room. Anything to get away from them and their tense vibes. I love Grandma, she's a serious badass, but I don't understand why she and Mom can't get along.

"Give me an update, sweetheart. What's going on in your life?" Grandma asks me once we're all settled around the table with our food. Her signature bangles clack on her wrists, just beneath the black cat tattoo of her familiar, Rosie, whom I haven't seen in years.

"Nothing, really. Same old, same old." I shrug. It's the same reply I have for her each month. I've been stuck in mud ever since I graduated high school. Seven years later and what do I have to show for it?

For the last thirteen years, from the moment my father died, my life has been one giant ball of nothing. I'm not human. I'm not a witch. I'm this *thing* in the middle. No friends, no social life, no professional life. I have nothing.

Her eyes are kind, however. No judgment, no disappointment, only a quiet understanding. "You are such a beautiful, creative, intelligent witch, Hazel. Never forget that."

Mom's teeth grind together the moment Grandma says witch. Is Grandma sincere in her words? Absolutely. Did Grandma use that word specifically to piss off Mom? Also absolutely.

"She's a beautiful, creative, intelligent *human*," Mom says.

Laura flops back in her chair with a groan. "Here we go! Only took two minutes tonight."

"I realize she's a human," Grandma continues as if Laura never spoke. "I also realize that Hazel is a grown woman and pretending she's not a witch is neither productive nor useful. I'm happy to support both of my granddaughters should they ever wish to explore that part of themselves. Is that truly so threatening to you, Sarah?"

The rickety chandelier flickers above us as Mom and Grandma stare at each other—waiting for the other to flinch first. Laura eats as if this happens all the time, but that's because it does. This bullshit happens every single month. Each time Grandma steps into this house, Mom ramps up her controlling monster persona and Grandma acts like the only joy she gets in life is from poking our mother until she breaks.

"My daughters will have nothing to do with that life," Mom says. "Not if I have anything to say about it."

Crack!

One of the light bulbs shatters in the chandelier in a swirling haze of . . . is that water? Laura and I gape at the splattered mess of glass and water all over the once perfectly set table.

And it's as if something breaks in me, too. What is the rest of my life going to look like? Am I going to live with my mother until I'm old, regretful, resentful, and cruel?

Until I become her?

My gaze lifts to the woman herself, watching her as she stares at Grandma. The anger in her eyes, the anger in her heart . . . I'm already so angry. I can't become her. I don't want the anger to eat me alive.

"And what if I *do* want something to do with that life?" My voice is steadier than I expected.

My mother's head turns toward me cinematically slowly, like something from a horror film. I ignore the "Ooooh" from Laura.

"You don't know what you're talking about." The house—full of noises, always talking and creaking—goes eerily quiet with Mom's words.

"For the first time, what if I do?" I pause, practically shaking in my chair. "God, Mom, for the first time I know exactly what I'm talking about. I need this. I need to be able to explore every part of who I am without fear of you burning me at the stake!"

"At the stake? Do you think that's cute, Hazel?"

"To be fair, it's pretty funny." Laura shrugs as she pops another piece of bread into her mouth. While the backup is appreciated, I want to do this on my own.

I stand slowly, rage boiling underneath my skin until it's practically tumbling out of me alongside my words. "I want the ability to choose the path my life will take. I can't know if magic is that path unless I try."

"Fine." Mom's eyes narrow. "Make your choice. But no daughter of mine will practice the craft while living under my roof."

Her response stops me, cooling the heat burning my blood. I knew I was letting her control me for far too long, but this?

"You'd kick out your own daughter?" My voice wavers.

She nods once. "I'd do anything to protect you."

My hands smooth over the white tablecloth, the slight embossed flower texture rippling under my fingers. Do I want to practice magic so badly that I'd risk homelessness? I have some money saved, but I'm an unemployed loser with no friends and no college degree. Homelessness is a real worry here.

Is it worth it?

I nod.

"I'll be out in an hour."

CHAPTER 2
A PROPOSITION

I'm like a hummingbird as I flit around my room, trying to gather anything I could possibly need while also trying to pack light. I certainly didn't expect to push my mother with an ultimatum, but kicking me out with no notice? Nice, Mom. Love you, too. I didn't realize our relationship was this bad, but maybe I should have.

I pick up my sketchbook, taking just a beat to look it over. I couldn't go anywhere without this, even if I'm going underneath a bridge. Where *am* I going? A hotel? I don't have a friend I can crash with.

The dark walls seem to remind me only of my mother's dark, golden-eyed stare. The way she was both furious and broken. They close in on me as I fill my purple suitcase.

"Sweetheart, let me."

I turn to Grandma, standing in my doorway. She places her hand on the leaves of an aloe plant sitting on my desk and snaps her fingers. My drawers fly open, the contents of my room reorganizing themselves and flying into my suitcase one by one.

"Oh," a gasp wrenches itself from deep in my gut.

Magic.

I barely remember magic being used so freely.

I missed the smell of it. It's the crisp scent in the air right before it rains. The slight tension, the sharp, refreshing moment before the downpour.

She crosses the room, narrowly missing a flying shirt, and sits on the creaky bed. "I have a proposition for you."

I sit beside her, an older sketchbook landing in the suitcase with a thwap.

"I own the apartment above my shop. If you would like, I'd love for you to stay there." She smooths her hand over the floral bedspread.

Huh.

I guess I shouldn't be shocked she's offering to help, but I didn't think she'd offer to have me stay *there*. The magic shop. I've heard it referenced before, of course, but I don't remember it. I assume Laura and I have been there before, but any time I try to picture it, my brain fogs over like early morning mist.

I know how much she loves antagonizing my mother, but this is more. This is different. Battle lines have been drawn and she's taking in a traitor. "Thank you, Grandma. I'd love to. Are you sure my things will fit? How big will my room be?"

"Sweetheart, do you . . . Oh, how precious. I don't live above the shop. I own the building and rent out the apartment upstairs. My previous tenant moved out a few weeks ago, so you'll have more than enough space."

My own space? I've never had more than just a bedroom to myself, and Laura has such a big personality, I always felt like anything I had was really hers.

"You're going to love it," she continues. "Although I'm not entirely selfless. I would appreciate your help in the shop, since I'll be letting you stay in the apartment rent-free."

"There's the strings." I smile. "I'd love to help in the shop."

She nods, snapping her fingers once more. My suitcase disappears.

"You have to teach me how to do that!"

"That's the entire point, dear. I'm going to teach you how to do that and so much more."

More? My heart flutters at the thought. That's all I want—*more*.

"I'll meet you outside." With that, she leaves me alone in my empty room. The room I grew up in. My sanctuary for the past twenty-five years.

I'd be lying if I said there wasn't the smallest pang in my heart at the thought of leaving here. Despite everything, this is home. The place my father called home.

But it's time.

I memorize each creak and groan of the staircase as I make my way down. The noise has returned to the house, if slightly muted. Anywhere else will always seem too quiet.

"Will you at least let me come over once in a while?" Laura stands in the way of the old wooden front door.

My stomach twists at the expression on her face. I hate leaving her with Mom. I hate knowing that even though I'm getting out, Laura isn't. I may only just be coming around to it, but this life we live isn't normal, and I know Laura needs to get out just as much as I do. But I need this. I have to do this for me. And Laura will have to take that step on her own, just like I am.

"Of course. You know I love you, right?"

"Yeah?" She brushes an imaginary piece of lint off her shirt. "As you should. I won't make you go out with me tonight, but tomorrow. You promised."

Shit, I completely forgot. After moving out on her with no notice? There's no way in hell I'm getting out of this.

"Yeah, I promised. I'll drive."

She squeals, giving me a big hug. "You won't regret it!"

Oh, I will. I always do. But I don't regret the opportunity to make her happy, to make up for leaving her. I squeeze her heavily perfumed self a little too tight and release.

"I'm only a text away, and you can visit whenever you want. I mean it."

"I know. Go on, Grandma's waiting."

I turn to the interior of the house one more time. I don't know if I'm expecting my mother to be there—leaning against the staircase or walking into the kitchen—but she isn't. Just the house, groaning and creaking its goodbye.

An ache settles low in my rib cage. Maybe she really does hate magic more than she loves me.

The irony of all this? Grandma's shop is just a few blocks away. Our house is in the village of Chagrin Falls, just a couple streets over from the town center where Grandma's shop stands. Despite the closeness, I don't expect to return my mom's house for a while. Not after the way she looked at me.

I walk out onto the front porch and find Grandma tapping her foot at me with a smile. I fall in step beside her as we walk through the cool fall air to the store.

I only look back at the white Victorian house once.

There is no better place than Chagrin Falls, Ohio—the most New England town you can find outside of New England—in the fall. The leaves are a rainbow of reds, oranges, yellows, and greens and the air has that crisp warmth to it that can't be replicated. Leaves crunch underfoot as we walk, the stars and light from the windows of our neighbors lighting the way. There are no streetlamps in the neighborhood, just in the town center.

Grandma is silent during our walk, something I appreciate. My head is swimming with the implications of everything that happened tonight. I know I've done the right thing, but this is going to impact my relationship with my mother for the rest of my life.

"We're here," Grandma says as we approach the brick building. The Cat's Cradle is dominated by a large, frosted bay window that doesn't allow you to see much farther than the hanging herbs just inside. Pumpkins line the green door for Halloween.

Her shop rests right in front of the town gazebo, in the middle of a row of shops and restaurants. Even from here, the scent of magic in the shop is overwhelming and it pulls me. Like my body wants to take me there, needs to be there. Instead of entering the shop, Grandma opens the private door to the apartment, and we climb.

When I step inside the apartment, my breath leaves me in a whoosh. I'm standing in the kitchen, the floorplan completely open. The only rooms with doors are the two bedrooms and bathroom. The main wall of the apartment is exposed brick, where a nice-sized TV resides. My eyes jump from place to place, unable to settle on one thing.

"Where did the furniture come from?" I ask, taking in the tasteful fluffy couch and armchairs.

Grandma raises a brow. "I'm a witch, sweetheart. Plus, renting out a partially furnished apartment means I can charge more."

That's my grandma—ever the businesswoman.

"The apartment is guarded by spells, so there's an extra layer of protection. I've left the keys on the counter, but I'll show you how to unlock the door without using them. The shop opens tomorrow at nine a.m., so I expect you downstairs at eight thirty sharp. Bring a list of anything you need for the apartment, and I'll help you out. Once you start getting paychecks you can handle the rest yourself."

"Paychecks? I thought the apartment was my paycheck."

"You need independence. Getting a paycheck will help with that until you find out what you want to do. There's a whole world out there you know absolutely nothing about. It's time you learned."

Well, damn, Grandma. Don't pull any punches.

"Thank you."

She smiles, pulling me into a hug. "I'll see you in the morning. Rest, my dear."

With that, she's gone and I'm alone in my apartment.

My. Apartment.

A place that is *mine*. I wander to the window, looking out on the sleepy small town that I've called home for so long. It's only a new perspective, but my hands are trembling with excitement. This is exactly what I'm meant to be doing.

Running to the bedroom, I flop on the familiar floral bedspread and can't hide my beaming grin. This may be the best night's rest I've had in years.

CHAPTER 3
THE CAT'S CRADLE

The shop calls much stronger this morning. It's a gentle caress on my skin, crawling up my arms and leaving the little hairs standing on end. After sucking down a delicious cup of coffee, I walk down the back stairs.

My hand lingers on the door. I may have moved out last night, but this right here—this is the true point of no return. There's still the slim possibility that, if I turned around now and begged for days, my mother would forgive me. But, if I go inside . . . my relationship with her will never be the same.

Deep breath in.

Screw it.

I open the door and step in. A sense of calm, of relaxation, immediately takes me over. That, and the smell of burning incense.

"Good morning, sweetheart!" Grandma chirps from her chair. The stairs seem to have dropped me right into her curtained-off office, if you could call it that. It's more like a private garden room —complete with hanging potted plants and ivy twisting around the windowsills—with the biggest armchair I've ever seen in my life. I actually have to look for her in the mass of cushions.

"Good morning, Grandma," I reply, closing the door behind me.

"You're exactly on time. I love a punctual woman," she teases, standing from that absolute cushion monstrosity. "Let me give you a reminder tour?"

A reminder tour?

Before I can question it, she takes my hand in hers, the almost twenty bracelets around her wrist jangling. With a wave, the curtain blocking off the room pulls away and I'm hit with memories I didn't even know I had. I'm left barely standing, my legs wobbling beneath me. I remember running between the bookshelves with Laura, giggling and making a mess. I remember creating little 'potions' in the largest cauldron we could carry, throwing in whatever we thought looked good. Daddy caught us right before we lit the entire building on fire.

Dad. How could I have forgotten him?

"Steady on your feet, my dear," Grandma says, wrapping her thin arm around my waist. "Memories can bowl you right over if you let them."

"I just . . . Why didn't I remember?" I ask, blinking a tear out of my eyes. The weird fog. Anytime I tried to imagine this shop, I'd get stopped by some veil. I just accepted it as another thing that didn't make sense, but something caused it.

"It was a decision made by your mother, and that's all I'll say about that."

I snort. Of course it was my mother. Who else but her? What else has she stolen from me? Stealing my life, my future, my decisions wasn't enough, apparently. She had to steal my memories of the one person who actually loved me? She'll be lucky if she ever sees my face again.

Grandma places a cool hand on my arm. It's like I'm burning from the inside out with white-hot rage. "The past can't be changed. Instead, let's reacquaint ourselves."

I nod, stepping with her further into the space.

It's exactly the same as my new memories suggest. Clean, but weathered in a comforting way. The smell of old book pages, leather spines, incense, and herbs permeate the very walls. It's like Grandma intensified—I love it.

"Over here are the books. Spellcasting, potion-making, gardening, the history of our line. Everything is here." Grandma has wrapped her arm around mine as she points.

"The history of our line?" My interest is immediately piqued. I know almost nothing about the Pruitt line.

"I figured you might be interested in that. You can peruse these books as much or as little as you desire. If you have any questions, I'll answer what I can." She pulls me further along the shelves. "Ingredients are over here, but I would prefer you ask me before taking anything. More often than not, I'll give you ingredients from my own garden. This stock is for customers—plus, mine are better."

"Keeping the good stuff for yourself? I approve." I brush my fingers along a long ivy plant.

She lightly slaps my arm as we halt in front of the counter. It's glass, with all manner of crystals and jewelry on display inside. An ancient cash register sits on top. "Don't sass your Grandma. Now, this is you."

"I'm not a counter."

"You're also not funny, sweetheart."

"That hurts."

"You'll be working up front. I don't expect you to be able to answer every question you're asked right away, of course, but I expect you to handle each customer with the grace they've come to expect at The Cat's Cradle. Understood?" She may be small, but my grandmother makes an imposing figure when she wants.

I nod. "Yes, ma'am. But what about magic?"

"Let's see how you do today. Then we can discuss a training schedule if you're still interested."

A mass of black fur jumps onto the counter in front of me. Rosie, the ancient creature, somehow still has all the energy of a youthful kitten. She caused too much trouble scratching the furniture during Grandma's visits, so I haven't seen her in at least three or four years. Her fur has only grayed a little bit and she still has a small notch in her left ear from a fight with a stray.

"Hello, you." I scratch lightly under her chin until she hisses and jumps into Grandma's arms.

"Be good." With a conspiratorial smile, Grandma and her little demon cat head back into her curtained-off room, leaving me alone in the shop.

I don't want to be good. I'm like a kid in a candy shop. Must touch. Must touch everything. My feet carry me—completely on their own—to the ingredients as I dig through all that lies before me. Crystals, herbs, candles, books, little wooden totems—oh my! How much of this is legitimate? Do some herbs and crystals really help focus a spell or is this mostly just for show?

The scents are overwhelming. It's as if I've been in the kitchen all day as flecks of sliced herbs stain the pads of my fingers. I'm building piles of my favorites from each category almost subconsciously. The books spill out behind me.

The bell rings and I look down at the mess I've created. Grandma is not going to be happy about this.

"Welcome to The Cat's Cradle!" I say, hoping that Grandma will rescue me. "What can I help you with?"

"You must be new," the older woman says with a smile. "Don't trouble yourself, darling. I'll just go back to see Elizabeth."

"Dotty, don't torture my granddaughter." Grandma emerges from her room with a flourish. Does she open the curtains with magic every time?

Dotty's eyes light up as she looks me up and down. The woman is, I'm guessing, around my grandma's age and has a matching sense of style. Boho chic meets old witch. Lots of bangles. "This is your granddaughter?"

"That's what they tell me." I shrug.

"Shush!" Grandma whacks me lightly on the arm. Then she takes in the mess. She shakes her head, but she can't hide the slight smile at the corner of her mouth. "I don't understand how you've managed to make an absolute mess in only a few minutes."

"It was an hour. I can do a lot of damage in an hour, Grandma." Do I have a sense of humor? That's new.

Dotty chuckles. "She's definitely your granddaughter, Lizzy. Why don't you give the girl a break and clean the place?"

"Because she needs to learn that I'm not here to be her maid. Cleaning it by hand will do her good. Now, come on back, I have our tea ready." Grandma pulls her friend into her room with a pointed stare in my direction.

Message received.

I regret my mess as my eyes travel along the shelves. This is not made easier by the fact that I barely know where anything goes. Grandma has everything labeled pretty well, but I genuinely don't know what lavender looks like.

I guesstimate where things go, and by the time I look at the clock again I've made it look halfway decent. Instead of worrying about my haphazard job at cleaning, I focus on the spellbooks:

Healing Herbs and Their Properties.

How to Conjure: Creating Out of Thin Air.

Household Spells for Beginners.

Ah—that sounds like a perfect place to start, since I am definitely a beginner. You're coming with me, gorgeous. I pull the book off the shelf and bring it to the counter, brushing dust off the cover. The back description reads in deliciously swirly writing:

As you begin your journey into magic, reach for Household Spells for Beginners. This tome is perfect for those who have a basic knowledge of the craft and wish to expand their skills. Want to learn how to clean your home in less than a moment? Make a delicious dinner for your family in a flash? Household Spells for Beginners is for you!

THIS IS THE BEGINNING OF MY JOURNEY INTO MAGIC. IT'S LIKE THIS book is made for me and I can't wait to dive in.

"Hazel?" Grandma's voice echoes through the shop. "You can

take your lunch break now. Only thirty minutes! Don't take anything from the shop to lunch with you."

So close. How did she do that?

"I'll be back for you," I whisper to the book and grab my jacket.

Turns out there is a *dynamite* sandwich shop on the corner that I have somehow never set foot in. I don't know what is in this marinade, but I want to bathe in it, or eat it every day for the rest of my life.

Or both.

I return to the shop holding my chocolate chip cookie with five minutes to spare. The household spells book beckons from where I left it on the counter, contents just waiting to be discovered.

Grandma would be pissed if I got chocolate fingerprints on it—so cookie first, book second.

"Ah, you went to You're Great in Bread," Grandma says from the stacks of potion ingredients, where she is probably fixing my clumsy attempt at cleaning. It seems her friend left during my lunch break.

"You should've warned me about this place. I may be addicted now."

"They do make a very good sandwich. You know, they buy their herbs from here." With a saucy wink, she waltzes off to her room.

Why am I entirely unsurprised she put some of her witchy woo-woo on it? I should've known there was no way this sauce was anything but magic.

I wipe off my hands and sit down behind the cash register. I'm ready to dig into this damn spellbook as if my life depends on it.

Hell, maybe it does.

I crack the cover and . . . *oh*. Warmth spreads from the tips of my fingers to my toes. Thunderstorm crackles scent the air and a smile breaks across my face. I'm supposed to be here, in this moment. I'm supposed to be learning magic. God knows how I know that, but I do.

The first page says "Cleaning Spells." I could've used this a couple hours ago. Maybe someday I'll get to the point where I can do these spells nonverbally, but for now it looks like I'm learning Latin.

"Grandma, you got any dust I can borrow?" I yell across the store.

Her snort, and an equally sassy meow, rings through the shop. "You do realize you're in a magic shop with a plentiful offering of old books?"

I walk over and grab the oldest looking book I can find—um, heavy much?—and lug it back to my counter. It smells of *old*, and has a layer of dust so thick I could write messages.

I turn to *Household Spells* and read through the page. According to this, I just recite the words and then poof—magic happens. Seems a little too easy, but let's give it a try.

"Purgomundus Purus," I whisper. I'm not sure what I expected to happen, but it wasn't a whole heaping pile of nothing. One speck of dust could've wiggled.

"Purgomundus Purus," I repeat, louder this time. Okay, there's the wiggling. Still not clean.

"Purgomundus Purus." Did a few specks disappear? "Purgomundus Purus!"

"If it were just reading and repeating, witchcraft would be much easier," Grandma says as she emerges from her Grandma-cave.

I sigh. She's right, of course. "Practice makes perfect?"

"Exactly. All skills take time to master, including witchcraft. You may have been born a witch, but you aren't a spellcaster yet. It'll come with time."

"How much time?"

"Patience is a virtue, sweetheart." She settles her bangle-clad hand on mine, giving it a squeeze. "Try deep breathing, emptying your mind completely, and then try the spell again."

It's not like I've ever been known for my patience. Granted, I've never been known for anything.

I close my eyes, inhaling as deeply as I can. The smells of the shop fill my nose—herbs, dust, and a light layer of cat—and I allow the warmth and pull of the magic to fill my lungs. I exhale.

"Purgomundus Purus." The magic, the warmth, flows through me and into the world like a wave.

"You're a natural after all. Open your eyes."

I open to find the entire store, not just my book, has been wiped clean.

Oh.

Maybe I can do this, maybe I'm meant to do this. My eyes sting as I take in what I've done. I've never felt like this. Like I'm finally doing something with my life, not just stuck in the rut my mother forced me into. Controlled me into. Manipulated me into.

I'm finally someone.

"Customer," Grandma says, right before the bell above the door rings.

I'm distracted by customers for the rest of the afternoon, but the sense of pride never leaves me as I help each person.

"Do you teach your art class tomorrow? That's Saturdays and Wednesdays, correct?" Grandma asks as we close the shop at the end of the day.

A slight smile graces my lips. "Yes." My classes have been my only opportunity to get out into the world. My only connection to life around me. I suspect the only reason my mother let me teach them was because they didn't pay me. No money, no independence.

She nods. "You can have Saturdays and Wednesdays off, then. We're closed Sundays as well. I know your class is only an hour or so on those days, but it's good to have time off. And tomorrow we can discuss a training schedule. It's best you get started with magic quickly if that is the path you're going to take."

"Can I . . ." Deep breath. "Can I take *Household Spells* with me tonight?"

Grandma clicks her tongue, unable to hide her slight smile.

"While I don't want you getting into the habit of taking things out of the shop and leaving them upstairs, I'll make an exception tonight."

"Sounds good. I appreciate everything you're doing for me."

"I would do anything for you, your sister, and your mother. I know that I don't particularly help with reducing tensions in our family . . ."

I raise a brow.

"Hush. I have my own reasons for my actions. One day I'll have to get over my own issues and act like an adult, I suppose. But, not today." She laughs.

I hug her tightly, pretending I'm not ridiculously intrigued by what she just said. I'm not opening that can of worms.

Not tonight.

CHAPTER 4

BEBE

The moment my key turns in the front door of my apartment, I'm hit with a wave of belonging. Maybe it's because my stuff was magically arranged just so, or because it's close to the shop, but this place is *mine*. There are even fluffy blankets.

Fluffy blankets!

I don't know exactly where they came from, but I can't find the power to care.

I wander into the living room, still marveling that this place belongs to me. The exposed brick wall, the comfy cream-colored couch, it's all mine.

I pull *Household Spells* out of my bag and place it on the coffee table for future perusal. I plan to spend all night wrapped up with a cup of decaf and this book.

Ring, ring.

Where did I leave my phone . . . ? I pat around my jeans, over the couch cushions, and finally find it tucked underneath the spellbook.

Laura? I didn't expect her to reach out this quickly after I left.

Oh, wait. I promised her I'd go out tonight. I completely forgot! Crud.

"Hey sis," I say, flopping onto the couch. Maybe she forgot and I can have a date with my fluffy blanket after all.

"Are you ready?" Laura replies. The sound of her flicking through clothes hangers filters through the phone. Nope, she definitely didn't forget.

I take a deep breath. "Today was my first day working at Grandma's shop. I just got home."

"Hazel, I'm not an idiot. You can't get out of this. Get sexy, I'll be there in an hour. Remember, you promised to drive." And with that, she hangs up.

Get sexy? I don't even know what that means. I walk over to the closet in my bedroom and stare at my clothes. I'm flying blind, here. Maybe someday I'll find a spell called Perfecto Outfit Immedius, but for now, I'm on my own.

It seems the best I have is a low-cut v-neck black shirt and tight —can I actually fit these over my ass?—skinny jeans. A little black eyeliner around my green eyes and mascara, and I'm ready to go.

Of course, Laura will say something along the lines of, "Are you seriously going out like that?" I'm used to it by now. She means well, and it's that fact that saves her.

While I don't have many reference points outside of old episodes of *Charmed*, I suspect our sisterly relationship isn't entirely normal. When Dad died, Mom changed. She distanced herself while also controlling our every movement. Skinned your knee and needed a hug? You'd get a Band-Aid and not even a kiss on the head. Wanted to go to a slumber party? Absolutely not. We were locked in the house and she threw away the key. That meant the emotional stuff fell to me. I was the one who soothed every nightmare, who taught Laura how to use a tampon; I spent my entire childhood trying to preserve hers.

The outcome? Laura gets out into the world more than I do because I cover for her, but she's also a little immature, if I'm honest.

A few raps on the door interrupt my internal monologue.

"It's annoying how inherently sexy you are without even trying.

Did you even spend more than three minutes on your makeup?" Laura says instead of a greeting as I open the door.

She means well. But she and I both know I look nowhere near as good as she does.

"I think I spent five?" I give her a warm hug. She is wrapped in some too-tight contraption of a dress in a forest-green color. It makes her golden-brown eyes look even brighter, like liquid gold. Although that could be the masterfully crafted eyeshadow.

She scoffs. "Bitch. Let me see the place."

I move to the side and allow her to step in.

"Ugh! This is all yours?"

"Yep."

"Such a bitch." She smiles at me.

I wrap my arm around her waist. "Did you want to go to whatever awful place you're planning on taking me? Or would you like to gape at my fabulous apartment and call me a bitch a few more times?"

"Is that a trick question? Because I'm enjoying the gaping," she replies with a smile, perfect white teeth glinting.

"Come on, commence your torture."

"You have fun every single time we hang out. I don't know why you put up this charade, but you're only hurting yourself," Laura says with a nod as I lock the door.

I silently roll my eyes and follow her down the stairs to the road.

And then I see it. My feet stop on the sidewalk. *Oh God, she didn't.*

"Laura . . ."

She turns to face me. "I know you hate my car, but I couldn't very well borrow Mom's when both of you refuse to speak to each other. And you won't get your own, so here we are."

I glare at the Pepto Bismol-pink Prius sitting at the curb. I'd rather rip each of my fingernails off than be seen in her ridiculous car. The car I forced Mom to get for Laura so she could go to college.

She only gave in on the condition that Laura would live at

home, and that I wouldn't take classes myself. Giving up my college education for my sister? All in a day's work.

"I hate you a little bit more every time I see this thing."

A roll of her eyes is her only reply.

I get behind the wheel of the Pink Puke Mobile, resigned to my fate. I am the Queen of the Barbie Car.

I HATE IT HERE.

Laura talked me into coming to the 'hip' new bar called Matchstix in Lakewood. It's obnoxiously dark—and worse, filled with people our age. *Human* people.

"You're here to spend time with your sister amongst the living. We'll eat a burger, have a drink or two, and then go back to your apartment to watch a stupid movie together," Laura says, taking my hand in hers. "I promise I won't torture you for long."

I take a deep breath. "Fine."

I'm not antisocial per se. I just don't see how I'm supposed to connect with people when I don't even have a connection with myself.

Good job, Hazel, very poignant.

We walk over to the corner booth and sit. I watch Laura scan the crowd hovering around the bar. She's single again and I can tell she's on the prowl for her next victim. So much for spending time together.

I can't really blame her, though. Finding a connection with someone would be wonderful.

Sometimes I hate how easy it is for Laura to make connections, regardless of how fleeting. She doesn't keep guys around for longer than a month or two, but at least she's out there.

"I see a group of handsome guys!" Laura says with a squeal. She casually flits her eyes to the bar.

"You always do," I tease, but I follow her gaze anyway.

The breath whooshes out of my lungs. My heart stops beating in my chest. The entire world quiets as if someone pressed the pause button on reality. Or like someone slipped noise-canceling headphones on my head.

It's the eyes.

The *eyes*.

The dark brown, almost black, eyes I've been drawing for weeks now. They've plagued my dreams, dominated my sketches, and now they're here. Watching me.

They belong to a strong-jawed, lanky man with tousled brown hair and bushy eyebrows.

My whole body flushes, heat burning my cheeks so quickly I have to raise a hand to check I didn't catch fire.

"Something catch your eye?" Laura's voice is way too proud. Little brat.

Do I tell Laura? Tell her that he's . . . I don't know what he is.

"You told me to look, so I looked." I break eye contact with the mystery man and focus back on Laura. If I told her, she'd try to convince me he's my soulmate or something stupid like that. Best to keep her in the dark for now.

Thankfully, the waiter saves me. I don't dare look back at the bar as I order a Coke.

"Why didn't you order a drink?" Laura asks, having ordered herself a Slinky Orgasm or an Over The Ass Slap or whatever the hell drinks are called these days.

"Because one of us has to drive home. If you wanted us to drink together we could've ordered a ride share or something instead of driving the Pink Puke Mobile."

I don't mention that I don't like drinking because I hate feeling out of control. Laura already knows that.

"Will you please stop calling my car the Pink Puke Mobile?" Laura crosses her arms. "It's just pink."

The waiter drops off our drinks and . . . ew. Laura's drink is the same shade of pink as her car and it's making me want to barf. I have no idea how she can drink that.

"Cheers to not talking about my car anymore?" Laura asks, raising her drink.

I snort. "Cheers to that, I guess."

"Refills are courtesy of those guys at the bar," the waiter says as he brings a second round, despite us only having taken a few sips. His finger points right toward Brown-Eyed and Bushy-Eyebrowed and his two friends.

Am I blushing? Yuck.

Laura bats her mile-long eyelashes at the group of guys. "Wow, how generous."

I can't help rolling my eyes as two of BEBE's—Brown-Eyed and Bushy-Eyebrowed—friends wave back enthusiastically.

"You have issues. Why can't you just find a nice boy and settle down for longer than two minutes?" I wince the minute the words leave my mouth. I sound way too much like my mother.

"*You* have issues. Why can't you get out of your hole and actually meet a guy?" Laura snaps.

You could hear a pin drop.

The urge to comfort her, to smother my own emotions, is too strong to ignore. Despite the fact she hit the nail on the head. But I *am* out of my hole, and I'm working on making a real life for myself. Finally.

"I'm sorry." I always apologize first.

She sighs. "Me too. That was uncalled for. Let's order our burgers and work on this whole hangry thing, hmm?"

"Yes! I'm starving!" Deflection is my super power. I've never held Laura accountable for the things she says to hurt me, and I'm not going to start tonight.

"*Hey*." A shaking voice interrupts my internal innuendos. It's not BEBE, but it's one of his friends. One of his slightly tipsy friends, if the wobbling is any indication.

His gaze is firmly planted on Laura so I let her take over. I need a burger and I need it now. In my face.

With an approving nod from Laura, I stand and make my way to the bar.

I lean over the side to get the waiter's attention. "Hi!"

He waves a hand at me as he chats up a *very* attractive guy with the roundest ass I've ever seen. I'm not even mad that he's taking his time.

"It may be a minute," says a calm voice that floods over me like an ocean wave.

I freeze. Without looking, I know exactly who that voice belongs to. I don't know if it's a witchy moment or what, but I know that voice belongs to BEBE. Almost as if I've heard his voice my whole life.

I force a cough, trying to reanimate my body.

I can definitely talk to the man whose eyes have haunted my dreams for weeks. This is totally normal.

"It happens. I'm just hungry." Very normal response, Hazel. Good job.

BEBE's lankiness shouldn't work for him, but all those long limbs are drawing me in. I want to know how many times his arms could wrap around me. Probably fewer than I'd want.

No. I barely know him and I don't need to be thinking about anything wrapping around anything.

"I was promised mozzarella sticks myself, but Benji seems to have forgotten that." He motions over to the tipsy boy still leaning precariously over my giggling sister.

"Why are my attempts at enjoying food being thwarted by bubble butts and fluttering eyelashes?" I grumble.

His eyes bug out of his face as water shoots from his mouth like a hose set on high. It takes a few moments for BEBE to stop hysterically laughing.

I'm definitely blushing again, basically on fire. No wonder my mom never allows me in public. She may have been right this whole time.

Thankfully, the almost-death-by-laughter of BEBE has roused the waiter's attention and he appears in front of us.

"How can I help you?" the waiter asks, eyeing his wet counter.

Is teleportation out of the most embarrassing moment of my life on the menu? "Two cheeseburgers, please."

"Absolutely, sweetheart. And you?"

"May I have two orders of mozzarella sticks and another round of drinks, please?" BEBE asks politely, still chuckling a bit. Must he draw out my embarrassment so?

"Will do." The waiter writes down our orders. "Sorry for the delay."

"No problem." I wink. I was aiming for funny, but I'm pretty sure it just came off creepy. But the waiter gives me a fond smile regardless. He's getting a very large tip this evening.

Oh Lord, the innuendo. Jesus take the wheel.

"It was nice to meet you," I mumble in BEBE's general direction.

I turn to go back to my table, alone with my sister where I belong, when a gentle hand touches mine for a brief second. I almost jump at the electric buzz that surges through my skin.

I stare at the point of contact for a beat. Two.

That is not normal. But, what about this evening has been?

"I'm sorry if I embarrassed you. I didn't mean to, you just took me a bit by surprise there. If it helps, no one has made me laugh like that in a long time," BEBE says so sincerely I swear a piece of my heart melts off.

"You're welcome?"

"I'm Noah. Noah Rogers." He extends his hand.

"Hazel Hollis," I reply. My fingers wrap around his and the same buzz skitters across my skin, raising the little hairs on my arms.

What *is* that?

"Would you want to wait for our food together?" Noah asks. "Benji just went through a really nasty break up, and talking with your friend is the most I've seen him smile in two weeks."

I turn to my sister and it's quite apparent she's barely even noticed my absence. The bitch.

"My sister," I correct, sitting down. "Until our food arrives."

Another reason I don't go out in public very often is I have no idea what to say to people. I have barely any idea what's going on in popular culture, and I'm sure Noah would be super freaked out to hear how I cleaned the store today by murmuring some Latin-adjacent gibberish.

What do I even talk about? What do people talk about when they can't stop staring at the other person's mouth?

Pretty lips are so pretty.

"Tell me a bit about yourself, Hazel."

The dreaded question. Hi, I'm Hazel and up until yesterday I lived at home with my Mom. I was also unemployed and I come from a long line of witches that I don't know anything about because my mom refuses to say anything. Nice to meet you.

"There's not too much to tell. I'm one of those sheltered, boring people who should be studied in a lab somewhere."

Was I raised in a barn? How was that answer better?

Thankfully, I get a deep, gorgeous laugh in response, not the awkward exit I was expecting.

He leans in, accentuating the lean lines of his shoulders and torso. "Unless you spend your time staring at the wall, there's always something to tell. What do you do for fun?"

"How dare you guess my favorite hobby on the first try?" I need to rein in this new desire to be funny. It's not working for me. "I enjoy painting, that's what I usually do when I'm not working in the shop or teaching."

Noah perks up like a golden retriever. "Where do you teach? I have a cousin who's an elementary school teacher."

"Oh, God no. Not with children." I shudder at the thought. "I teach a couple of sketching classes at the community center on Saturdays and Wednesdays."

"Wow, my artistic ability begins and ends at stick figures. You must be talented if you teach."

"I'm a volunteer. And you know what they say—those who can't do, teach." I let out a self-deprecating chuckle.

He shakes his head. "I don't believe that for a second. You're talented, I can tell."

Oh, hello cheeks. I almost forgot you were on fire.

"What about you? Tell me about you."

He smiles and takes a sip of his drink. Is he as nervous as I am? I've never made anyone nervous before.

"I'm just normal, I guess. I work at a publishing house in the city. Shit, that's a tougher question than I thought." He scratches his stubble thoughtfully and I swoon a little.

I bet I would get a delightful case of stubble burn on multiple parts of my . . .

Oh my God, I'm a literal virgin. Where are these thoughts even coming from?

"Two cheeseburgers for you, sweetheart, and two orders of mozzarella sticks for you." The waiter places our plates in front of us.

Thank *God*. I needed the rescue.

"Thank you." I smile and pick up the plates.

Am I lingering a little to see if he'll ask for my number?

It's strange because I don't like being around men—talking to them, flirting with them, being in their general vicinity.

You have dreams about someone's eyes for weeks and an electric current up your arm when you touch them and suddenly you act like an idiot.

"Could I maybe . . . ?" His hand scrubs his face a little and—God, it shouldn't be as endearing as it is. "Would it be all right if I called you?"

I put the plates back down and stretch for his phone, which he delivers quickly with a grateful smile. I punch in my number and hand it back, only slightly shaking.

CHAPTER 5

HOT MESS HAZEL

"Hazel?"

I jerk my head up. One of my Saturday morning students stares at me like I'm from outer space. I haven't been able to get Noah off my brain since I walked away from him last night, and it's impacting my class.

"I'm sorry," I reply, heat flaming my cheeks. "Can you repeat the question?"

I saddle up behind her, looking over her sketch. We're focusing on drawing a bowl of fruit in the middle of the room. Not my most inspired lesson, but certainly a classic.

The man to her left leans over with a conspiratorial smile on his face. "Selma thinks her apple looks like a dead president. I'll give you five bucks if you can guess which one."

"Ted!" Selma exclaims, swatting him lightly. "Ignore my husband, Hazel. I just wanted to ask you about the holiday schedule."

A smile crosses my face as they bicker back and forth. They're pretty adorable.

My phone buzzes in my pocket so I leave them to their teasing with a promise to text the schedule over, a gentle ache in my chest.

> Unknown Number: Hi, Hazel. This is Noah from yesterday.

> Unknown Number: I was wondering if you'd like to grab lunch today?

Oh, well that's surprising. I didn't expect to hear from him again, despite him asking for my number, and certainly not so quickly. I was actually pretty damn sure I burned that bridge all the way down with my bubble butts comment.

He must be a masochist.

> Hazel: Hi! I'm teaching today, so I don't get much time for lunch. Maybe we could do something else a little later?

I need to find out why I've been dreaming of his eyes. I need to find out why I get that electric buzz when I touch him. And the only way I'm going to do that is by spending time with him.

And then I can run away before I inevitably embarrass myself beyond redemption.

> Noah: Absolutely. Dinner?

> Hazel: Let me know when and where, so long as it's after five. I'll meet you there.

Put the phone away, Hazel—you have a class to teach.

I wonder how obvious it is that I'm talking to a boy. A very cute boy.

Oh dear.

My cheeks almost burn my palms as I touch them. No one has ever made me blush like this.

I'm not liking the sneaky look that Selma and Ted are giving me.

You don't know my life, cute old people.

TWO HOURS IS *NOT* ENOUGH TIME TO GET READY FOR THE FIRST DATE you've ever had. Twenty-five years old is also way too old to be having your first date.

Thanks, Mom. Your societal repression is really working in my favor.

I wore my only 'good' outfit the first time I met Noah, so what the hell am I supposed to wear now?

I could potentially call Laura, but that's a can of worms I'm unwilling to open. Not to mention the fact I barely got the wench out of my apartment this morning. Inviting her back would be dumb.

It would be very dumb.

Damn my lack of friends.

Wait a hot damn minute. What did I wear to Laura's high school graduation? I frantically dig through the closet and—yes! A dress! It may not be the sexiest thing that ever existed, but it's form-fitting and black.

It's only through the magic of a curling iron and an unused dress that I look somewhat presentable.

This may not be an absolute disaster. No, this will probably be a disaster—but I'll look decent during said disaster.

Passable. I'll look *passable* during said disaster.

Noah asked me to meet him at some Italian place I've never heard of before, which makes my palms sweat just a little as I clench the steering wheel of Grandma's car. I don't like going to new places as it is. I don't know if it's the lack of knowledge of where I'm going or what, but I always end up getting there at least fifteen minutes early.

Hence my arrival at—gasp—an *adorable* little restaurant a grand total of twenty minutes before six o'clock.

I blame the extra five minutes on my first date nervousness.

I can do this. I breathe in, breathe out.

Breathe in.

Breathe out.

I haven't told anyone about this date. Not Laura, not Grandma when I asked to borrow her car, and—well, there's nobody else other than them.

I step out of the vehicle. Come on, Hazel. Get it together.

The restaurant, Georgio's, is even cuter on the inside. It's the epitome of a perfect date restaurant. The scent of garlic bread gently wafts through the air—mmm. The place has the air of the quaint Italian restaurants of New York City. The walls are beautiful red brick and the tables are draped in soft, cream-colored tablecloths and adorned with tea light candles. The space is open, the tables framing the giant brick oven in the back.

My mouth waters as I snap back to reality. I'm about to eat all the bread.

All. Of. The. Bread.

"Hazel?"

I turn to Noah, who is standing up from one of the more isolated tables.

Oh, my memory didn't do his lanky gorgeousness any justice. Tonight he's wrapped up in a forest-green sweater that does terribly beautiful things to his dark brown eyes, and crisp slacks.

"Hi Noah." I smile, walking toward him slowly. I'm not about to move too fast and fall on my ass.

Which totally hasn't happened before. Multiple times.

"You look beautiful," he says once I'm closer, pulling out my chair. I didn't realize guys who pull out chairs for their date still exist.

"Thank you. You look very handsome," I reply because I have no filter. And it's true.

I try to cover the dark blush on my cheeks by hiding behind my menu, but I can still see the grin that breaks on his face.

So maybe I don't regret saying that too much.

"I'm glad we get to do this. Thank you for coming to dinner with me," he continues after a couple seconds of menu perusing.

I'm looking for the most carb-loaded item on this menu, and the fact that I'm at an Italian restaurant means I'm in heaven.

"Thank you for inviting me."

My cheeks—my cheeks are burning.

"How was your class today?" he asks, relaxing his lanky limbs into his wooden chair.

It's like he's an octopus or something. But, like, a sexy octopus.

I place my menu down. "I teach two classes on Saturdays, a shorter morning class and then a longer afternoon class after lunch. They both went well. The Saturday classes are my favorite."

"Why's that?"

I smile. "You're going to judge me, but it's because those classes tend to be filled with couples. Specifically, older couples. You can tell they're there because they want to spend time with each other. They aren't there to make the best work in the class, or to lord their prowess over other people. They just want to enjoy their time together."

When did I become such a sap?

"That's sweet," he says with a smile so earnest I actually believe he means it. "What's different about your other classes?"

"Wednesday is aspiring art students day," I reply with an over-dramatic shudder.

He laughs, the sound tickling along my skin. I could quickly get addicted to it. "It's like you just said Frankenstein's monster or something. Are they really that bad?"

"Yes, they are completely and totally that bad."

"Maybe you'll let me come by sometime. It sounds like this is something I have to see."

"Oh!" He wants to come to my class? No one has ever been interested in my classes. Or my art in general, if I'm honest. A little ball of emotion wedges in the back of my throat despite how I try to swallow it away. "I can't imagine you'd have much fun. But, of course, you're welcome to come by."

"Good evening. May I get you something to drink?" The waiter saves me from my awkwardness. Thank you, generic young man with white shirt and black tie.

Noah gestures for me to go first.

"Water and a Coke, please," I reply. Still no drinking for this lady.

"Make that two."

"Fantastic. Would you enjoy bread on the table while you peruse your menus?"

It's almost insulting that he has to ask.

"Yes, please!" I say, possibly too enthusiastically. The waiter nods politely and departs while Noah chuckles.

Yep, I definitely asked for bread too enthusiastically. Although, really, is there such a thing as too much enthusiasm for bread?

Especially garlic bread.

Noah shifts in his chair, a hint of nervousness showing through. "Okay, I have a serious question for you."

Uh oh.

"Shoot."

"Pineapple on pizza. Delicious or sin against God?" The corner of his mouth ticks upward and warmth fills my chest. He smiles in this easy way that speaks of a purity I don't know if I've ever experienced. Not since Dad died, at least.

"I wouldn't say it's a sin against God, but it's definitely not my first choice. And you? Delicious or sin against God?"

He shrugs. "Trick question. It's only okay if you pair it with jalapenos for that sweet and spicy kick."

A small, genuine laugh escapes me. "Noted."

"Have we looked at our menus?" The waiter returns, turning our attention from each other. I miss the way his gaze feels on me. I miss the eyes that have haunted me for months.

I watch him as he orders, not paying attention to what he's saying. I'm surprised by how easy it is to be with him. I'm awkward as usual, sure, but there's something comforting about being around Noah. Something safe. Familiar.

I order too, and the waiter leaves with a smile.

"Tell me a story," I blurt out. There are all these little pieces that make Noah who he is, and for some reason I want to collect all of them.

He quirks one of his bushy eyebrows. "A story?"

"A story." I push my hair behind my ear. "Something about you."

He sighs, scrubbing at his stubble. "Okay. This isn't a story, but, I don't like bars. I realize we met in one, but I was basically forced out. I much prefer being a homebody."

"I hate them, too. My sister, Laura, forced me into it using familial guilt. I would much rather be home sketching." Or would I? Maybe that's just what I've been conditioned to think. I cough. "What do you do when you're being a homebody?"

"No judgment?" He asks, nervous smile wavering just a touch.

"Never." I pause. "Well, unless you torture people or something. Then I'll judge you a little."

He levels me with a mock glare, brown eyes flashing with mischief. "No torturing. I'm a bit of a nerd, actually. I collect and build minis for *Warhammer*."

I have quite literally no idea what that means, and it must be obvious because Noah chuckles a bit. His curls bounce with the laughter.

"It's okay if you don't know what I'm talking about," he continues. "It's a relatively niche hobby."

I prop my chin on the palms of my hands. "Tell me all about it."

The surprise in his eyes makes my chest tighten. Maybe no one has ever expressed interest in his hobbies either. Maybe we have more in common than I expected.

"Okay." His smile is bright, almost overpowering his face. "Yeah, I can do that."

～

IT'S NOT THAT I DOUBT SEX COULD EVER BE AS GOOD AS THIS PASTA, but how good could sex really be? Sex wishes it was as good as pasta. This pasta specifically. Creamy alfredo, moist chicken, and perfectly tender noodles. I'm in heaven.

"I'm glad you like it," Noah says, breaking the comfortable silence. Both of us were far too enraptured by dinner arriving to continue the pleasant conversation.

I lift a brow at him as I finish chewing my food. "What makes you think I like it?"

"I like to think I can tell when a woman is enjoying herself . . ." he trails off and wow, was I unprepared for that. "You're also making pretty positive noises."

"Whoops." I smile sheepishly. My heart beats unevenly with every second of uninterrupted eye contact.

"No, it's nice. Too many people are scared nowadays to show actual emotion. I like knowing that you're enjoying the food." He rubs the back of his neck. "Is that a weird thing to say?"

If only you could hear my inner monologue, BEBE. You don't know weird.

"Not at all. Are you enjoying yours?"

"Yeah, of course! Nonna Ricci's recipes are always the best."

"Nonna Ricci?"

"Oh, yeah." He swallows a forkful of pasta. "My friend from last night, Benji, his Grandma owns this place. I basically grew up here."

He brought me somewhere this special? For a first date? My heart clenches just a tad.

"Does that mean you're going to get a big hug from an Italian woman at some point?"

His eyes flit toward the kitchen. "Uh, that's actually entirely possible. I don't think she's working tonight, or I would've already seen her."

"I'll try not to get jealous."

He smiles cautiously. Wait. He has a little dimple in his chin that comes out when he smiles. Swoon.

"You've got nothing to be jealous about."

At this point I may just melt.

"So, when you say that you grew up here. What do you mean?"

"My parents worked a lot when I was younger—they both had demanding careers. So I would often get dropped off here with Benji, and Nonna Ricci would make us an after-school snack. We'd help her clean off tables and play boardgames in the back room."

"That's so sweet. It sounds like she means a lot to you."

His eyes go soft as he smiles down at his plate. "She does. I didn't have any grandparents, so she basically adopted me as her own. She's an amazing woman."

I reach for his hand and the moment I touch his skin, the electric pulse shoots up my arm. I can't hide the gasp this time.

"Do you slide your feet on the floor before you touch me?" He chuckles. "You're always shocking me."

He feels it, too? I gotta figure out what this is. I've never had this with anyone else. Maybe there's something about this in the books at the shop?

"I guess I'm just a little staticky." I shrug. "Um, you mentioned you work at a publishing house last night. Does that come from a love of books?"

Look at me forming legitimate sentences like an adult while changing the subject. I'm so proud of me!

"Yes, but I'm a writer, actually. I'm not anywhere as good as the people we publish, but it's something I enjoy doing."

"Uh huh. I'm an artist. I know impostor syndrome when I hear it. You're probably better than you think."

He chuckles, a light flush staining his cheeks. "I try."

"Can I read something of yours sometime? I figure it's only fair if you plan on crashing one of my classes." Who is this bold bitch and where has she been my whole life? I could've used her around.

The bushy eyebrows raise. My dear BEBE. "I guess that's fair, yeah. Are you sure? It's fantasy and the world-building is a bit excessive, and I'm pretty sure I just info-dump at the beginning for thirty pages."

Shit. He's adorable.

"Painting for writing. That's the only deal I'll take."

"Noah!" An older feminine voice with a touch of an Italian accent calls.

I turn toward the sound.

Approaching us is a tiny woman who must be Nonna Ricci. I'd bet all the money I don't have on it. She's wearing a white chef's coat slathered in old red sauce stains and her gray hair is up in a hairnet. Her arms are open, already anticipating a hug.

Noah shoots me a smile as if to say "whoops" and scrambles his long limbs out of his chair to stand and embrace her. I suppress a chuckle at their height difference. In paying attention to his lankiness—what up, Octopus Daddy—I've accidentally ignored his height. I can't even guesstimate, but he seems to clear six feet with inches to spare.

"Who is this?" The question from Nonna Ricci is accompanied by an elbow nudge into Noah's side.

I stand, because I'm apparently meeting Noah's surrogate grandmother now. I'm prepared for this. Totally.

"I'm Hazel, it's nice to meet you." Before I can stick a hand out, I'm swept into a bone-crushing hug. I'm much closer to her height, so I'm not breaking my back in half like Noah was.

"I'm Nonna Ricci—and I am so pleased to meet you, Hazel. Noah hasn't brought anyone home before."

"Nonna!" Noah's face is bright-ass red.

Is it bad that I'm okay with it? Considering how red I've been in the two interactions we've had, it's about damn time he gets embarrassed. Plus, he's somehow even more attractive when he's embarrassed.

Nonna just grins at me, patting my shoulder. "I hope you enjoy the food. I'll talk to you later, Angelo."

"Angelo?" I ask as Noah and I sit back down.

"Angel. She calls Benji and I that."

If anything cuter happens on this date, I think I'm actually going to self combust. I'm a witch, I could probably do it.

Noah insists on paying the bill, despite me trying to pay for myself. It's only after that I remember I haven't been paid yet.

Thank God chivalry isn't dead.

With a wave to Nonna Ricci—plus at least five to-go boxes for her "Angelo"—Noah escorts me out with a hand on the small of my back.

"I had a really nice time, Hazel," Noah says as we walk to my car.

"I did, too. Thank you for inviting me. I think I may be full for days." That's such a lie. I'll be craving ice cream by the time I get home.

"Nonna Ricci's pasta can't be beat. Everyone should experience it at least once."

I laugh, rubbing my arms. I wish I'd brought a light jacket. "It better not be the last time I get her food. I don't think I'll be able to look at alfredo the same way again."

His eyes—almost midnight-black in the autumn evening—regard me as if I've said something momentous. "I hope it's not. I hope you come back."

I stop in front of my car and turn to him. The air grows thicker with each breath until it's like I'm suffocating in his gaze. He's pulled in by invisible strings, until my back is against the vehicle and his body is so close a buzz simmers underneath my skin like a gentle tickle.

"I'll come back." The words seem so much louder in the quiet bubble we've fallen into.

Noah's hand grasps mine, the electric current almost familiar—comforting—now, and brings it to his lips. The gentle rasp of his stubble contrasts the smoothness of his lips as they press against my skin.

Legs? I don't have legs. I just have jelly. Thank God I'm pressed against this car or I would've fallen down.

"I'll call you?" he asks, keeping my hand in his.

I nod, not trusting my voice.

"Goodnight, Hazel. Let me know you got home safely, okay?"

I nod again, vigorously. Embarrassingly vigorously. Just like I do everything. Just call me Hot Mess Hazel.

CHAPTER 6
ROSES

An entire Sunday lies before me, and I have nothing to do. No one to answer to, no one to please, no one. I can do whatever I want.

And I want magic.

The smell of it, the way it flows over my skin, the all-encompassing *warmth* of it. There is no comparable feeling. There's nothing on this Earth that can recreate the overwhelming sense of peace and calm.

And I've only done one spell.

Household Spells for Beginners sits on my glass coffee table, beckoning me like an old friend. My hand skitters over the old leather.

"What new things can you teach me? What doors can you open for me?" I ask the air around me. I shake my head.

Air can't answer.

This time I'm going to read more of the set up, and not just jump into the first spell I find. I want to do this right. The font is swirly, exaggerated, but still surprisingly legible. The pages crackle as I turn them.

This version is well loved.

Before you embark on your magical journey, it is imperative that you prepare your space. While spells don't require an altar—and many witches don't use one once they become more connected with their magic—it can be a grounding space for the new witch. Create your altar with your magic in mind. Candles, herbs, and crystals can all enhance your own connection to magic and your element. Experiment and find what resonates within you.

ALTARS? ELEMENTS? CRYSTALS? I'M NOT EVEN PAST THE FIRST page and I'm already in over my head. I wish I had some basis of understanding, some bulk of knowledge I could pull from, but I'm just shooting in the dark. All because of whatever happened to my father. All because my mother couldn't handle it and decided the best way to move forward was to cut us off from a huge part of who we are. To isolate us.

A frustrated growl rips out of me. I'm so *sick* of being isolated and small.

I need help. I need guidance.

I need Grandma.

My hand blindly searches along the couch until I find my phone threatening to fall behind the cushions.

> Hazel: Grandma, I wanted to try out my spells but the book says something about an altar? And elements?

I will be entirely unsurprised if she tells me to wait until Monday to discuss training, as she called it. But I want it now. Despite not understanding half of what this page says, I feel a pull in my gut. The breeze from the open window ruffles my hair.

> Grandma: Meet me downstairs in half an hour.

That's even better than I was expecting.

I jump up from the couch and bound into my bedroom, brushing the tangled mass that is my hair.

Grandma is fantastic, but she can also be savage. It's where Laura gets it from.

I grab my keys from the counter and wander downstairs to the shop a few minutes early. Even with the lights off and the silence hanging in the air, the store is still warm and inviting. With all the occult items in here, and considering how I'm terrified of my mother's basement, which contains no witchy things, I'd expected it to be scarier.

My fingers trail along the candles. Scented and unscented. Is my magic more an unscented candle or a scented candle?

That's something I'd never thought I'd consider.

The book said to find what *resonates* with me. How do I figure out what resonates with me? Is there a tingly feeling? A little witchy voice in my head that will tell me which one is right?

"Starting without me?"

I jump so high I swear I float a little at the proximity of Grandma's voice. I turn to find her right behind me, a twinkle of mischief in her eyes.

My hand lands on my chest, feeling the erratic beat. "You scared the shit out of me, Grandma."

She *tsks* at me. "No one should be able to sneak up on a witch. But we'll fix that."

Thanks for that.

"Before you start your altar, you need to agree to a training schedule," she continues. "Practicing with spells on your own is all well and good, but without true training you won't get far. Are you willing to agree to three times a week?"

I nod without thinking about it. I don't need to think about it. I want to train and I want to learn. I want everything I missed out on. The frustration from earlier threatens to bubble up again, simmering slowly under my skin. I didn't miss out on anything, it was stolen from me.

If I don't see my mother again, it'll be too soon.

"Where did you go?" Grandma asks.

I shake my head, trying to physically dust off the anger. "It doesn't matter. I'll train three times a week. What do I need?"

She raises a skeptical eyebrow, but doesn't say a word. She gestures to the candles I was looking through.

My fingers trail over them, and I eye the different sizes and colors, breathe in the different scents. My hand stops on one. It's unscented and carved in the shape of a large white rose.

When I was four years old, it was my first Valentine's Day with a little sister. Admittedly, I didn't love that the attention of my parents was now split between the two of us. I was very happy being an only child up to then. My father noticed—of course—and asked me to be his valentine. He brought me home a big, fluffy bouquet of roses and took me out to dinner.

Just the two of us.

These are the candles I want. Roses, for my father. For the man who saw his daughter for who she was, and provided what she didn't know how to ask for.

"This one."

"A good choice. Color is important to candle magic. White represents new beginnings, which this certainly is for you. Take a few and put them in here." She hands me a small bag.

I put four of the candles into my bag and continue toward the herbs, like the book said. Unfortunately, there are even more choices here.

Awesome.

Each herb is labeled with an explanation of its magical proper-ties. Oh Grandma, you saint.

Angelica, protects the home and garden.

Chamomile, attracts money, protects the home, and aids meditation.

Yellow Dock, aids in spells for happy homes.

That seems like the perfect mix for me. A few sprigs of each go into the bag.

"Does a coffee table count as an actual altar, or do I need something fancy?" Possibly a stupid question, but my only experience with witch-craft is sneaking old episodes of *Charmed* when Mom was asleep.

Grandma snorts, following behind me. "An altar is what you make it. Some are more simple, using coffee tables and such. Some get custom altars made. It's quite unique to the person."

Not entirely helpful, but it works. My feet carry me through the aisles, and I hope something will speak to me.

I stop at the crystals. They're bound to be helpful, right?

Onyx, for focus and discipline.

Amber, for warmth and well-being.

Sodalite, for insight and clarity.

Quartz, for manifesting and improving the power of the other stones.

Two of each make their way into my bag.

An itch crawls along my spine, telling me to go back upstairs. That I'm ready and it's time. All I have to rely on is my intuition, so I lift my gaze to Grandma.

"I think I'm ready?" I can't help the question. It was meant to be a statement, but I'm fully prepared for her to tell me I've missed something imperative.

She wordlessly gestures for my bag, and slowly goes through the items as I shuffle from foot to foot.

After what feels like three thousand years, she finally nods. "I think this is a good starting point."

My breath escapes in a relieved whoosh. My instincts may be able to carry me through the awkward beginner stage better than I initially thought.

"You can go upstairs and experiment on your own for today. Training starts Tuesday. Tuesday, Thursday, and Sunday will be our schedule, each evening after dinner." She smiles. "Now go. Have fun, and I'll see you first thing tomorrow."

I kiss her cheek and turn to leave without a second look.

There's a chill in the air as I open the apartment door. It brushes past me purposefully, reassuringly. It raises goosebumps on my skin and settles my nerves all at once; my head is clear.

Thank you, whatever that was.

Settling down on the couch, I empty the contents of my bag on the coffee table. I'm not sure how to arrange the items, so I guess I'll just figure out what looks good to me. I place the spellbook in the middle and arrange the four candles around it in a circle. The crystals go between the candles, and the herbs surround the book.

It's rough, but it works. I light the candles using an old matchbook I found in the kitchen cabinet and open the book.

Dishes taking up too much of your precious time? Instead of leaving them in the sink to 'soak' overnight and hoping someone else tends to them—clean them in a flash!

WELL, THEN. I HAVE A DIRTY COFFEE MUG FROM THIS MORNING, SO why not?

"Purgo Catino," I say. Of course, nothing happens.

Nothing happened the first few times with the other spell. What was it that Grandma told me to do? Breathe, relax, let the magic guide me.

Or something. I wasn't listening when she said it before.

I close my eyes and breathe. The scent of the herbs fills my nose and I lift my hands to feel the gentle heat from the candles.

"Purgo Catino," I repeat.

I open my eyes to a clean mug.

CHAPTER 7

MONDAY ALWAYS COMES TOO SOON

Noah: Thinking about you this morning. When can
I see you again?

A text from Noah wakes me up better on a Monday than coffee ever could. It's a butterfly-esque fluttering in my lower belly that has me betting I could float through the rest of the day. Caffeine just doesn't do the same thing.

I take a sip of the rich, over-creamed liquid I brought in a mug from upstairs. I'm sorry coffee, my love. I didn't mean it.

I wipe off the glass countertop, clearing some of the dust that settled over the weekend. I was literally just in here last night and there's already dust.

Hazel: I'm pretty flexible. When are you free?

That's a lie. I can't even do the splits without wanting to cry. Laura, on the other hand, did gymnastics for years and can still do a jump-up-in-the-air-and-do-some-twirls-or-something handspring.

Noah: Can I see you tonight? I have a favorite
bookstore I'd love to take you to.

A favorite bookstore? He may be actual sunshine in human form. Granted, he's a writer, so I'm not surprised his kink is books, but I can absolutely get on board.

> Hazel: That sounds perfect. Send me the address and we can meet after work.

Speaking of books. Is there anything in one of these books about the electric current between Noah and I? Or about my dreams? Dreaming about moments that didn't happen surrounding my father's death sounds pretty witchy woo-woo to me.

I'm too chickenshit to ask Grandma. I want to know about the dreams, but I don't want to know. My throat closes up at the thought of actually verbalizing it, not to mention what Grandma would think.

As far as Noah goes, I'm scared partially because I'm convinced she'd know exactly what it is, and partially because I know for a fact she'd have questions about Noah. And I'm enjoying keeping his existence to myself for now.

Laura will sniff him out sooner than later anyway. Hell, she was there when I met him. I'm surprised she hasn't sniffed him out already. She's like a bloodhound when it comes to men.

My eyes flit over the books on the shelf. What am I even looking for? *Electric Currents Between Random People*? I'm sure there's a book with that title. Definitely.

Ugh.

Rosie jumps up on the shelf in front of me and knocks a book toward me.

The Women of The Pruitt Line. Well, hello there. Who are you?

I scratch behind her ears until she purrs, pull the book off the shelf, and examine the back. A comprehensive family tree with biographies of the Pruitt line all the way to Salem.

We came from Salem?

How do I know *nothing* about my family history? Rage boils in my chest, threatening to burn up my throat and into my mouth.

A breeze rustles my auburn hair as I stand there attempting to control my breathing. Breathe in, breathe out.

Traitor. Liar. Controlling bitch.

"That's something every Pruitt woman should read," Grandma says, interrupting my thoughts. "We have a very interesting story."

"Do we? I had no idea." Venom drips from every word as I clutch the book to my chest as if it were my very life in my hands.

She sighs, putting her hand on my arm. Her bangles jangle with the motion. "You have every right to be angry. You have every right to feel the way you do. Just remember not to let the anger eat at you. Anger can turn us into someone we no longer recognize."

I nod, walking back to the counter. Do I want anger to eat at me and twist me into something evil and bitter? No. But damn is it an uphill battle right now.

The book makes a *thunk* as I drop it on the counter next to the cash register. It's heavy and imposing, the leather cover decorated with flowers and embossed cursive text.

The pages slightly stick together as I open the book. It's been a while since anyone has read it. With delicate motions, I turn to the first real page.

Elizabeth Pruitt, 1672–1692

THAT NOW ALMOST FAMILIAR SCENT OF A FRESH RAINSTORM WASHES over me as I look at the name. Magic. As if her very essence has been shared with me through these pages.

The official beginning of our line, or at least the first record of it. It all starts with Elizabeth.

Is Grandma named after her? I always thought my middle name came from Grandma, but does it come from this woman?

I settle on my bar stool and prepare myself for the story of Elizabeth Pruitt, first of her name.

CHAPTER 8

ELIZABETH PRUITT

ELIZABETH PRUITT WAS BORN IN SALEM, MASSACHUSETTS IN 1672. SHE IS THE FIRST DOCUMENTED CASE OF WITCHCRAFT IN THE PRUITT FAMILY LINE, AND AS SUCH IS CONSIDERED THE ORIGINAL MATRIARCH OF THE FAMILY. SINCE ELIZABETH, EVERY FEMALE BORN HAS BEEN BLESSED WITH MAGIC.

HER PARENTS WERE GEORGE AND DOROTHY, AND IT IS UNKNOWN IF EITHER POSSESSED MAGIC. ELIZABETH NEVER MENTIONS IT IN HER JOURNALS—SHE ONLY SPEAKS OF HER OWN EXPERIENCES WITH MAGIC, STARTING AT THE AGE OF TWELVE. IT'S BEEN ASSUMED THAT THIS CORRESPONDS WITH HER FIRST COURSE.

THESE JOURNALS ARE PUBLISHED SEPARATELY.

HER FAMILY WAS SEEMINGLY RESPECTED IN THE COMMUNITY AND HAD MORE THAN ENOUGH TO PROVIDE FOR THEMSELVES. AS THEIR ONLY CHILD, ELIZABETH DESCRIBES HERSELF AS BEING DOTED UPON BY HER PARENTS AND HAVING A LOVING, YET FORMAL, RELATIONSHIP WITH THEM.

AT TWELVE, ELIZABETH BEGAN EXPERIMENTING WITH HER NEW BLESSING OF MAGIC. IT FIRST MANIFESTED IN THE FORM OF TELEKINESIS, LATER REDEFINED AS A SPECIAL CONNECTION WITH THE AIR ELEMENT. SHE EXPANDED HER SKILLS QUICKLY, COMING UP WITH MANY OF THE SPELLS STILL USED TODAY.

When Elizabeth was seventeen she met James Lawson, who was a traveling merchant. Their courtship was a quick affair and they were married within the year. Elizabeth describes him as her "true love" in her journals and their connection as "like the buzzing of bees."

Around the time Elizabeth was nineteen, whispers about witchcraft were growing. Elizabeth was unaware of anyone else in Salem having powers, but never discussed them with anyone. It has been revealed by looking at other journals from the time that there were, in fact, other witches. It's unsurprising they did not reveal themselves—presumably an attempt to protect their lives and families.

At the same time, Elizabeth became pregnant with her only child, a daughter she would name Abigail. Because of the growing fear and resentment of witchcraft, Elizabeth had her daughter in secret and swore James to an oath that if Elizabeth were to be arrested, he would take Abigail and leave Salem forever.

It was this oath that saved the Pruitt line.

Elizabeth was formally charged in 1692; her accuser was never revealed. Because of the promise James made, he left immediately with the infant Abigail, and Elizabeth was able to spin the tale that he left her because of the accusations against her.

No one ever learned of Abigail's existence.

Elizabeth was burned at the stake in 1693 Upon her stake, she swore that with each woman, her line would strengthen. This oath has held, as each generation has built upon the foundation she laid.

James and Abigail learned of her fate a few years later when James came through looking for news. He never remarried.

CHAPTER 9
OPENING THE FLOODGATES

I'm a ghost as I go about the rest of my day.

Elizabeth was *murdered*, her child ripped away from her, and James was forced to live the rest of his life alone.

Raise a child alone.

And what of Abigail? She never even got to have any sort of relationship with her mother. I may be livid with my mother, but at least I have memories of her. I can go yell at her right now if I want to.

I kind of want to.

Elizabeth would never treat Abigail this way. Dad would never treat me this way. I hiccup as a frustrated tear slips down my cheek.

"The past is the past. All we can do is learn from it," Grandma says, taking the book from where it rests on the countertop.

"I suppose."

She sighs as she places the book back in its original spot on the shelf. Rosie jumps onto her shoulder from her perch. "It's an awful thing that happened. There are other awful things that happened to our family, and there are beautiful things that happened to our family. Just like every other family in the world. If anything, sweetheart, remember that. Remember that we have a limited time on this Earth, and we can't always control how our stories turn. All we can do is try to do our best to enjoy the time we have. Spend time with the people we love. Do the things that make us happy."

She's right. As usual.

That's what I'm doing now. Spending my time learning magic, spending time with Laura and Grandma, and hopefully spending time with Noah. Compared to spending all my days and nights catering to Laura, catering to my mother's emotions, and sketching? It's not even a contest.

"Do you have questions?" she asks. "Now that you've gotten a small taste of magic, and of our family history?"

A frustrated chuckle forces its way out of my overstimulated body. "Only about a million."

"Come. Let's go sit down in my office and discuss some basics, so you're ready for your first magic lesson tomorrow."

I follow her lavender- and smoke-scented, muumuu-clad form through the curtains into her plant sanctuary. She gestures to one of the plushy armchairs and I sink into the green paisley one.

"Okay, first." I sit as straight as I can, unleashing the bottled-up rambling. "What in the heck is the deal with the elements thing? I keep seeing it referenced everywhere. Are we talking about the periodic table or what?"

"I'm surprised you remember the periodic table, considering how you did in chemistry." She eyes me over the lip of her teacup. "No, not those elements. The basic elements of life: fire, earth, water, and air. Every witch connects with one element, and that is how the majority of their magic is harnessed."

"How do you find out what your element is?"

She places the steaming cup on its matching saucer. "Usually after puberty the element will reveal itself. If a witch is being nurtured and properly trained this can happen quickly; if magic is being repressed it can be a lot more difficult to connect."

Add that to the list of things I'm fucking pissed at my mom about. "Mom's element?"

"Water. If you remember the light bulb incident from last week . . . it exploded in a bunch of water." A sad smile stretches across her lips. "She used to make these beautiful water orbs full of light in the evenings. When she and I would have picnics outside to watch the stars."

It's impossible for me to imagine them as mother and daughter. As a loving family unit. Part of my heart breaks watching my grandma hurt.

She shakes her head. "Anyway. It makes sense that you have not connected with your element yet. You wouldn't know to look for it, and you've been repressing your magic. I'm sure once we start training it will come to you quickly."

"What about Elizabeth? How did her magic come to her when she didn't know what she was? And are you named after her? You don't talk about your parents much, why would they name you after someone who had such a horrible life?"

"I should've known better than to open the floodgates with you," she chuckles, no actual annoyance in her tone. "Elizabeth wasn't actively repressing her magic, she just didn't know it existed. You have to take into account that magic was something people were more aware of at that time, even if it was for negative reasons."

Okay, yeah, that makes sense. I lean back, folding my knees up to my chest. Maybe I understand the plushy chairs now.

"As for my parents." She pauses. "They weren't bad people. Just not people meant to be parents. They loved me as much as they could, but the only reason they had me was to continue the lineage. Duty called and they answered. It's why they named me Elizabeth. My mother used to say that I carried the future of the line in me."

"That's a lot of pressure."

"It certainly was. Then I met . . . Well, I had your mother, and I didn't want her around that. So she and I stole away to a small town in Ohio and made a life for ourselves. Almost like James and Abigail in a way."

I know not to ask about my grandfather. Even Mom protected Grandma by not talking about him. Whoever he was—is—he is a non-starter.

"And on that note." She slaps her knees. "You should go upstairs early. You certainly won't be able to concentrate after all that, and it's only an hour before closing."

"Are you sure, Grandma? I don't want to leave you to fend on your own."

"What, with all of the customers chomping at my curtain?" She smiles. "Go. Do something that makes you happy."

I plan on doing exactly that.

CHAPTER 10
BOOKSTORE BOYS

The bookstore is in a tiny building in Shaker Heights. Walking in, the floor is worn wood covered in multiple rugs that lead into the main area of the store. Skylights illuminate walls literally covered in books. The ceiling is painted a silky black.

Wait, was that a cat? This place has a *cat?*

That's it. I'm living here.

I should get a cat. Lord knows Rosie would probably enjoy the company. Although Grandma mentioned once that socializing adult cats can be a real bitch.

But really—what is a witch without a familiar?

"Hazel!" I turn to Noah as he walks in the front door. "Hi!"

I have to do my damnedest not to melt into a puddle. It may be a losing battle. His shaggy brown hair is especially tousled today, as if he's spent all Monday running his fingers through it.

I'd rather it was me tousling it.

"Hey!" I reply with a smile.

With a confidence that I really appreciate, he wraps me up in his arms. I barely meet his shoulder, my face pressed instead into the soft fabric of his cream-colored sweater. The electric shock is more of a gentle, consistent buzz under my skin as he holds me to him. His fingers tangle in my hair as I take a deep breath.

Bergamot, neroli, and green tangerine. And a hint of the weathered pages of a book.

Why in the shit am I able to identify those specific scents? It must be a witchy-herby thing.

"Have you ever been here before?" he asks as he pulls back from the hug. I was right, he can wrap those lanky limbs around me fewer times than I'd like.

"I haven't. Why don't you show me around?"

Okay, Confident Hazel. Don't know who you are, but I'm glad you've made an appearance.

He takes my hand in his, the gentle buzz still fizzling, and leads me toward one of the walls filled with books.

"What are your favorite genres? Do you enjoy reading?" he asks, long fingers thumbing through different titles.

Why yes, Noah, I love reading. Just today I was reading about the premature grisly murder of my family member.

That may be a little heavy for a second date.

Is perusing a bookshop technically a second date? Or is it just a hang? What's a hang? Is there a difference between a date and a hang? I'm so woefully unprepared.

"I love reading. I'm honestly all over the place. I've read thriller, fantasy, historical fiction, romance. It just depends on my mood."

"You've read thriller? I've only seen the music video."

A startled laugh escapes me. "A fellow lover of horrible puns, I see."

He nods, grin so large I could just melt. "Yeah, but I'm the same way with books. I love all those genres. What did you expect, really? Only a book nerd would work at a publishing house."

"You're in luck. I like book nerds."

He scratches the back of his neck as a slight flush darkens his cheeks. "I think new arrivals are over here."

Sunshine. In. Human. Form. What guy would willingly admit to being open to the romance genre, let alone reading it actively? I appreciate his open-mindedness. Maybe if this continues and I have to drop the witch bomb . . . Well, maybe he'd be open-minded enough to listen.

"Cat!" I say as said cat jumps up on a table next to us.

Very astute, Hazel. Good job.

He chuckles. "That's Tubbs. He's the owner's cat, but he comes to the shop every day. Total tease. He hardly lets anyone pet him, but he loves to be up in your personal space regardless."

Regardless of Noah's warning, I must try to pet.

I reach out slowly, allowing Tubbs to smell my skin. With a very melodramatic sniff—he's a little prince for sure—he purrs and rubs his cheek against my palm. I scratch behind his ear and down his neck as the purring grows into a steady rumble. It vibrates in my chest, helping melt any lingering tension from earlier in the day. Maybe I'm a cat person.

"I've never seen him do that," Noah says. "And I come here at least twice a week."

I meet his gaze and my cheeks heat at the pure awe in his eyes. Like I'm some sort of magical creature.

"I guess I have the magic touch."

He squeezes my other hand in reply and a new electric current travels up my arm to my spine.

Is it this intense for him, too? Or is it just like he explained—a little shock?

"I'd like to pick out and buy you a book, if that's okay. I'd buy you flowers, but I genuinely know nothing about them and according to Nonna Ricci there's this whole *language* with flowers." His cheeks flush as he presses on, not even taking a breath. "But, books, I know books. I understand books. I can convey what I feel with books. Not that I'm trying to . . . I just think it'd be a really . . . I would like to buy you a book, Hazel."

I'd listen to him ramble for hours.

"I'd love that."

His face lights up with a grin so large the dimple in his chin shows. "Let me go pick something!"

Without a second word, he runs off toward the classics. With a smile, I turn back to Tubbs and give him more scratches.

He wants to buy me a book. A book he picks. A warmth starting in my chest settles all the way to my fingertips. I like how he rambles, how he wants to do this thing for me that is personal. It's not flowers, it's not chocolate, it's a language that he speaks specifically.

I don't think anyone has put that much effort into getting me a present before. Certainly not my mother.

"Hazel!"

My head jerks toward the now somehow familiar tone of Noah's voice. How long have I been standing here scratching this spoiled cat?

Said cat *mews* in my general direction and hops off the stack of books he was happily snoozing on.

Noah jogs up with a small bag in his hand. He hands it to me, his foot nervously tapping on the ground. "I hope you like it."

"I don't think it's possible for me not to," I reply, honestly. With trembling fingers, I pull out a brand-new special edition of *Pride and Prejudice.*

"That's, uh . . . my mom's favorite book," he says. "She used to lecture me and my brother constantly on communication because of Darcy. Told me that, whenever I met a woman I liked, I should write her letters and overshare because being emotionally stunted would end with you being rejected in the rain." A smile grows on his face as he speaks about her. "Plus, your sister kind of gives me Lydia vibes."

Tears prickle in the corners of my eyes, blurring the black and floral cover.

Is this what being chosen feels like?

I swallow around the ache in my chest. "Thank you. I'll treasure it for the rest of my life."

～

MY NEW BOOK SITS HEAVILY IN MY PURSE AS NOAH AND I WALK back toward the bookshop from the ice cream parlor. I knew the moment he suggested it, I wouldn't be able to resist. Plus the walk gave me a minute to put the overwhelming emotions I don't have names for away.

Chocolate-chip cookie dough ice cream slides over my tongue and I suppress a full body shiver. It's the best kind of ice cream, and I will throw hands over this.

"May I walk you to your car?" Noah asks, licking at his mint chocolate-chip cone. The way he flattens his tongue as he . . .

Is it hot out here?

"Oh, I took a ride share," I reply. It would have been suspicious if I'd asked to borrow Grandma's car again and I wasn't ready for her questions.

He turns to me, forcing me to meet his dark brown eyes. I swear I could get lost in that purposeful gaze. "Do you want me to give you a ride home?"

I'd love to give you a ride.

Shit, Hazel, hold it together.

"Are you sure it wouldn't be too out of the way? I live in Chagrin Falls and I know you have work tomorrow."

Brick storefronts pass us by as we walk through the shopping district of Shaker Heights. People are out enjoying the fall weather with their dogs and families, laughter and barking filling the spaces in our conversation.

"I'd be happy to drive you. But, it's completely up to you. Whatever you feel comfortable with."

"Then I'd love a ride home."

We discard the remains of our desserts and he leads me to his car, opening the passenger-side door of the gray sedan. The car smells like him. An intense, unfiltered version of his scent—bergamot, neroli, green tangerine, and weathered book pages—that just makes me want to roll around on the leather seats, soaking it in.

Which would be very weird, so I don't do that.

He slides into the driver's seat with that quiet confidence I've come to appreciate. I'm honestly surprised his lanky features all *fit* in the car.

"What's your address?" He pulls out his phone. I tell him the address of the shop and he sets his phone on the holder on the dash.

He wraps his arm around the back of my seat as he turns his head to pull out of the parking space, and even the proximity of it causes anticipation to build in my gut.

"What plans do you have for the rest of the week? Anything fun?" he asks, the arm around the back of my seat coming down to the armrest between us.

It's just lying there, palm up. Almost like he's waiting for me to link our fingers together.

So I do.

"Not really. Just working in the shop and then teaching my class on Wednesday."

"The shop? I don't think you've mentioned the shop." He turns to me just a little, keeping most of his focus on the road.

Shit. How do I explain that I work in an occult shop without making myself sound like an absolute weirdo? Considering I *am* a complete weirdo, maybe I should just go with it.

"My grandma owns a shop in downtown Chagrin. It's called The Cat's Cradle. I work there during the week."

He shakes his head. "Never heard of it. Is it a pet supply thing? Is that why you're so good with animals?"

It would be so easy to lie to him. So easy to slip into being a normal human. And while I don't plan on telling him about the witchy thing for at least a while, that doesn't mean I want to be a liar. I want to be as much of myself as I can with him.

"No. It, uh . . ." You won't have a real relationship with him if you lie, Hazel. "Grandma sells a lot of magic things."

Descriptive.

His head cocks slightly. "Like, for magicians?"

This isn't going well. "I guess they could use some of it? But no. It's more witchcraft."

"Witchcraft?" He says the word slowly, as if he's making sure that's what I said.

"Yeah. Crystals, herbs, books. A bunch of other weird stuff, too."

I fully expect Noah to laugh, drop me off, and then block my phone number. I wouldn't necessarily blame him.

"Interesting. That's pretty unique. Do you believe in that?" His body hasn't tensed, he's still holding my hand. For all intents and purposes, he's remained perfectly neutral.

Despite it all, I'm not sure how to answer the question. Do I believe in the social media craze of healing crystals instead of medicine? No. Do I believe that humans can do witchcraft? Also no. But, do I technically believe in witchcraft and that I'm a witch?

Of course.

But, I'm not ready to tell him I'm a witch. I'm not ready to reveal a part of me that I'm only just now discovering. It's mine. At least for now.

"No. That's more of my Grandma's thing. But the store is warm and welcoming, and the people who shop there are kind. It feels like home."

His smile brightens the car. "That's really nice you have that. Everyone deserves somewhere that feels like home."

I squeeze his hand, the comforting electric fizz traveling over my skin. I could get used to this.

To him, and our electric connection.

The car slows in front of the shop as he pulls into a spot. The air is thick with expectation. Is he going to kiss me? Am I supposed to ask him to come up?

As if he knows, as if he can hear me, he gets out of the car and walks around to open the passenger door for me. Ever the gentleman.

The fall air ruffles the trees around us, creating a swirl of crisp golden and red leaves as he pulls me close. I lick my lips and his eyes track the motion, one hand on the small of my back.

His other hand cups my cheek, thumb rubbing along my skin.

The smallest spark zaps along the trail. I lean into the touch, eyes closing.

My eyes fly open at the first press of his lips against mine. It's tentative, questioning. His full lips press for just a second against mine before he pulls away.

A shy smile plays on his face and I want to kiss it away.

I just *want*. The very center of my chest aches and pounds like it's trying to leap toward him.

I lean onto the tips of my toes and press a kiss to the corner of his mouth. His smile grows as he nuzzles his nose against mine and sinks into a new kiss. His mouth is still soft against mine, gentle, as he guides me.

With every second, the awareness that it's Noah—my sweet, nervous-talking, bookish, *Warhammer*-mini-collecting nerd—heightens every single one of my senses. Everything is more. More than I've ever felt.

The hand on my cheek drags back, getting tangled in my tresses and I have to grab onto his sweater at the shoulders just to keep myself from melting into the ground.

Noah grips my hair firmly and tilts my head so he has better access, his teeth gently grazing my bottom lip. His stubble scratches against my skin, amplifying the electrical surge that's lighting my skin on fire.

He pulls just a little on the too-hard side and I accidentally moan into the kiss, unable to help myself. The sound pulls a matching groan out of Noah as he pulls my body even closer.

"Hazel."

I whimper at the way he says my name. Like he's desperately thirsty and I'm the only drink of water for miles. Like he's been denied food for days and I'm a thick, juicy steak.

"Yeah?"

"I should . . ." He licks his lips. They're rosy and swollen from kissing and I can't stop staring at them. "I should let you go upstairs."

The hands still desperately clinging to my body say otherwise.

"Why?" I'm still staring at his mouth.

He takes a deep breath, leaning his forehead against mine. "Because it's a weeknight and I have work in the morning. And if I follow you up there, I don't know if I'd ever want to leave."

A breeze rushes by us and I nuzzle further into his warmth, away from the cold.

"I want . . ." I trail off.

He groans again, the sound reverberating through my body. "I want, too."

I sigh, pulling away the smallest amount. "Next time?"

He smiles, arms unwrapping from around me to hold my hands. "Next time."

CHAPTER II
WITCHES ROLLER DERBY

"Hazel? *Hazel!*"

"What?" I lift my eyes from my phone. From the text I've looked at fifty times since I woke up.

> Noah: Good morning beautiful. Have an amazing day.

I've been daydreaming about my kiss with Noah last night since I saw that text. And apparently Grandma talking to me isn't enough of a distraction to pull me out of my musings.

"Your head is full of fireflies, sweetheart. What has you in the clouds?" Grandma asks, leaning against the counter.

I swivel to face her in my little chair behind the cash register. "I'm not ready to talk about it yet. But it's good."

She smiles, lavender and smoke filling my nose. "Every woman is entitled to her privacy. I'm glad you're finding things that bring you joy."

"I am, too." I take her hand, the bangles on her wrist jangling. "Have I thanked you lately for doing all this for me?"

"There's no need to thank me. I would do anything for you—for all three of you. However, if you wish to do something kind for your Grandma, I have an errand that needs doing."

85

Sometimes I wonder how fiercely grandma loves mom. That's her daughter, but I've never met two more different people. Two people who enjoy riling each other up as much as they do.

They'd do anything for each other—except fix whatever it is that broke them.

"Whatever you need."

"I have a few orders that need to be delivered. Luckily, I have a few items that are ready for pick up at the witches' farmers' market, so I was going to go there to make my deliveries. I was wondering if you'd want to accompany me and make the deliveries so I can do my other tasks."

"The witches' what now?"

Witches have gatherings like farmer's markets and I'm only finding out about this now? Do we have fashion shows? A bowling league? A roller derby team? A book club?

"Close your mouth, sweetheart. You're a beautiful girl, but not when you gape," Grandma says.

I promptly shut my mouth. "I'd be happy to join you, Grandma. Will we close the shop for the day?"

She nods. "We leave in an hour."

With that, she turns on her heel and heads for her office.

"Wait!" I have to ask; if I don't, I run the risk of being murdered. "Can we bring Laura?"

Grandma laughs. "If you can convince your mother."

The fact that we're in our twenties and have to convince our *mother* to let us out is ridiculous.

Screw it. I'm not going to continue catering to my mother's control issues. I'm going directly to Laura.

Hazel: Wanna do something witchy with me?

Laura: I don't even need to know what you mean.
I'll be there. When?

Hazel: One hour. Come to the shop.

Laura: Thank you.

"So, where are we going?" Laura bounces up to me and Grandma right as Grandma's locking the front door of the shop. It's a seasonably warm afternoon and my belly is full of You're Good in Bread.

Life is good.

Grandma raises a brow as she gives Laura a hug. "Hazel didn't tell you?"

"I apparently didn't need to. Laura dropped everything and came running."

Laura sighs. "I'm not that desperate, Hazel!"

"You had me fooled." I laugh at the way her eyebrows crease. She deserves the ribbing after all I do for her.

"Let's get going, girls. Into the car." Grandma shepherds us into her car, waving her hands.

Laura scoffs. "We aren't going by broomstick? How lame!"

I snicker from the passenger seat as Grandma narrows her eyes. Being the favorite is so much fun.

WE DRIVE TO AN ABANDONED FIELD IN THE LITERAL MIDDLE OF nowhere. There is nothing, not even a stray haybale or bouncing tumbleweed. Just space.

"Are you sure you have the right place?" I ask, eyes raking over the emptiness.

Grandma raises a brow as she parks the car. "Do you really think magical creatures would meet somewhere that allows anyone to stumble upon them?"

Okay, so that's a good point. Humans wandering into a witches' market would probably be very, very bad. Horrible. Salem horrible.

We exit the vehicle and Laura comes up close. I'm her safe space, always have been. We follow Grandma as she confidently strides forward.

"Here. Follow me."

And she vanishes.

"Did she just—?" Laura grasps my hand in surprise. "So fucking cool."

Hands clasped, we follow her exact path and step directly into the market. The sounds and sights are almost disorienting in their immediacy. Like walking through a soundproof door.

There must be at least fifty stalls surrounded by all types of people in all manner of outfits ranging from distinctly human to . . . what I can only describe as witchy. Flowing muumuu-type numbers that are oddly enchanting.

The sun shines on dirt paths and the scent of herbs and smoke fills the air. Someone has a fire going and—oh, is that pork?

"Holy. Balls," Laura gasps.

"I couldn't have said it better myself."

"Girls." Grandma calls our attention. "This is the market. Witches and wizards who have wares to sell will set up a stall, just like any farmers' market or art show in the human world. There are markets like this all over the world, and this one services all of Northeast Ohio. You can expect anywhere from forty to one hundred and fifty booths depending on the time of year. As it's fall, we're starting to get into the slower months."

We nod at her, my sponge brain absorbing any and all information she's willing to give.

"Now, you will be making deliveries. Throwing you in the deep end is the best way to get you to learn your bearings. If you have questions about where someone is—ask! Maybe you'll meet someone new. Here is your basket. I have my own errands, so you'll be on your own. I trust you both to represent the shop, and the family, respectfully. I'll meet you back here in three hours."

Without waiting for a response, Grandma turns and glides off in that way only Grandma can. I'm a little surprised she didn't disappear in a cloud of smoke, to be honest.

"Who's first?" Laura's practically bouncing as I lift the blanket off the top.

The basket is filled to the brim with wrapped packages, each labeled with a person's name. I peer at one. "Someone named Lucinda Vale."

"Badass name. Do you think there's other things in the world? Not just witches. Like, vampires, werewolves, leprechauns . . . ?"

"Leprechauns?" I chuckle. "That's where you go after vampires and werewolves? Leprechauns?"

We walk leisurely through the booths, dirt soft underneath our feet. Grandma's right, it gives off major art festival vibes. That pork scent only intensifies as we wind further into the maze of artists, farmers, and clothiers.

"I always liked the idea of leprechauns. Just doling out luck and happiness."

I wrap my arm around her, the basket securely looped around my other elbow. "Let's find Lucinda."

I can't help spending too much time at each booth. With every delivery it's like I'm discovering something new. Even if it's just lettuce.

I'm thankful I chose to wear sneakers today. I cast a glance toward Laura's ruined high-heeled boots with a wince. The dirt is solid, thanks to the sunlight, but it's still getting everywhere.

"I can try to fix them with a spell later?" I ask. Half of our basket of deliveries are gone.

She stops walking. "You could do that?"

I can't quantify the look on her face. Is it . . . jealousy? No, Laura has never been jealous of me in her entire life. "Probably."

Part of me—a dark, twisty part that I almost don't want to give voice to—enjoys that maybe she is jealous. Just once.

"Anyway." The look disappears from her face just as quickly as it arrived. Another of her famous talents. "I didn't know witches gathered like this. Mom made it seem like something to be ashamed of, that everyone was ashamed of it. But all I see is pride. Who's next?"

I nod, digging through the basket for the next delivery. "Ash Cedar."

"That sounds more like a scented candle than a person."

"Brutal."

Laura laughs. "Although not the weirdest name I've heard since being here."

A dark, decidedly male, voice chuckles. "It's a family name."

Laura and I turn toward the speaker. Ash Cedar leans casually against the side of his booth, a subtle smirk on his young, handsome face. Jet-black hair hangs over his bright green eyes. Standing to his full height, he rolls his large shoulders.

He's built like a dramatic lumberjack—if the giant house crest ring on his hand is any indication. No man without a flair for being extra wears a ring that big.

I smile. "Sorry about that. We're a bit new to the magical world. I have your delivery from The Cat's Cradle."

"Lucky me." He walks around the table toward us, gaze bouncing between me and Laura. "I can't say I don't prefer you both, but you're not Elizabeth. New employees?"

"We're her granddaughters," Laura snaps.

I raise my eyebrows. Laura usually loves hot guys with the dangerous lumberjack vibe. Her instant distaste is surprising.

He grins, teeth glinting in the sunlight. "Now I see. You're the elusive hermit grandkids. Anyone else would know the Cedar family."

Laura snorts. "Someone's far up their own ass."

"I know I'm good at what I do, Goldilocks. It's just a fact." He turns to me with one last wink in Laura's direction. "Thank you for bringing my package."

I shake off the tension and hand him the carefully wrapped bag. "Of course."

My gaze is caught by the wood carvings on the table before me. They're all different shapes and sizes—animals, buildings, everything.

"My family and I carve wood. Everything from talismans to altars," he says with pride.

"Wait." Laura snorts. "Your last name is Cedar and you work with wood? Really?"

A flicker of annoyance mars his face for a moment, but he quickly relaxes. "And what is it you do, Goldilocks? Prance around judging others?"

There's no way I'm sticking around for whatever this is. I squeeze Laura's arm and walk toward a woman spinning wool on an old-school spinning wheel.

"What are you making?" I ask, mesmerized by the soothing rhythm of her actions.

"It will be a cloak. I make clothes for the colder months ahead."

My eyes trail along her wares—some scarves, hats, and gloves —as the sound of the wheel spinning continues along.

She sighs, a sound full of emotional fatigue. "Mostly I'm distracting myself."

It's not until now that I notice the pain in her face. The creases in her forehead, the partially dried lines of tears on her cheeks.

Without invitation, I sit on the ground next to her. "Are you all right?"

"My son was injured in a daemon attack last night." Her fingers never waver in her work. "He should be okay—eventually. But, it was close."

A *daemon?* Those are real? Why haven't I read about them? Why hasn't Grandma mentioned them?

"I see the confusion on your face. As with all things, there is good and bad. It's what balances the universe, despite the pain the bad causes," she says.

"Are altercations with daemons common?"

She shrugs. "It depends. Some of us like to hunt them, like my son. Some of us may live our whole lives without facing one."

"Why does your son hunt them?"

"They do a lot of harm. Tear families apart, and my son is one of those people who can't let that stand. He's a good boy, if not a bit reckless."

My blood burns. Could it have been a daemon that killed my father? Killed my family's chance at a life together? "How do you find one? How do you hunt them? Who was it that your son fought?"

Her face hardens. "You are best not to ask such things, girl. Go home to your family and leave daemons like Botis to those who know how to handle them."

I won't learn anything more from her. But a name is all I needed.

Botis.

He might not be whatever killed my father, but he's a daemon who hurts people. Breaks apart families. Causes damage that lasts for generations. And I have no problem training up for the specific purpose of getting rid of creatures like him.

And if one day I meet the thing that killed my dad . . . Well, then I'll be ready.

I stand and brush the grass and dirt off my jeans.

Laura and Ash are still . . . I don't even know how to classify what they're doing. Staring at each other. Dick measuring. Eye fucking. Whatever. But our three hours are almost up and I don't need to stare down the wrath of Grandma.

"Laura! We're leaving!" I call to her.

Her head whips to me, blonde hair cascading around her face and shoulders. The surprise on her face is evidence enough that she's lost herself in conversation with Ash. With a pointed glare in Ash's direction, she huffs and joins me.

"Not a word," she grumbles, crossing her arms.

"Yeah, yeah. I won't mention whatever that was." I chuckle at her pouting. "Let's go back to the entrance. Grandma should be there soon."

"Don't tell Grandma about Ash! The last thing I need is for her to make assumptions and ask a bunch of questions. He's obnoxious and I have no intention of ever seeing him again."

"My lips are sealed."

We walk in silence through the rest of the stalls. Thoughts of Botis overwhelm me. Any other day I'd be poking and prodding

Laura about Ash, but I can't clear my head. It's like a puzzle piece that I've been missing.

I can *help* people. I can have a purpose. I can use that knowledge to find whatever it is that killed dad.

Maybe someday I can even bring closure to my mother. To myself. To Laura. Is this closure what's been preventing us from connecting as a family all these years?

If I avenged my father, would Mom embrace magic again? Could she heal in a way that could open a real door to us for a relationship?

That's the question. Do I have the opportunity to fix my family?

Even if I'm not sure of the answer, the possibility is enough of a reason to try. I may get hurt in the process, but as Grandma says: I'd do anything for my family.

CHAPTER 12

COTTAGECORE

Grandma invites Laura and I for dinner with her friends at her home before my first magic lesson. Which gives me time to decide if I want to ask her about daemons or keep that to myself.

Would she support my desire to hunt them? I honestly have no clue at this point.

Those thoughts are overtaken by curiosity as we turn onto a dirt path in the forest. I've never been to Grandma's cottage.

When Grandpa left, Grandma bought the house I grew up in for her and Mom. She stayed there when Dad moved in, and when my parents had Laura and I. But once he died, she moved out.

No one ever told me why she moved out, despite me asking almost every day for two months. All I remember is the silence as she walked out the door with her bags already in her little car.

I can taste the tingle of magic in the air as we approach the cottage, proving that Grandma gets no unwanted visitors.

The cottage itself is straight out of a fairy tale. It's a two-story white-brick with wood accents and ivy climbing gracefully up the sides. It's a secluded paradise surrounded by a garden the likes of which I've never seen. Herbs, flowers, vegetables. Many I couldn't name.

"Damn, Grandma, this place is *amazing*," Laura says with a gust of breath from the back seat.

That's an understatement.

Grandma chuckles, pulling up next to her home. "Thank you. I've taken a lot of time crafting my space."

As we step out of the car, the scent of chrysanthemums and pansies dances around me, mixing with the fall leaves that sway in the breeze.

"Come, come." Grandma opens her forest-green front door and herds us into the house. "This is home."

Home is the cottagecore house of most wannabe-fairies' dreams. I expect a bunch of forest animals to be cleaning around the next corner. The wallpaper is a floral pattern on a green that matches the front door. The furniture is cozy, a mix of creams, browns, and wood. I look for the stereotypical knitting basket and find Rosie sleeping on it.

"I expect you both to assist me in preparing dinner—and tea afterward," Grandma says as she walks into the equally floral kitchen.

"Are you going to teach us how to do it magically?" Laura asks, getting into Grandma's personal space.

Grandma grins, rolling up the sleeves of her flowing dress. "It's the only way to cook, darlings. I will not, however, incur the wrath of your mother any more than I already have today, so Laura, you're only allowed to watch."

The pout is almost legendary. Laura doesn't fight it verbally, however—she simply walks over to the table and sits in one of the antique wood chairs. That same look is on her face from earlier. I wanted to call it jealousy, but it isn't that. At least not completely.

Grandma motions me over to stand before what would seem to be an ordinary cookbook if not for the warm, shimmery undulations of power leaking from it. It laps at my skin like a gentle breeze. It draws me closer.

My hand, almost of its own accord, reaches forward. The leather warms underneath my fingers as I stroke the cover. It's similar to *Household Spells*, but older. Worn. Beloved.

Grandma smiles fondly, warmth in her gaze. "My grandmother gave me this book when I was around your age, Hazel. She and her mother wrote it together as she grew up. It has been added to by my mother and by myself, and your mother as well. It is time it sees additions from the next generation."

"I have no idea what I'm doing," I whisper.

She nods. "No one does at first. That's why you have me to guide you."

I stand at her side as the sound of Laura chopping vegetables floats over us.

The chicken rests in a deep roasting pan, surrounded by potatoes and broth. With a wink, Grandma lifts her hands and rhythmically moves them over the bird.

Nothing happens. Is she just messing with me? She has to be.

Wait. No. The bird is shining? With each wave of her hands, a new layer of magic coats the meal. I didn't realize I could *see* magic, but there it is. It's an iridescent shine, a little thicker than air. You wouldn't notice if you weren't looking.

Another flick of her fingers and the vegetables fly in front of my face and into the roasting pan. Herbs fly in from the other direction. She murmurs a few words, and everything glows with an earthy warmth. A sunshine warmth that reminds me of a summer day. A crackle disturbs the air and the glow fades.

She nods and places the pan in the preheated oven.

"And I'll be able to do that?" I ask in awe. The way she was so casual . . . It's strange watching someone use magic as if it were part of their very essence, while I've been kept from it.

Grandma nods. "You will soon find that magic is as easy as breathing. You can *both* embrace this part of you, if you so choose."

Laura plays with a lock of her hair, refusing to meet Grandma's eye. "I'll go set the table."

My eyebrows raise as she leaves the room. She's never seemed so young; even when she was a little girl she was always precocious.

"Laura, my dear," Grandma says, following her. "You said in the car you had questions. I'll tell you anything you'd like to know that is in my power to share."

A grin breaks on Laura's face. "Anything?"

I squeeze her hand as we sit down, happy to see her smiling again. "You'll regret that, Grandma."

We sit together around the dinner table as the scent of cooking wafts in. Rosemary, thyme, and sage.

"So, first of all." Laura's face is all business. "If there's a witches' market, then that means there's communication between magical beings that doesn't involve humans. So, cough it up, Grandma. How do you all stay in touch?"

Good question, Laura. Damn.

"Well, we certainly don't use pigeons. This is the twenty-first century, Laura. We use social media like everyone else."

"There's little witchy pockets in our apps?" I ask.

Grandma laughs. Laughs! "Of course not. We have our own apps."

Laura's head cocks. "Wait. What?"

"We have our own apps. For protection, of course. No one wants Salem to happen again, and privacy is quite limited on human apps. I can show you both after dinner if you'd like."

Laura and I are nodding vigorously before Grandma stops speaking.

"Is there a witchy counterpart to every app?" I ask.

"I'm sure we've missed a few of the more ridiculous apps. But witches must make a living, too. We have tech witches, artistic witches, medical witches . . ." Grandma trails off with a smile. "There's a whole world out there. A world that has pride and embraces who they are."

The anger that lives under my skin threatens to flare. I've been denied this world for over a decade. Who knows the person I could have been if I'd been raised in the magical world? Who would I be if my powers had been encouraged, not suppressed?

Would I have friends? A purpose in life?

Grandma's eyebrows furrow as she reaches across the table to hold my clenched fist. "Breathe. There is no future in anger, only more anger."

I lock eyes with her, allowing her calm breathing to regulate my own. I can only control my decisions going forward, not my mother's decisions in the past.

"*Anyway,*" Laura says. "Are there magical dating apps? Because if there are, I need to know about it yesterday."

I laugh despite myself. Of course that's where Laura's brain goes first.

"There are dating apps, yes." Grandma rolls her eyes. "I will *not* be walking you through those."

My phone buzzes and I sneak a look under the table as Laura and Grandma banter back and forth.

> Noah: I hope you're doing well today. I'd love to see you on Friday, are you free?

Does he have perfect timing or does he have perfect timing? My heart threatens to leap free of my chest and into my phone.

> Hazel: I am very free. What do you have in mind?

Very free? Yikes.

> Noah: It's a surprise. I'll see you after work.

"Earth to Hazel?" Laura smirks.

Grandma shakes her head, a fond grin on her face. She stands and leaves, presumably to check on dinner.

"Do you need any help?" I call after her.

"Don't change the subject! Who are you texting? Is it that guy from the other night? Tell me everything, and don't leave out a single detail."

Well, I knew this day was coming. I couldn't keep Noah a secret forever, but I thought I had more than a week, at least. Although considering how nosey Laura is, I'm lucky I was able to keep him to myself for this long.

"Yes, it's the guy from the other night."

Laura squeals. "I *knew* you liked him! Spill all the beans!"

The clinking of dishes comes from the kitchen as Laura and I bend closer together over the table.

"His name is Noah."

"Noah is a hot name, but we already know he's *adorable*. How many times have you seen him? Have you . . . ?" She waggles her eyebrows. "Y'know?"

"*Laura,*" I hiss. "We are in Grandma's house and she hears everything."

A cackle comes from the kitchen over the oven beeping.

I raise an eyebrow at Laura. We're literally in the house of a witch, did Laura really think she wouldn't eavesdrop?

A genuine smile breaks on her face. "You aren't getting out of this conversation so easily. I won't forget."

If only I could be so lucky. I expect I'll be subjected to a full interrogation at the soonest possible time. Laura has never been able to ask me about a guy before—she must be practically salivating.

"As I was saying earlier," Grandma interrupts. "All magical apps can be found through the magical app store. Salem. It's impossible to find without another witch assisting you. You will now find it on your phones."

"The fun I'm going to have on the dating apps," Laura sighs wistfully. "If only you could be my wing woman."

A jolly knock patters the front door, saving me from Laura's imaginings of two sisters on the prowl.

"Coming in!" a familiar voice announces as the front door opens. Grandma emerges from the kitchen to greet four women around the same age as her. I recognize one as Dotty, the woman who came into the shop on my first day.

"Ladies, I'd like to introduce you to my granddaughters—Laura and Hazel. Girls, this is Dotty, Vera, Natalie, and Penny."

They're like the magical *Golden Girls*. Each one dressed more witchy than the next. It's a sea of silver-blue hair, chunky necklaces, and flowing, floral dresses. It's muumuu manor over here.

Dotty smiles at me, earrings clacking. "It's nice to see you again, dear."

Grandma claps her hands. "Let's eat!"

THE HEADLIGHTS OF GRANDMA'S CAR SLICE THROUGH THE NIGHT AS Laura and I sit in silence. She lent us her car, saying that one of her ladies would drop her at the shop for training so I could take Laura home first. I think they just wanted to gossip alone over tea for a little bit.

Grandma's car is doused in her scent—lavender and smoke—and it stings my nostrils with its intensity.

"Well, now that we're alone . . ." Laura was gazing out the window, but now turns to me. "I want the rundown on Noah."

I smile despite myself.

"Look at you," her voice is laced with awe. "You really like him."

My cheeks heat. "Yeah, yeah. What do you want to know about him?"

Laura huffs. "Literally anything! Where does he work? How many times have you gone out? Is he a good kisser? Have you let him bend you over your kitchen counter yet? Does he have any cute friends that don't drink as much as that one at the bar?"

Jesus.

"He works at a publishing house in Cleveland. We've gone out twice." I give her a pointed look. "I'm not setting you up with one of his friends."

"Way to ignore the actual questions I want answered, Hazel."

I sigh. "He's a wonderful kisser."

The shit-eating grin on her face is practically too big for the car.

"Calm down." I laugh. "You look ridiculous."

"I'm just excited for you. You've lived like a nun for the last twenty-five years and you deserve to have someone in your life who makes you happy." If I'm not mistaken, there's a little bit of guilt in my sister's eyes as she says that. "Even if you won't give me all the juicy details."

"In my defense, for the first thirteen of those years I thought boys had cooties."

Laura smiles. "Some boys do. Which is why you always use a condom."

"LAURA."

"Am I wrong? I'm not wrong. Sexual health is an important part of becoming sexually active. I had the exact same sex talk as you did and I'm telling you, surprise to literally no one, Mom left out a lot."

I'm going to drive us into a tree to escape this conversation. A really old, big tree that would kill us instantly.

"I'll drop you off at the shop, you can walk home," I say.

Laura's eyes drop to her lap, fingers twisting in a lock of her golden hair. "Are you never coming home again?"

It's the same reaction she had at Grandma's. The way she shrinks into herself, becomes almost timid . . . It's unlike her. Laura is loud, in your face, beautifully brash. And it scares me.

Is my being gone changing her?

"It's complicated. I have a lot of anger, and honestly, it's pretty obvious that Mom does, too. I think the space is good for us right now."

"She misses you. She refuses to talk about it because she's just as stubborn as you are, but she does miss you. She worries about you."

My throat constricts as my eyes prickle and burn. My emotions are a jumbled bundle of cords that I can't untangle. Anger, sadness, love—I can't make sense of it.

"I didn't say that to . . ." Laura pauses. "I don't want to guilt you into trying to talk to her. I just wanted you to know that she's not the stone wall she pretends to be."

I sigh. It's not her fault that she's caught in the middle of me and

Mom. She's never been in the middle of us, if anything I've always been in the middle. The protector. I can't be that person anymore, though. I can't protect Laura for the rest of her life. I have to start protecting myself.

"Laura, I love you. While I'd do anything for you—honestly—leave this alone."

"But Hazel—"

I cut her off with a hand on hers. "Leave it alone."

She nods, squeezing my hand.

The headlights illuminate the town square, and the gazebo covered in leaves in front of the shop. I park in the open spot right in front, giving her hand another gentle squeeze.

"I love you, too," she whispers.

Once we're on the sidewalk I pull her into a hug, the cold fall air chilling my bare arms.

"Do you want to stay the night? Slumber party?"

Despite knowing I can't protect her, I don't like the quietness. Part of me needs to know she's okay. Even though there's a risk that letting her into my space will eventually make it *her* space.

She shakes her head. "No. I need to go home. I'll text you tomorrow though, and I'll insist on a slumber party another night this week. Okay?"

"Okay, Laura."

I stand outside the shop, watching her until she turns down a side street.

I didn't get to ask Grandma about daemons, or anything, really. But for now, I'm much more concerned about Laura herself, and how every interaction with her is just a bit more awkward. A bit more uncomfortable.

I hate it.

CHAPTER 13

WATER, EARTH, AIR, FIRE

I push thoughts of Laura out of my mind and run upstairs to change into workout clothes. Which I only have because Laura went through a six-month yoga phase and insisted I do it with her. She bought me the clothes to guilt me into it.

I'm not sure what 'training' consists of, but considering witches all seem to wear flowy muumuus, I'm guessing jeans would not be the correct choice of clothing.

I descend the metal stairs at the back of the building and enter the back door of the shop. Grandma's office is empty, so I pull back the curtain.

The entire shop is cleared. The bookshelves are pushed against the walls and the counter is moved to the side.

In the middle of the clearing is Grandma, putting the finishing touches on her space. She's still in her flowing dress from dinner. I look down at myself.

Maybe the workout clothes were unnecessary.

"Before we begin," Grandma says, "you should know that magic training requires time and devotion. It is not a few words and a flick of the wrist like it was with that beginner spell. You must agree to dedicate yourself to this."

"I agree," I reply easily, quickly. "When do we start learning about fighting?"

Her face scrunches up. "Fighting? Fighting offensively takes years of practice. You don't even know the fundamentals of magic yet. One step at a time or you will trip over your own feet. If I'm to teach you, you will agree to the pace of training. You will not go searching for trouble. Promise, or go back upstairs."

Her tone brokers no argument.

"Okay, I promise." I can't meet her eyes.

Her gaze burns a hole in my skull. I can feel her searching my face. She doesn't trust me, doesn't believe me.

I wouldn't either.

"All right. Have you tried to connect with your magic, uncover your element?"

No, I've been daydreaming about kissing Noah.

"What's your element, Grandma?" I deflect.

"Earth." Her postures straightens with pride. "You've seen my plants. There's a reason why I'm known across the state for my herbs."

Huh. "I've never thought about that before."

"How do your spells manifest? How do they happen for you? What happens to your body, to the world around you? What do you smell, what do you sense?"

I stand in silence. I don't know.

"Does the ground shift beneath your feet? Do you feel the condensation in the air? Does it whip around you? Does heat lick up your spine? What do you *feel*, Hazel?"

A frustrated growl rumbles out from somewhere in the very pit of my body. "I don't know!"

She's not even pushing that hard but it feels like an attack on me as a person. On my inability to do something I was born to do. I don't know how to connect to my magic, and I think some part of me expected to pick it up in a snap—to inherently know exactly what to do.

Sure, I can move some dust. But if I can't connect to my element, then what am I doing?

Despite my outburst, her eyes remain kind. "Your homework will be to pay attention to the world around you as you interact with it. For now, we're going to focus on connecting with ourselves through meditation. That is how we can peel back the layers of stress and noise. We will connect to ourselves, and then to our element."

I fidget, my toes digging into my sneakers. I know I'm impatient. I also know that I apparently can't do anything without *connecting to my element*. It'll cause me more grief in the end if I don't commit and do this the right way. That's the only way I'll get further in my training and eventually take on daemons. And find out if one killed my dad.

So I can kill it.

"Okay."

"Sit," Grandma says, gesturing to the pillows in the center of the room. I follow her guidance, sitting opposite her with my legs crossed.

She holds her hands out and I take them. She leaves them between us, squeezing me slightly. A wave of calmness rushes through me at the motion.

"Center yourself. We start with the toes. Be aware of them, how they feel—and only them. How does the pillow press against them? How does the weight of your body feel on them?"

Okay, Grandma. Someone has some serious meditation chops.

"Then, the ankles. Breathe in, relax the muscle as you breathe out."

She addresses every inch of my body until I'm such a relaxed, blissful puddle I could fall over and go to sleep.

A breeze ruffles my hair and passes through me, into my bloodstream. It is the very essence of my ability to live, to thrive.

"How do you feel?" she asks.

A soft smile breaks. "At peace."

"What did you feel?"

"A breeze that calmed me." My eyes open.

"There was no breeze, Hazel." Her eyes twinkle. "I think we've found your element."

CHAPTER 14
FIVE HOURS AND TWENTY-SEVEN MINUTES

My foot taps against the counter rhythmically. My date with Noah starts in exactly five hours and twenty-seven minutes. And each second crawls slower than a tortoise. I have been waiting months, years, eons to see him.

Okay, it's only been a few days since our last date at the bookstore, but *ughhhhh* this Friday is dragging.

Grandma's suspiciously quiet in her little hidey-hole with Rosie and there hasn't been a customer in an hour.

I want to read another book—hopefully about daemons—but just because Grandma is quiet doesn't mean she's not watching. She knows all. And I don't want her to know this. Especially since I promised her I wouldn't go searching for trouble.

But I can't ignore the pull in my stomach telling me I need to keep working toward my goal. And the books have what I need.

I hop off the stool and meander my way toward the books, running my fingers along the spines. *The Women of The Pruitt Line* sits in exactly the same spot as last time, waiting for me to continue along our family tree.

Maybe one of my ancestors fought daemons and I can find some clarification that way?

Nestling the book in the crook of my elbow I allow myself to linger, eyes dancing over the spines. Spells, how-tos, alchemy, gardening, histories . . . fiction? Grandma wasn't lying, there seem to be magical writers and novelists.

Maybe the magical world could use one more artist.

Warlocks, Daemons, And Other Evil Beings.

Bingo. That's the book I want. That's the book I can't have. Slipping it underneath *The Women of The Pruitt Line*, and then another book underneath and pretending I grabbed it by accident wouldn't work either.

Grandma's too smart.

I'll come back for it when the time is right. When I know more about my element and more about witchcraft. When I know what I'm doing well enough to not get hurt and not alert Grandma.

I'm not going to risk my lessons for anything. Not yet.

CHAPTER 15
ABIGAIL PRUITT LAWSON

ABIGAIL PRUITT LAWSON WAS BORN IN SALEM, MASSACHUSETTS IN 1691. DESPITE BEING BORN TO ELIZABETH PRUITT, A KNOWN PRACTITIONER, ABIGAIL WASN'T EXPOSED TO THE CRAFT PERSONALLY. ELIZABETH SENT ABIGAIL AND ABIGAIL'S FATHER, JAMES LAWSON, AWAY WHEN ELIZABETH WAS CHARGED WITH WITCHCRAFT. ELIZABETH WAS BURNED AT THE STAKE BEFORE ABIGAIL'S SECOND BIRTHDAY.

JAMES LAWSON TOOK ABIGAIL TO NEW YORK AND RAISED HER THERE BY HIMSELF AS A WIDOWER. JAMES'S FAMILY WAS FROM NEW YORK, SO ABIGAIL WAS SURROUNDED BY FAMILY DESPITE NOT EVER GETTING TO KNOW HER MOTHER. ABIGAIL WAS CLOSE TO HER AUNT, CHARLOTTE, AND HER GRANDPARENTS, BERNARD AND VICTORIA.

WHEN ABIGAIL WAS TEN YEARS OLD, SHE ACCIDENTALLY LEVITATED FOOD WHEN SHE WAS HUNGRY. IT WAS THE FIRST MANIFESTATION OF HER MAGIC. JAMES WAS AWARE OF ELIZABETH'S POWERS, AND HAD BEEN WARNED BEFORE HER DEATH THAT THEIR DAUGHTER MAY SHARE THIS GIFT. ELIZABETH GAVE HIM A LETTER AND HER JOURNALS IN CASE ABIGAIL SHARED HER MAGIC.

THIS LETTER WAS ADDRESSED TO ABIGAIL, APOLOGIZING FOR HER ABSENCE AND EXPLAINING THE FOCUS ON SECRECY. THE JOURNALS OUTLINED EVERY SPELL OR DISCOVERY ELIZABETH HAD MADE

SO ABIGAIL WOULDN'T HAVE TO DISCOVER EVERYTHING ON HER OWN.

THESE JOURNALS BECAME THE BASIS OF OUR MODERN UNDERSTANDING OF MAGIC, HERALDED GLOBALLY AS THE FIRST RELIABLE RECORDS ON ELEMENT MANIPULATION AND EARLY SPELLWORK, AND IS WHAT ABIGAIL BUILT UPON DURING HER LIFETIME.

UNTIL HIS DYING DAY, JAMES PROTECTED HIS DAUGHTER AND ENCOURAGED HER HONING HER CRAFT. HE DIED OF OLD AGE WHEN ABIGAIL WAS FORTY YEARS OF AGE.

JUST AS ELIZABETH SWORE, ABIGAIL'S POWERS WERE MORE ADVANCED THAN HER OWN AND ABIGAIL TOOK TO THE CRAFT QUICKLY. WITH HER MOTHER'S JOURNALS AS GUIDANCE, ABIGAIL BECAME A TALENTED DAEMON HUNTER AND SPELLWEAVER. SHE DEVELOPED THE TECHNIQUE OF 'SCRYING'—USING MAGIC TO TRACK SOMEONE OR SOMETHING—AND USED IT TO PURSUE DAEMONS ACROSS THE STATE.

IN 1713, WHEN ABIGAIL WAS TWENTY-TWO YEARS OLD, SHE MET CHRISTOPHER BECKETT. IN HER OWN JOURNALS, WHICH WERE CONTINUATIONS OF HER MOTHER'S AND ALSO PUBLISHED SEPARATELY, SHE DESCRIBES HIM AS THE LOVE OF HER LIFE. THEIR CONNECTION WAS "BUZZING AS IF LIKE THE BEAT OF THE WINGS OF A BEE", AND THEY WERE WED WITHIN THE YEAR.

ABIGAIL WENT ON TO HAVE THREE CHILDREN—CHRISTOPHER, JAMES, AND ANNABELLE. ANNABELLE WAS THE ONLY CHILD TO INHERIT THE CRAFT.

ABIGAIL DIED OF DISEASE IN 1756 AT SIXTY-FIVE YEARS OLD, HER HUSBAND HAVING DIED A FEW YEARS PRIOR. ABIGAIL LIVED TO SEE HER LINE CONTINUED, TO MENTOR HER OWN DAUGHTER, AND TO SEE THE FIRST OF HER GRANDCHILDREN.

CHAPTER 16

STREEMZ AND CHILL

I close the book on Abigail Pruitt and sit back on my stool.

Scrying.

That's how I can track Botis, and that's how I can face whoever —or whatever—killed my father. Once I learn some offensive spells, so I know how to actually defeat those things. But that's details.

I have the beginnings of a plan, and that's enough.

And it's all the mental energy I can devote to it right now, because I get to see Noah in an hour and my heart is beating a million miles per second.

Just the thought of him—of our *spark*. The way his hand tightens in my hair and pulls just this side of pleasurable. I suppress a shiver.

I shift on the stool, a gentle ache settling low in my belly. I can hardly wait.

My phone buzzes on the counter, practically jumping across the glass.

Laura: Are you seeing Noah tonight?

It's the first time she's reached out since I watched her walk out of my car—even though she promised to text me the next day—and toward her house. What used to be our house. What's now their house.

> Hazel: I am. But if you need me, I can reschedule with him.

The ache doesn't like that plan, but the ache can wait a day.

> Laura: It's not an emergency. Enjoy a night with your guy. Can I see you tomorrow before your classes? Maybe we can get breakfast?

> Hazel: Absolutely. Pick me up at nine?

> Laura: I'll see you then.

She's too formal. Something has been wrong ever since our tense discussion in the car. Even mentioning Mom briefly caused a shift in the dynamic. I'm glad she's at least willing to talk, willing to reach out and try to mend this. Mend whatever *this* is. It's like she's on one end of a giant chasm and I'm on the other, and the chasm is our mother and our magic.

My head swims. It's too many emotions for one person to contend with at a time.

I can't focus on the shit with Laura until I see her tomorrow. There's no way to plan for where her head is at, and focusing on it will only freak me out.

For now, Noah. Noah is my focus.

THE TOE OF MY BLACK KNEE-HIGH BOOT TAPS AGAINST THE sidewalk as I wait outside the apartment for Noah to arrive. I pull my red leather jacket closer around me. I'm ten minutes early, as usual. Grandma left over an hour ago so there should be no awkward run-ins. At least not today.

The village is alive. No one can resist Chagrin Falls on a gorgeous fall evening. Children run after their dogs and couples lean close as they sit at the outdoor tables of their favorite restaurants. Teenagers huddle together giggling as they move in packs eating ice cream cones.

Despite never joining in, I find something oddly peaceful about observing the world around me. Watching people live their lives, seeing the everyday moments. At this point I've turned people-watching into an Olympic sport.

My head turns as Noah's car pulls up and comes to a stop in the parking space in front of me. The grin on his face is blinding, raising the hairs on my arms. My fingers itch to reacquaint themselves with his deceptively soft brown locks, to have him wrapped around me in every way possible.

"Baby," he says, exiting the car. He's directly in front of me with two steps of his long legs, and soon has me in his arms, nose buried in my hair.

Thank God he's holding me up because *baby* mixed with the electric current surging through my body at his touch has my knees weakening. Legs are jelly. I'm someone's baby.

I'm Noah's baby.

My arms tighten around his neck, pressing myself to every lanky inch of him as his scent—bergamot, neroli, book pages, and green tangerine—fills my lungs. I breathe in deep.

He pulls back just a hair, eyes meeting mine, nuzzling my nose. "Missed you."

Could he be any sweeter? My God.

"I missed *you*."

"I have two plans for the evening, depending on your comfort level." He doesn't release me from his hold, for which I am thankful. "I made up a picnic basket. If you'd like, we could go to a picnic area in the Metroparks and watch the sunset. Or we could take the picnic basket upstairs or to my place, and we could watch a movie on Streemz."

Did he just ask me to Streemz and chill? I thought that only happened to girls on social media. I'm not mad about it though.

"A night in sounds perfect." I smile, disengaging from the hug and taking his hand. We get the picnic basket from his back seat, and I lead him upstairs to my oasis.

Thankfully the place is reasonably tidy.

Noah's breath leaves him in a *whoosh*, hand squeezing mine as his eyes dart around the space. He places the basket on the counter and walks further in, not releasing me.

"This place is fantastic, Hazel." He turns to me, eyes glittering in the low lamplight. "It's artistic and cozy. Safe. Just like you."

Something has to be wrong with this guy. He's always saying the right thing, always positive, but I don't get the willies. There's no nagging punch in my gut telling me that he's fake or shady or just trying to get in my pants.

There's just the electricity. And the electricity feels *good*.

"Thank you. I'm looking forward to seeing what you packed."

He grins, opening the basket. "I'm going to be honest. I can't cook, despite Nonna Ricci trying to drill it into me. I burn just about everything. But, she helped me make this."

"You got her to help you?" I can't take the astonishment out of my voice. I can't hide the surprise, the disbelief, the sheer obviousness that no one has ever done something like this for me.

Melted. I have melted. I am puddle.

Noah's brow furrows just a little, two small lines forming in the middle of his forehead, and he comes to me. My thumb reaches up and smooths out the crease, hand settling on his cheek.

His head dips, lips pressing gently against the very tip of my nose. "I'd risk burning just to see you smile."

Fucking writers, man. They know exactly how to turn you into goo.

How do you even respond to that? Those brown-black eyes—with that little green star in the corner of the right one—are threatening to swallow me whole, and I want to be devoured. I lift onto the very tips of my toes and press our lips together, trying to convey what I don't have the words to express.

It's been quick. Frighteningly quick. There is still so much more to unpack, to unearth, to learn about Noah. But the buzz.

The buzz. The electricity. The current.

The current demands. Reassures that this is right, that we are right, that we are everything.

I haven't felt judged. I haven't felt repressed. There is no controlling nature, no dislike of who I am as a person. Each layer I reveal, each part of myself I show him, is accepted with enthusiasm.

He groans. "Hazel."

It's the same way, the same inflection, as when he kissed me for the first time. An awe—a reverence that I've never experienced.

"Noah." I smile, tongue darting out between my parted lips. His eyes track the motion, keeping me pressed against all the lanky angles of his body.

"What the hell are you doing to me?"

I have no idea, but I'm enjoying every damn second, you sexy octopus.

"Kissing you," I reply instead. "Would you like me to stop?"

He shakes his head, returning his mouth to mine. His movements deepen, teeth nipping at my lip to coax me into opening to him. I lead him toward the couch, pulling those long limbs on top of me the minute I hit the cushions.

My fingers get what they've wanted since the moment I saw him as they finally tangle into his brown curls. So soft.

His stubble rasps against the skin of my neck—kisses rain down on a path toward my collarbone. Legs are tangling together and hips moving, finding a rhythm.

A high-pitched moan escapes me on a particularly perfect movement of his hips.

"Hazel." His voice is broken like he's been gargling rock salt twice a day since he last saw me. Chest heaving, he stares at me. His body is completely still otherwise, just staring at me with lips turned rosy from kisses and lip gloss.

"Yeah?" I don't like the talking. I want more of the kissing.

His head drops onto my chest, forehead pressing right in the center. "You're driving me crazy."

"Is that a bad thing?"

That earns me a grin, a dimple-in-the-chin grin. My favorite.

"I'm gonna put my cards on the table, okay?" He stays tangled with me, forearms holding his weight. "I'm falling fast, faster than I ever expected. And I feel like it's reciprocated. Despite that, I—shit."

I nod, one hand coming up to caress his cheek as he speaks.

He exhales. "Can we eat dinner and watch a movie?"

"Absolutely. And Noah?"

"Yeah?"

"It's more than reciprocated."

His smile is everything, a light that fills up even the darkest parts of my aching soul. He's sunshine and I've been in the dark too long. I'm unwilling to let go of our spark, the gentle buzz that's been dancing along my skin, so I follow him as he sits upright.

He doesn't seem to mind as he wraps me up into his side, where I fit perfectly. I thought maybe he'd be tough to cuddle with, considering all his million lanky limbs. I thought he'd be bony or sharp, but he's comforting as he snuggles around me.

"What kind of movies do you like?" I ask, handing him the remote. I need to peel back some of these layers, see the full picture that is Noah.

He turns on the TV, navigating to Streemz. "I can watch anything with a good story. While I tend to gravitate toward sci-fi, I like a good romance every now and then. How does that sound for tonight?"

"That sounds lovely."

The sectional couch is wide enough for both of us to lie together horizontally, which is how we end up a few hours later. Belly full of handmade gnocchi with pesto, buzzy cuddles, and a cheesy romantic comedy? This may be the perfect evening.

My eyelids are heavy. The electric shock has dulled into a

soothing hum that relaxes each and every muscle in my body. I snuggle further into Noah, pressing my face into the soft skin of his neck.

His hand travels up my back and into my hair, stroking the strands in a slow, gentle rhythm.

Goodnight world, it's been real.

～

I'M FLOATING. MAYBE. WEIGHTLESS IN A WAY THAT MAKES ME FEEL like I might fall at any moment.

I throw an arm out as my eyes open, finding Noah carrying me through the apartment. I must have actually fallen asleep on the couch during movie night.

I'm such a butthead. He came over to spend time with me and I fell asleep!

"Hey," I say as he awkwardly opens the door to my bedroom with his foot.

He smiles, meeting my gaze. "Hey, you."

A wave of sleepiness threatens to pull me back under, the comfort of the evening settling a little too easily into my bones. But not yet. Not yet.

"Will you stay?"

Sleepy Hazel is even more loose lipped than Normal Hazel. Considering that wasn't a very high bar to begin with . . . this is not a good development.

He hesitates, arms tensing before he places me on the floral bedspread. I've seen him embarrassed, nervous, but I've never seen him uncomfortable. Not until now.

"I want to." He sits, hand reaching for mine and wrapping around it. "Does this feel a little too . . ."

"A little too what?" I prompt after a second, sitting up.

He shrugs, obviously struggling for the right word. "Easy? I've never connected with someone so quickly."

I have no frame of reference. The only real relationship I've gotten a look at was my parents and they were—God, they were *devoted*. Devoted isn't a good enough word. Words can't encapsulate the way my father would look at my mother. It was as if she hung the moon, the stars, and resided among them.

"My dating history isn't necessarily what I would call extensive." Or existent.

He chuckles. "I find that hard to believe. You're the most amazing person I've ever met."

Warmth blooms in my chest, filling my body with a lightness. He thinks I'm amazing?

"I like you a lot, Noah." And it's true. Despite his hesitance, and his worry that things are too easy, I enjoy being with Noah. It's calm, reliable, and I may or may not want to rip off his clothes and attack him.

He leans his forehead against mine with a sigh. "I like you, too. I should just shut up, shouldn't I?"

I shrug. "A woman you think is amazing is inviting you to spend the night with no expectations. Unless . . . unless you want to talk about it. I want to be there for you." I don't have any experience with being someone's partner.

His shoulders drop, a sheepish smile on his face. "I honestly think I'm just nervous as fuck. Do you still want me to stay, or have I successfully put my foot in my mouth?"

"I'd watch you do that," I reply before I can stop myself.

His bushy eyebrow quirks. "Do what?"

"Put your foot in your mouth." I break off with an embarrassed grin. It's not my fault that the thought of him contorting his body in weird ways is attractive to me. He could eat a piece of cheese and I'd find it attractive.

"What the fuck, Hazel?" he wheezes in between uncontrollable laughter. "You're such a fucking goofball."

"Guess that foot is in my mouth, too."

Oh. Oh God. I said that. That thought went through my brain and got cleared for take-off.

"For the record, I'm not into feet. Just in case you were trying to, I don't know, work it into conversation," he says with a wink.

I bury my face in my hands. "You can go and never speak to me again. I completely understand. This has been lovely."

One minute I'm safe in my little finger cocoon, and the next I'm being attacked by tickling. My hands fly from my face to protect other vulnerable places as Noah descends. The room is filled with giggling and laughter as he breaks down every single defense I have.

"I concede!" I whine, ribs aching. Too much laughing.

It's only when he stops that I realize how close we are. He's fully on top of me, legs tangled together. I can feel every single inch of him pressed against me.

And a bunch more inches that have made an appearance.

Whatever fatigue was clinging to me is thoroughly shaken off, replaced by a warm ache low in my belly.

I'm a woman possessed as I pull him down and seal our mouths together. Despite his earlier reservations, he seems to have no problem responding. His big hands wrap around my waist, and he *drags* our hips together in a move that is completely unexpected from a guy who spends his free time in a bookshop.

I'm not complaining, though, because along with that he's *moving*. It's a slow pulse in exactly the right spot to make my eyes roll back in my head.

His mouth is harsh, demanding, and taking all that I can give to him. The friction sends little waves of electricity along my arms, making me more and more sensitive to every touch.

There is no doubt I will have intense stubble burn, and I'll relish every second of it.

"You taste delicious," he says into my neck.

I squirm, running my fingers through his hair and tugging. The groan I get in response curls my toes.

I want more of that sound. I could probably get off on that sound alone.

Before I can recover my wits his hand roughly grabs my breast, catching the very tip between his spread fingers.

Despite the fabric separating us, I arch and moan. The noise is inhuman. It's a pure animalistic noise of pleasure.

"Fuck, that was hot." His hand moves, massaging me through my clothes.

A voice in the back of my head reminds me that he wanted to wait. He wanted to talk. He wanted to go slow.

Shut up, voice, can you not see I am very much enjoying myself?

He matters more.

Ugh. *Bitch.*

"Noah," I say, scratching along his scalp.

His eyes—which were firmly planted on my chest—meet mine. "Yeah? You okay?"

"I, um." Courage, Hazel. "I'm great. Perfect, actually. You just . . . Earlier you wanted to take things slower?"

"Shit, you're sweet." He presses a quick kiss to my lips that has me chasing after him. "You're right, though. I want to do this right."

"I want to do this right, too. I like you, Noah. I know-ah I just said that, but I mean it."

"Did you just use my name as a pun?"

"Yup. Figured you should know what you're getting into."

"I'm into you."

A dorky grin breaks on my face. "Cute."

"Will you be my girlfriend?"

My heart soars out of my chest and into the sky. I'm lighter than air as I soak in the blinding sunlight that is Noah Rogers. I want to live in this moment, catalog every single detail so I can play it over and over again in my mind. Right now, everything is perfect.

I smile. "Absolutely. Will you stay tonight so I can sleep in your arms?"

He returns my smile, the little dimple in his chin peeking through.

"Absolutely."

CHAPTER 17

EARLY START

Sunlight dances off little specks of dust in the air as my eyes blink open. I'm cocooned in Noah's arms, his fingers splayed possessively across my chest and belly. His front pressed against my back provides that steady hum of electricity that I've come to crave.

His nose drags slowly along the back of my neck—achingly slowly—alighting every single nerve. They seem to converge in my core, an ache building in my lower half that grows with every second.

"I could get used to waking up to you."

Shit. His just-woke-up voice is way too sexy for me to handle.

I really hope he doesn't expect me to respond, because words—what are they?

Instead, I roll my hips, pressing back into his body. Hopefully that encourages less words and more touching.

His hands grip tighter, almost bruising, pulling me impossibly closer.

"And here I was trying to be sweet."

Sweet. HA! He knows what he's doing and it ain't sweet. Right now he is the farthest damn thing from it.

My alarm chimes, pulling me out of the haze of want. Why in the hell did I set an alarm?

Laura. I promised Laura I'd meet her for breakfast. I can't blow her off.

"As—" Gulp. He's perfectly lined up with my ass, a slow grind that has me struggling to breathe. "As much as I'd love to continue this, I have to meet my sister Laura."

"When?" he all but growls in my ear.

Where has dominant Noah been? Because I can absolutely get on board with this.

I clear the sleep from my throat. "Nine."

I turn in his arms to find his eyes darting around the room, presumably looking for a clock or some indication of what time it is. It allows me a few seconds to absorb Morning Noah. The tousled brown locks are at prime messiness. Despite holding me all night, his hair tells a story of tossing and turning. His bushy eyebrows seem even larger—taking over his eyes, which are narrowed to block out as much sunlight as possible. Even so, his brown eyes sparkle in a way I've been unable to capture in the millions of times I've tried drawing them.

Right. I almost forgot that I've been drawing his eyes for months before meeting him, like a complete creeper. I hope those drawings are very deep in a drawer somewhere.

Noah finds his phone and tosses it toward the end of the bed. "Fuck, it's after eight."

I giggle at his annoyance.

He grins at me. "How did you sleep?"

"Perfectly. And yourself?" My hands crawl up his chest and up around his shoulders. If it were up to me, I'd stay right here forever.

"Better than I have in a long time."

"I really should be getting ready. Laura will kill me if I'm late." I make no move to get out of bed. My brain and my body are not on the same page.

"Probably," he agrees, nosing my neck. "And then you have class, right?"

Damn. I forgot about classes today.

"Yep. What about you?"

"I'm going to focus on writing today. And then hopefully take my girl out to dinner so we can spend some more time together. If you'd like?"

More Noah time? I'm nodding before he finishes the question.

"Good. Let's get out of bed, then. Don't want you getting killed before I see you again."

~

ONE ADORABLE KISS LATER, I'M ON THE SIDEWALK WAITING FOR Laura. I'm wrapped up in a midnight-blue sweater and my favorite jeans. They're basically threadbare at this point, but there's no replicating how perfectly lived-in they are.

I can just barely smell Noah on my skin, and I want more. Maybe I'll steal a hoodie or something. Anything to keep a small piece of him with me when I can't see him.

"Hey!" Laura calls. I turn as she walks toward me. She's wearing a sage-green long-sleeved crop top and tight, high-waisted jeans. It's showing off her abs and perfect boobs.

"Hi!" Despite my jealousy at just how perfect she is, I missed the crap out of her. I pull her into a hug, the scent of her newest favorite perfume filling my nose. She changes scents just as often as she changes clothes and I've lost the will to try and keep track.

Despite the closeness, her shoulders are stiff. She doesn't fully surrender to the hug.

She pulls back; her eyes trail me from head to toe. "Did you spend the night with Noah?"

Bloodhound. A freakin' magical bloodhound.

"He slept over," I admit. There's no point in lying, she'll sniff it out. "But nothing happened."

"I believe you. Let's go. You can tell me about it when we sit down." She reaches for my hand, and we link fingers to walk to the restaurant.

Early Start Diner is right across the street from Grandma's shop and it's our favorite breakfast place. It's an open room, a counter with bar stools separating the dining area from the kitchen. It's surprisingly rustic—like we're sitting in a country house kitchen waiting for our entire family to eat breakfast together.

We're seated at a table by the window, looking out at the village gazebo and Grandma's shop. The sunlight streams in, lighting up the wooden table and reflecting off the glass cups.

"So he slept over and you didn't fuck him? Whose decision was that?" Laura asks when the waitress leaves with our orders.

I'm so unused to being the one in the hot seat. Laura is usually the one with the boyfriend, and I'm asking the questions. "I'm pretty sure you didn't invite me to lunch to talk about my lack of sex."

"Excuse me for trying to bond first." Something is happening in that head of hers and I still don't know if she's ready to share.

"I'm sorry," I say. "What's going on?"

"Nothing!" She snaps, refusing to meet my gaze. She picks at her nails instead.

I lift a brow at her, giving her the *I don't believe you* face.

She exhales. "Things have been different since you left. I just wanted to spend some time with you."

I've been so focused on me and figuring out my shit that I've left Laura in the dust.

I've always prioritized her, and while I need to get a better balance on that, I can't abandon her in the process.

Having a life is hard.

"I know, and I'm sorry for that. I want to spend time with you, too." I reach my hand out, but she doesn't take it.

"So, uh." She takes a sip of orange juice. "Why didn't you fuck him?"

"Laura!"

"What?!"

At least she's acting more like herself. That doesn't mean I want to talk about sex with her though. "Did you check out Salem? The witchy app store?"

"Duh." She gives a skeptical squint in that I-know-what-you're-trying-to-do-and-I'll-allow-it-for-now way. "There's two dating apps I found. Meow and Lock & Key. Meow seems to be more hook-up based, while Lock & Key is more serious."

I would bet the whole ten dollars in my bank account that she's only on Meow.

She flips her blonde hair over her shoulder. "I'm on Meow, of course."

Knew it.

"Any viable candidates?" I ask.

Before she can answer, a beautiful blueberry lemon muffin, scrambled eggs, and a bowl of fruit are placed in front of me by the server. I am in heaven. The waitress also places a fruit bowl and cinnamon sugar oatmeal in front of Laura.

"Turns out that, magical or not, dating is a mess. Lots of fuck-boys, but considering I'm not looking for a husband I don't really care."

I nod, stuffing egg in my mouth.

"Hazel?" Her voice is doing that scared thing that I really hate.

"Yeah?"

Her eyes flicker between mine—looking for what, I don't know. She doesn't seem to find it as she just shakes her head.

"Never mind," she whispers and goes back to her oatmeal.

I wish things weren't so weird between us.

I'm determined to figure out why. I will fix this.

CHAPTER 18

KEEP MOVING FORWARD

My classes are canceled. Apparently there was a water main break in the community center and they're using the weekend to fix it.

Which means I'm tip-toeing around the shop, looking for a book about scrying while Grandma sits in her office. I have no doubt Grandma has some sort of magical security system—she's too savvy not to. Which means I have to be careful.

Scrying: How To.

Gotta love obvious titles.

I wonder if this is like that scene in *Indiana Jones* where an alarm will go off in Grandma's head the moment I move the book from its place on the shelf. Should I try to replace it with a vase?

She's too smart for that. What's my excuse for picking this book up?

I've seen scrying described in popular culture—movies, TV shows, etc.—and I wanted to see if it was the same? It looked interesting? I want to keep an eye on my family because of what happened to Dad?

Too close to the truth.

While I run the risk of losing my lessons, I can't sit back and do nothing. I have to prepare in every single way I can until I'm ready to fight daemons.

I run my finger up the spine and tip it toward me. It falls into my hands like a snowflake. Easy. Now the real question is: Do I read this down here, or try to smuggle it up to my apartment?

Reading it here is less suspicious than trying to run away.

I really am overthinking this. I need to calm down and just read the damn book instead of standing here like a tree. I'm bound to grow roots at this rate.

I take the book to a comfy green floral chair in the corner. This is still technically my day off and I'm not going to tempt Grandma into getting me to work by going near the counter. After another uneasy glance toward the office, I crack open the book.

Scrying is an ancient form of calling visions forth. In this book, we discuss the many different ways scrying can be, and has been, used in witchcraft. This includes tracking, future predictions, and receiving messages.

So not as straightforward as I thought. But you have to start somewhere, and I can't just ask Grandma without risking my progress.

Scrying can be used to find persons or things. Focusing on the person or thing is sometimes enough for the talented witch, but having something of value related to the person or thing is preferred. By taking a crystal, your personal item, and a map, you can create a vision of the location of whatever you're looking for.

Simply swing the crystal from a string over the map while holding the personal item. Clearing your mind through deep breathing and meditation can be helpful if scrying proves difficult.

SEEMS SIMPLE ENOUGH ONCE IT'S LAID OUT. I CAN PRETTY EASILY snag something of Noah's or Grandma's to practice. I know I'm nowhere near ready for something like Botis—which is good, since there's no way I'd find anything of his lying around.

I'll have to practice sometime soon, when Grandma isn't in the shop and I'm not spending time with Noah. Or training. Or trying to figure out what's going on with Laura. Or avoiding Mom. Or teaching my classes.

I exhale. Good luck to me.

"Hazel!" Grandma's voice calls.

Shit. I run to the shelf, deposit the book back in its original spot, and jog back to her office.

"Yep?" Am I a little breathless? Yikes.

She eyes me. "You had to know I would ask."

"Ask?" I'm screwed. "Ask about what?"

"The boy you're dating, of course." A soft smile breaks on her face. "I heard you and Laura discussing him at my cottage the other night."

I try to suppress the breath of relief. Noah is safer than scrying for daemons. "Right. Noah, his name is Noah."

"Mm, Noah. Strong name. And he's good to you?"

I nod. Noah is one of the few people in this world who's genuinely been good to me. Better to me than Mom by a long shot.

She smiles. "Stop looking like I'm going to interrogate you. I'm not Laura. I just needed some sort of gossip to bring back to the ladies."

"Thanks, Grandma." I turn to go.

"One last thing before you leave." She stands, Rosie hopping off her shoulder and onto the chair. "Every magic lesson will be attended. No absences for dates."

CHAPTER 19

WHAT'S YOUR FAVORITE COLOR?

I think I have an addiction. An actual, gives-me-the-fidgets addiction.

And the name of that addiction is Noah Rogers.

I'm tapping my fingers on my arm as I wait outside the shop for him to pick me up, my body itching for the electric buzz. It's that moment after being shocked, the loss of sensation after being over-whelmed.

I really should try to figure out what the hell that's about. That and the eye drawing. There's something going on, and I've been too focused on Noah to figure out what that is.

Grandma knows about him now. Maybe it's finally time to ask her.

I gnaw at my bottom lip, a cool fall breeze raising goosebumps on my skin despite my thick sweater. If I could live somewhere where it's perpetually fall, I would be a happy lady.

Give me all the pumpkin spice. In my face. All the time.

Speak of the sunshine devil himself, Noah's car pulls up right in front of me in a repeat of last night. Before he can get out I bounce over and jump in the passenger's side.

No words are spoken as I soak up the fact that *he's here*, and I wrap my arms around his neck. It's an awkward angle since he hasn't had time to take off his seatbelt, but we make it work.

His lips are just as soft and full as I remember as they softly caress mine. The fidgeting is gone, replaced by the soft comfort of being in Noah's presence.

"Hey," I whisper, breaking the kiss but keeping the contact. It may be difficult for him to drive with me wrapped around him like a jellyfish, but I may just have to let him figure it out.

"Hey." He chuckles, pressing one last quick peck to my mouth. "How are you?"

Mmm, how I love that electric buzz. "Really good now. How about you? Did you get any writing done?"

"If you mean scrolling social media, doing a bunch of research, cleaning my apartment, and doing literally anything other than writing—then yes. I got a lot of writing done."

A *giggle* escapes my mouth. It's a high-pitched noise that makes my cheeks flush in embarrassment. I don't giggle. Laura giggles, I guffaw like a chicken.

"Where are we going?" I ask, momentarily distracted by how he drives. One hand is confidently draped over the steering wheel and his forearm is on the armrest in the middle. He's fascinating.

And hot. Did I mention hot?

"I owe you that picnic. Plus it allows us time to really get to know each other without the distractions of a restaurant."

I don't know if anyone has ever put this much effort into getting to know me. When I'm with Laura, we talk about Laura. When I'm with Grandma, we talk about magic. When I was around Mom, we didn't talk at all. I don't think any of them could tell you my favorite color.

My chest aches a little at the knowledge that he wants to know me.

～

WE PULL UP TO A SECLUDED SECTION OF THE METROPARKS JUST AS the sun is setting. The reds, yellows, and oranges of the sky blend with the matching colors on the trees.

A babbling brook can be heard to my right, just out of sight. I instinctively turn toward it. Maybe I'm having a witchy nature moment, but I'd like to sit by it. If I start chanting and dancing around in a circle, I hope Noah doesn't film it before he runs away.

He takes my hand and thankfully leads me straight to the little river, spreading a red plaid blanket on the grass.

"Did Nonna Ricci help you again?" I ask, sitting on the blanket. It's surprisingly plushy.

Noah sports a guilty smile as he pulls takeout boxes out of the picnic basket. "I told you I can't cook!"

I laugh as he hands me a white plastic fork. "I just don't want her to think I'm dating you to get to her food. It's a perk, but not the sole reason."

"Not the sole reason?" A cocky smirk ticks up the side of his mouth. "What are the other reasons?"

I could mess with him. Use the opportunity to razz him. But there's something in his eyes, a quick moment of doubt that tells me I shouldn't. Tells me that he needs reassurance and is hiding it behind a smile.

"You're kind, funny, handsome, and . . . you make me feel seen. You make me feel like me."

Oof. Way to lay it on thick there, Hazel. My cheeks burn at my admission, eyes downcast toward the food. Maybe if I don't make eye contact with him, he won't address how I've laid myself bare before him.

He clears his throat, the sound jarring in the silence that has fallen. "I can't remember the last time I've . . . Hazel, look at me?"

His hand gently covers mine so I'm unable to fidget with a stray thread. Rude.

With a deep breath, I finally meet his gaze to find those brown-black eyes kindly regarding me.

"You make me feel like me, too."

Oh. My heart pitter-patters at his words.

"I want to know more about you," I say, spearing a piece of steamed broccoli from one of the takeout containers. "I like learning more about you."

Please take the spotlight off me, thank you.

He sighs, spearing his own piece of—what is that? Chicken parmesan? Thank the Lord above for Nonna Ricci. "What would you like to know?"

Do I detect some reluctance? Here I was thinking I was the only one with skeletons in my closet.

"Whatever you want to share. I don't mean to be all up in your business, I just want to know more."

"No, no, I know." He sighs again, chewing his food slowly. "I just hate pity, and my life tends to get me pity."

I cock my head in confusion without thought. I would've never imagined the word pity would be associated with him. "But you're always so happy, so sunny."

"I've learned some tough life lessons, and one of them is that life is short. Enjoying every moment is important to me."

"That's an incredibly healthy way to deal with trauma. I just drown myself in anger and regret." I nervously giggle. It's true, though.

He chuckles—a low rumble that vibrates through my body. "That happens, too."

"That's a good start. Tell me something else." I nudge his knee with mine. "Even if it's just your favorite color."

"My favorite color is blue."

"How utterly basic of you."

"My brother killed himself five years ago." His hand ruffles his hair, shaking slightly before he drops his eyes to the food in front of us.

That stops me cold. My fork hovers mid-air, noodles of some sort dangling precariously. I'm grinding my teeth in an attempt at holding my mouth shut for fear of gaping at him like a fish.

Get it together, Hazel. You can't act like a dumbass.

I bring the food to my mouth, chew, swallow. Take the few moments to calm the fuck down.

"I'm sorry. Losing him must have been awful." Normal response achieved.

I hated pity when my Dad died. Granted, I only had a handful of friends from middle school at the time, and they got bored of my grieving process very quickly. But still, the pity was the worst. The false understanding. The look on their faces.

Like I was a broken thing with no hope of ever becoming a whole human again.

Although, in their defense, I never did.

He smiles. It's a sad thing that looks so foreign on his face. "There's . . . there's a lot of feelings I have about losing him the way I did. The way he did things. How I could've changed things. But, that's a very long conversation."

"I don't want to be that person who says they get it. Because that person sucks and sometimes you just want to be allowed to feel like shit. And I've never lost someone that way. But my dad died when I was twelve, so I get losing family."

Instead of responding, he holds his arms open to me. Maybe he knows that saying sorry only goes so far, maybe he has no words at all. But this is better.

I snuggle into his chest, receiving his warmth—his electric current—like a balm on a topic I've never been able to discuss.

Maybe being in a relationship isn't about finding someone who completes you. Maybe it's about finding someone who's broken in the same ways you are. Finding someone who knows what you need because they know how you feel. How you've felt in your darkest moments because they're their darkest moments, too.

"I love fall," I whisper into Noah's flannel shirt. "It's my favorite season."

"I love summer. I like the heat."

"That's because you're hot."

He snickers into my hair, pressing a kiss to the very top of my head. "And you're perfect."

"Not perfect," I insist. "I'm pretty weird, honestly."

"Exactly. I don't like you in spite of you being weird, I like you *because* you're weird. It's my favorite thing about you." He pauses. "That, and how you never make me feel like I need to be anyone but myself."

"Because I want you, Noah. I don't want anyone else."

Once the food is gone—eaten mostly by me, because Nonna Ricci is a goddess—Noah leans back, pulling me with him as we watch the sun dip below the trees. We lie like that, quiet and calm, as the stars twinkle awake on their midnight-blue pillow.

I am safe.

The electric current has other ideas, however. Noah's fingers travel a path up and down my spine and with each sweep, the electricity crackles against my skin. Being this close to him, with his scent in my nose and his warmth underneath my cheek, I can't help but want more.

More closeness, more heat, more *Noah*.

I pull myself up so I'm hovering above him. His eyebrows draw together slightly, confused by my sudden movement. His shaggy curls are off his face, highlighting his eyes. He must have shaved a few days ago, as there's a light stubble on his cheeks. I take a moment to appreciate him in this moment. Appreciate how vulnerable we both were, and how safe we both are.

He opens his mouth to speak and I descend. Instead of surprise, Noah adapts immediately, wrapping his fingers in my hair. Pulling me closer until I can barely breathe.

I don't need air, I just need Noah.

"Maybe—" I gasp as Noah pulls my earlobe between his teeth. "Maybe we should continue this elsewhere."

Blown-out pupils search my face with a lazy smile. "I'd follow you anywhere."

～

THE DOOR SMACKS AGAINST THE WALL WITH A *THWACK* AS NOAH and I stumble into my apartment, glued to each other. As soon as it's closed again, my back is against it as Noah tears at my clothes.

Too much fabric. There are too many barriers between us. I want skin.

I need skin.

My fingers steal under his t-shirt, bunching the fabric underneath his arms until it won't go any higher without his assistance.

He breaks away to rip the shirt off and pull mine off with his, just to return moments later.

A moment of insecurity at being exposed like this threatens to overwhelm me, but he grounds me. "You're beautiful. So beautiful, Hazel."

Then he nuzzles his nose against mine and takes my lips again.

I suck on his bottom lip, pulling the kiss-swollen flesh into my mouth as my hands roam over new territory. His chest is dusted with dark brown hair that tapers as it travels down his chest to his toned abdomen, to disappear into his jeans.

Obviously they have to go, too, if I'm going to follow that trail.

I should feel inexperienced. I shouldn't know what to do. But Noah guides me in an effortless way, allows me to explore and find what feels good.

His hands haven't been idle. He's grasping at whatever part of my body he can reach. One moment he's tangling his fingers in my hair, the next he's bruising my hips with his grip.

I want to press against those sore spots tomorrow, loving the reminder of his desperation. How much he wants me. I want to leave my own marks.

"You're delicious," he murmurs against my lips. "Up."

He grasps the back of my thighs as I jump into his arms.

A fresh wave of heat floods my body at the action. That was *hot.* He drags me deeper into the apartment and deposits me on the kitchen island. The height makes it so much easier to get my hands all over him.

My legs wrap tightly around his waist, pulling him closer. Chest to chest, I heave for every breath. The air is thick and my head is fuzzy.

Big hands drag up my back until they reach my bra. With a deftness I'm bowled over by, he flicks my bra open and drags it down my shoulders.

The entire world is still in this moment—the moment Noah sees me for the first time. The moment anyone sees me for the first time. I attempt to lift my arms to cover myself, but he shakes his head. Puts my arms back around him.

With the same awe and reverence he always has for me, he runs the tip of his finger along my collarbone and down the middle of my chest.

"Hazel, you are the most gorgeous woman I have ever seen." He says it so obviously, as if there was never another option. As if there never will be another option.

And I believe him.

"You're not so bad yourself," I reply. I have to force some levity into the situation, force away the stinging in my eyes from his sincerity.

If I don't, I'll fall in love.

He cups my breast suddenly, squeezing just right. My head falls back as his dips forward to take my nipple in his mouth. I gasp as his teeth graze the very tip.

I'm a liquid puddle of need.

"*Noah*," I beg.

Two black eyes meet mine. The sight of him with his lips wrapped around me stops whatever train of thought I had.

A smirk is his only response. Cheeky son of a bitch.

His fingers pluck at the button of my jeans, but he stops before unzipping. Why has he stopped?

I lift my hips to encourage him, practically ripping my jeans off for him. He pulls them off my legs and kisses my ankle, slowly traveling up my skin.

Each kiss is an electric shock to my core. I'm shuddering by the time he reaches the top of my thigh.

"You're sure? You want this?" he asks, lifting his head a fraction of an inch.

He asks me this *now*? When I have no words left to let him know just how much I want this? The audacity of this man!

I nod ferociously instead, lifting my hips again in what I hope is an obvious desire for *more*. Whatever more is. I may never have personally experienced more, but I know I want it.

Seemingly appeased by my body's response, he pulls off my underwear and buries his head between my thighs.

The squeal I emit makes me happy there's a brick wall between me and the neighbors.

My body falls back on the kitchen island, the marble cool against my overheated, sweaty skin.

Noah throws my thighs over his shoulders as he eats me within an inch of my life. His tongue dips inside and my back arches at the breach. My hands bury themselves in his bushy curls. The answering groan vibrates through my entire body, making me clench around his tongue.

"*Noah.*"

"Fuck, I love how you say my name," he says, nipping my inner thigh.

"Love how you taste." He bites my inner thigh. "Love how you move."

I'm only able to whine in response to his praise, pulling his head from my legs and back to my cunt. I'm so close. So, so close. I just need a little bit more and I'll be right there.

He chuckles but obeys my request, lapping at my clit. His fingers have a bruising hold around my thigh and I want more. More marks. More proof of his passion on my skin.

"That's it, baby. Take what you need. Take it."

Holy hell.

One finger enters me, and my body explodes like a firework. The orgasm is sudden and overpowering. My back arches almost painfully as my shoulders lift off the island. It's as if I've been electrocuted. The current has made my nerves almost raw. My whole body is floating as magic and sex and electricity course through me.

I am powerful.

I've had little moments of exploration on my own before, but it never felt like this.

It's only as I come back down I realize that I really was floating. Levitating. Channeling magic in the most intense way I ever have, and I hope to God he didn't notice.

He rises, hungry gaze roaming my naked body, and adjusts himself in his pants. The obvious sign of his continued arousal is threatening to tear his jeans in two.

I'd rather it tear me in two.

"Help me up?" I ask, comforted by the fact that he isn't asking about the floating.

He takes my hands and pulls me to sit up, a smug smile breaking over his face.

"Bed?" I ask, wrapping my legs around him once more.

He's proven he can carry me and there's no way in hell I'm going to be able to walk anywhere. Not with the mind-blowing orgasm having turned my brain into goo, and the stubble burn already aching between my legs.

"Anything you want. I'm yours, Hazel." He lifts me gently. A moment of connection in the middle of the passion. It's so uniquely us.

"I'm yours, too, Noah." Because I am.

He kisses me once more, allowing me to taste my release on his tongue. It shouldn't be as hot as it is, and yet I'm practically rubbing myself against him like a cat by the time we make it to the bedroom.

I've completely surrendered to this dynamic. The inherent knowledge that he's going to take care of me. He can do with me as he pleases because I trust him to make me feel good. To protect me.

I bounce twice on the bed before he crawls up my body, reconnecting our lips. My nails dig into his shoulder blades, leaving little crescent moons on his skin.

It satisfies a primal urge inside me. I want to know he's marked.

To know if anyone were to see his back, they'd see that he's taken. That he's mine.

Apparently I have a possessive streak—who knew?

The button on his jeans presses painfully into my bare skin, which is raw from his stubble. I hiss into his mouth at the unwanted friction.

"Shit, yeah, let me take care of this." In a moment he's standing at the foot of the bed and he's pulling his shoes and socks off.

An improvement to be sure, but not what I wanted. My bottom lip sticks out at his reduced speed.

"Something you want?" he asks with a quirked, bushy brow.

Okay, Hazel, you need to turn the tables because this man has way too much damn confidence right now.

I stretch on the bed, wiggling my naked hips a little more than necessary. He catalogs the movement, licking his lips.

"I don't know, Noah. Is there something *you* want?"

Nailed it.

His eyes hold mine as he pulls off his jeans and boxer-briefs in one go.

Every part of Noah is long.

Every. Part.

I make grabby hands until he comes back, enveloping me in his warmth, his scent, his comforting buzz. Every point of contact sends a little electric shock, until I'm practically vibrating with the desire to cement our connection.

To get my brains fucked out.

"You'll tell me if you don't like something?" The words leave his mouth in heavy gasps. He's at the edge of his patience, and frankly so am I.

I nod, sinking my nails into his ass. "Now, please."

Should I have told him that I'm a virgin before this moment? Probably. Am I going to tell him? Later. Possibly.

"Wait. Shit. Condom?"

"Birth control."

He lines up and, with a deep breath, pushes in. I whimper at the pinch, biting his lower lip.

My mind expands.

I can *feel* what he feels. My walls clamped around him, my skin against his, the sting of my fingernails digging into his sides. It's as if it's happening to me—at the same time I'm feeling everything that's actually happening to me.

It's overwhelming. It's intense.

It's *hot*.

My entire body is like an exposed nerve and I need him to move. I want him to move. *Move.*

The first drag of him as he pulls out punches the air from my lungs. I'm only able to wheeze when he buries himself to the hilt. His pace is slow, controlled, and it only serves to jack the electric current up to an all-encompassing buzz.

"Fuck, you feel good," he says, grasping one of my hands above my head. He buries his face in my neck, biting and sucking the skin there.

I refrain from telling him I know, because *I know*. I know exactly how I feel and I know how he feels and I just . . . *shit.*

"Harder!" I manage to exclaim. I don't know who wants it—if he wants it, I want it, or both of us do.

The scent of sex fills my nose, the taste of it fills my mouth.

The build-up can only go for so long, the waves can only crash for so long before they break. And I'm going to break in two.

"Suck," he says, pressing his thumb to my lips. I hollow my cheeks around the digit before he quickly withdraws it.

His spit-soaked thumb finds where we're joined and rubs in gentle circles just as he hitches my leg over his elbow. The new angle causes him to hit a spot that Laura told me *definitely exists*, and my consciousness shatters.

Waves of electricity and satisfaction roll over my skin in a delicious mix as my back bows as much as Noah's grip allows. I feel him, too.

I feel how my orgasms trigger his, which triggers more of mine. How I milk him dry.

I lose consciousness.

My eyes flutter and everything has changed. I'm on my side and Noah faces me, running his fingers over my cheeks.

"Hey, there you are," he says, a relieved exhale escapes his kiss-bruised lips. "Kinda lost you there for a second."

A dopey smile breaks my face. I may be a little cock-drunk. "How long was I out?"

"Maybe a minute. Long enough for me to worry, but not long enough for me to call an ambulance."

I nuzzle into the perfect chest before me, an arm instantly wrapping around my back. "You're just that good, I guess."

"*Me?* How about you?"

"Beginner's luck." I smirk, snuggling further.

He pulls back with a confused head tilt. "Beginner's what now?"

Right. I didn't tell him about that. Well, no going back now.

"You were my first." I can't help but cringe, looking up at him from under my lashes.

"Shit, Hazel!" His hands are soft, caressing me, looking me over. "Did I hurt you? If I knew . . . I could've been softer, slower. I should have prepped you."

I hush him with a finger on his lips. "It was perfect."

"But—"

"It was perfect. Now hold me and tell me you enjoyed it, so I don't get a complex."

He chuckles, bringing me back into his chest. Into his safety.

CHAPTER 20

THAT ELECTRIC SPARK

It's torture kicking Noah out of my apartment in the morning, but I was told I'm not allowed any absences. And I'm not risking pissing Grandma off.

Despite my desire to lie on top of Noah like Rosie the cat and refuse to let him leave.

Once I *finally* get him out of the door, I change and bounce downstairs to the shop. I'm practically dancing through her office and into the main area of the store.

Grandma, however, stands straight with her arms folded across her chest. Her stare stops me in my tracks.

"You are five minutes late."

Shit.

My gaze falls to the floor. "I'm sorry, Grandma."

I see her shoes as she approaches me. "I don't mean to be a taskmaster. I just want you to learn all that you've missed, and I suppose I'm motivated by more than a little guilt."

That captures my attention. I lift my eyes to meet her blue ones, laced with turmoil. "Guilt for what?"

"Many things," she huffs a laugh that has more stress than levity in it. "For now, tell me about the past few days. Have you had any manifestations of your element? Have you been meditating?"

I open my mouth to say no, and then . . .

Oh shit. It happened. I manifested my element last night. When Noah was . . .

My cheeks heat so quickly I'm almost lightheaded.

I levitated while he was . . . while I was . . . Not the image I want in my head while trying to have a conversation with my grandma.

"I levitated once."

She smirks. It's an evil, knowing grin that I very much do not appreciate. Lock that shit up, Grandma, I'm not talking about this with you.

"That would confirm that your element is air, like I assumed earlier. It makes sense for you." She nods, winking at me. Ew.

I lift my chin with the little dignity I have left. "So what does that mean?"

"It means we have made a wonderful step forward. Sit down. Let's meditate and see if we can further connect you."

We sit as we did in our other lessons and go through the relaxation process. Contracting and releasing every muscle in our bodies until the world is calm and still.

"The air," she whispers into the silence between us. "It is your connection. It runs through every part of you and re-centers you. It takes you back to this place, to this level of relaxation and calm. The air is in the breeze as it sweeps over your skin. It is how we breathe, how we live. Feel it as you drag it into your lungs, as you release it back into the world."

I am weightless. Air rushes through my body in my bloodstream. It is the very essence of my ability to live, to thrive.

"How do you feel?" she asks.

I smile softly. "At peace."

"You're levitating. You have found your center, your connection."

I open my eyes to find I'm a few inches off the pillow. And I am at peace.

"Grandma, I have a question for you." Peace loosens my tongue apparently. "It's about Noah."

"You can ask me anything," she says with the kind of composure I can only dream of having. She's the epitome of calm, cool, and collected. I doubt the woman has ever been surprised in her life.

"When I touch him . . ." My cheeks heat at the very thought of his touch. "Ever since the first time, it has been electric. Literally electric. There's this connection between us. It started as a jolt with every accidental brush, but now it's grown. Sometimes it's a gentle hum, and sometimes it's a strong buzz. Do you know anything about that?"

Grandma's eyebrows jump into her hairline as every single candle extinguishes simultaneously. Her mouth drops.

"Grandma?" I ask after a few long moments of silence.

She shakes her head, her eyebrows coming down but not hitting their normal height. "Give me a moment."

The pillow is suddenly beneath me as I drop painfully onto my tailbone. I've come down and not just physically. Despite how amazing the electricity feels, her reaction can't mean anything good. Grandma has never been speechless.

A sniffle snaps my gaze back to her face. She's . . . crying? A few tears roll down her smiling cheeks.

Wait. Smiling?

"Grandma, please," I beg, grabbing her hands. "You're scaring me."

She pulls me into a hug, grasping me close to her. "I'm so happy for you."

"What?"

"Oh, sweetheart." She leans back to smile at me, choking on a sob. "You've found your soulmate."

Grandma's words reverberate through my head for what seems like hours.

Soulmate. Soulmate.

Soulmate.

It doesn't even sound like a word anymore. But it is. It's the word to describe Noah.

Soulmate. Mate of my soul.

Grandma brushes a lock of auburn hair from my face. "My joy is truly indescribable, Hazel. You deserve a world of happiness."

"Sorry, Grandma, I'm still kind of wrapping my head around this whole thing," I reply, a hysterical screech in my tone.

I think my brain may explode. I think my brain *has* exploded, because there is no way this is actually happening.

Grandma meditated me into a coma and this is some sort of magic-fueled hallucination.

I could really use a fuzzy blanket right now.

"You've read some of our history—is this really that much of a surprise to you? How did Elizabeth Pruitt, her daughter Abigail even, describe their relationship with their husbands? They described their bond as *buzzing like bees' wings*, sweet girl, for a reason. And that's because electricity hadn't been invented yet and it was the closest description they had. It's a unique blessing Elizabeth passed on to her line, along with her magic. We are able to find the person who fits us like a puzzle piece."

The paragraphs I read come swirling through my mind like a windstorm. It was there, for me to see, all this time. If only I had paid attention.

"I've been drawing his eyes for months," I blabber. "I only just met him, but I knew his eyes already."

Her smile is kind, eyes full of tears. "That doesn't surprise me. You have always had such a beautiful connection with your art. It makes sense that your magic would speak to you through it."

She's got a way with words sometimes. The urge to flee lessens as I absorb some of her joy, her glee.

"A unique blessing for our line?"

She nods. "Something you'll learn as you submerge yourself in our world is that the Pruitt line is well respected for a reason. We are the only ones who can find our soulmates through the electric touch."

"Was Dad . . ." I gulp down the lump in my throat. "Was Dad Mom's soulmate?"

I know the answer before Grandma can nod her head. "Their bond was special. It was a blessing watching them grow in their love for so many years."

"Grandpa. He left when Mom was so young . . . He couldn't have been?"

"No, Grandpa wasn't my soulmate. While I loved him with my whole heart, I have not been blessed with finding mine." The sadness in her eyes pulls fresh tears to my own. "He came quite close, though."

My arms are around her before I consciously decide to hug her. Her embrace is a balm on my frayed nerves.

"Don't be sad for me, sweetheart. I mourned long ago, and I can find joy in watching my beautiful girls finding their love. Now, you must tell me all about Noah. I also expect to meet him shortly."

I chuckle—it's a watery, happy, emotional thing. "It may be a little soon for meeting everyone."

"Nonsense." She shakes her head, wiping a tear from my cheek with her thumb. "He's family now."

Jesus. That hits me like a gut punch. I would love to have Noah in my life for as long as I can, of course. It's not the concept of forever with him that scares me . . . It's the fact that I could lose him. Just like Mom lost Dad.

"Here is your homework for the next week," Grandma says, drawing my attention back from that destructive line of thinking. "You're coming with me to the market tomorrow, but in your free time you should connect with your element. Work on what that looks like to you. Spend some time in nature. Listen to the wind. Come back on Tuesday and we'll take another step forward."

"Yes, ma'am." We stand and a wave of fatigue rolls through me. I turn toward the back of the shop, toward my bed.

"And Hazel?"

"Yes?"

"I expect to see Noah in the shop this week."

CHAPTER 21

THE CLEARING

The next day, the market smells exactly the same. That nature-y, herby scent that I've begun to associate with witches.

Witches like their damn herbs.

There are fewer stalls this week, but not by many. It seems as though some business owners rotate out depending on what they have available.

Unlike last time, I stay by Grandma's side as we meander past the people going about their days. She walks through and the crowd parts almost unconsciously.

Apparently she acts like a queen everywhere, not just with me and Laura.

A group of kids bowls past us, one rebellious little troublemaker directing at the front. The four of them weave through the crowd with a practiced ease that screams familiarity. They've been in these crowds for their entire lives.

"Carter, stay within the barriers!" a woman calls after them from her booth. With that she turns back to her customer, seemingly unbothered.

My heart pangs. Even before Dad died, I don't remember coming to the market. Would Laura and I have grown up running through the legs of other witches if my mother had allowed it?

Grandma swats my hand lightly. "Keep up!"

I divert my gaze from the children and follow her to a stand with a woman selling specialty tea. The two of them duck heads and are instantly cackling like old hags. I roll my eyes with a fond smile.

"Carter?"

I turn back to the woman. Her eyes scan the crowd for the children. They're nowhere to be seen.

"Give me a moment, Grandma." I pat her on the shoulder and walk in the direction the children went earlier.

The wind whips hair across my face as I pass through the people, looking for any trace of the group. I run out of stalls soon enough.

I have to be close to the barrier at this point. It's invisible, but the magic is palpable. The barrier itself is some sort of ancient magic to repel humans and evil intentions.

The field has entirely run out and I'm standing at the edge of a dark forest. The kids wouldn't leave the barrier, would they? They couldn't have been older than ten, so not rebellious teenagers looking for danger.

A chill travels down my spine as I watch the darkness underneath the canopy of leaves. There couldn't be danger out there, could there? I look back toward the market.

I could very easily grab Grandma, tell her that—what? I have a *feeling*? That something in my gut is screaming at me to find those kids before something awful happens?

I turn back to the trees. The wind whispers through the leaves with an ominous whine.

I step forward.

Where's the person throwing popcorn at me, telling me to get out of here? I could really use that person.

Leaves crunch underfoot as I walk as softly as I can manage. The world darkens with each step, the air closing in on me until there's no sound at all.

Not an owl, a squirrel . . . Hell, I'd take a rat right now.

The silence follows me like a bubble, encasing me in nothingness as I keep moving forward. Can I turn back yet?

No. Not yet.

A branch breaks.

My head perks up, turning toward the sound. It's to my left, off the path. Please tell me these kids aren't dumb enough to go off the path in a creepy-ass forest.

I turn and tip-toe until . . . Oh, shit. I duck behind a tree and peek.

In a small clearing is a child—Carter, I believe—and what *is* that?

A hulking creature with long, sharp horns looms over the child. It's swathed in a thick black cloak that conceals most of its body, but I see the flash of claws in the dim light.

The poor dear has the nerve to stare right back at it. Whatever *it* is.

I could go get Grandma. I *should* get Grandma. But my feet are rooted to the spot.

Where are the other children? I flick my gaze over the trees and —there! A pink sneaker pokes out from behind one. They haven't abandoned their friend.

I have to respect that, despite the fact at least one of them should've run back to the market.

Okay, Hazel. How are we handling this? I'm the only adult in the vicinity and despite me probably being less trained than these little kids, I can't let them get hurt.

With a deep breath, I step out from the tree line. "It's time to go, Carter."

Maybe I can convince this daemon I know what the hell I'm doing. I assume it's a daemon, I have no idea.

That's not comforting.

A dark, twisted laugh escapes the creature. It turns to me, red eyes burning into my skin. "We're simply playing, sister. Are you here to join us?"

The thing's fangs glint in the sliver of sunlight breaking through the canopy above us. Long and bright white.

Cool.

I'm super dead.

I gesture to the child, waving him over to me. If I can get him behind me, maybe he can get away and get help. Real help. Not whatever I am.

Carter makes a break for it and the daemon allows it, a twisted smile on its leathery skin. It's difficult to see, with the shadows of the trees playing across its face.

"I would much rather play with you, anyway, sister." It holds a hand up to me, a snake slithering along its palm.

Oh I am royally screwed. Royally. Screwed.

"Go," I whisper.

The sound of running feet fills the space and I exhale. Probably prematurely. But at least they got away.

"A Pruitt witch approaches and doesn't have the decency to say hello?" it continues. "No introduction?"

He knows who I am? Why do I feel like I've walked right into a trap? It's not even funny how out of my depth I am.

I channel my inner Laura. False confidence is better than none at all.

"I'm Hazel." I step fully into the clearing. "And yourself?"

"Botis. I was hoping to run into you."

Botis. Daemon.

The name that I've been obsessing over for a week, and here he is.

I wanted time. Time to learn how to defend myself, to learn how to defeat a creature like this. To learn how to get information out of daemons. Because there is a chance—albeit a small one—that this thing knows what killed my dad. I had a plan and now it's all gone to absolute shit.

Grandma's meditation techniques go through my head. I can't have a panic attack about how I wanted things to go and how I'm going to die right now.

"I've heard of you."

The grin on his face spreads, fangs practically jumping out of his mouth. "You flatter me, Hazel."

"Trust me, that wasn't my intention." Hell, yeah. There's that false bravado.

Strong arms cross against his chest, claws poking out of his long, black sleeves. "You snap like an animal caught in a trap."

"Only one of us kidnaps children, so who is the real animal here?"

A stinging slash as bright as the sun breaks against my cheek, pain following immediately after. He hasn't moved an inch, yet hot droplets of blood roll down my skin.

"You talk too much," he growls. His voice is an evil mix of animalistic growl and human lilt. "An unfortunate trait you witches tend to share."

Yes, I'm buying time, asshole. My hand touches my cheek and I wince. The cut is deep.

"I can honestly say that's the first time I've ever been accused of that."

"I have a message for the Pruitt witches."

"And here I have nothing for you in return. How rude of me." My entire being is vibrating with the knowledge that I'm going to die right now.

"I don't mind, sister. Besides . . ." A sickening, face-splitting grin breaks on his face. "The message isn't *for* you. You are the message."

Oh, shit.

I close my eyes as my entire body slams against a tree. Pain splinters from my back down every single nerve. I'm held aloft against the tree as if pinned by a thousand nails.

I open my eyes to the sound of boots crunching across the leafy bed of the clearing. He approaches, red eyes blazing with the promise of exactly what he's going to do with me.

I don't expect mercy.

"No words now? No smart comments?" He *tsk*s. "So disappointing."

"Let me down and I'll tell you exactly what I think about you." Blood drips from my mouth, spotting the leaves below.

He chuckles. It's the confident chuckle of someone who enjoys playing with their food—and lucky for me, I'm the meal.

One sharpened talon trails along the exposed skin at my navel where my shirt rode up. It's like a fancy knife, so sharp the slice doesn't start to bleed until a few seconds after. The snake's tongue gently flickers at a droplet.

"There's a beauty in marring skin with no scars."

"What do you hope to accomplish by killing me? You'll only piss off a bunch of powerful women who will kick your ass."

He laughs. "I doubt they'll ever find me. I'm doing this . . . Well, because I was asked to, and it was too tempting an offer to refuse. This quarrel isn't mine. I have no intention of sticking around for the aftermath."

"You're someone's errand boy? I should've known. You don't have main character energy." If I'm going to die, I'm going to piss him off enough that he makes it quick.

His talon slices in a thin line down my right arm—straight through the vein, if the blood gushing out is any indication.

My head is lighter and I don't know if it's spinning or if the earth is moving a bit faster. The taste of blood is metallic on my tongue.

"Draven was right about you lot. Talkative, cocky, and weak."

Draven? Who is Draven?

"Draven the one who pulls your strings?" My voice is tired. My eyelids are heavy but I force them open.

"Draven—" his voice drops and he gets right in my face. The stench of blood lingers on his breath, "—is the one who will destroy your entire family. Too bad you won't live to see it."

My body flies off the tree and slams back into it. Pain blooms at the back of my head.

Again.·

And again.
And again.
And again.
"Hazel!"
Mom?
The world goes black.

CHAPTER 22

NOTHING

The light is what wakes me. It burns even with my eyes shut.

Voices follow. Grandma, Laura, Mom.

Mom?

Despite their heaviness, I blink through the pain and open my eyelids. I'm in Grandma's cottage, presumably in her bedroom. The floral wallpaper extends to this room, which is about the same size as my bedroom in my apartment.

"She's awake," Laura says, a mix of relief and something else in her tone. She's standing in the open doorway, soon joined by both Grandma and Mom.

Grandma approaches first, sitting down next to me on the royal-purple bedspread. Mom lingers in the doorway. If I thought she was closed off the day I left, well, she's outdoing herself now. Her shoulders are square, her posture rigid. She's barely even looking at me.

"How do you feel, sweetheart?" Grandma asks. She waves her hand over my face, a healing warmth emanating from her spread fingers.

I instinctively lean toward it, as if it can burn away the pain. "Like shit." My voice is hollow and breathy.

Laura snorts from the corner of the room. "No shit, bitch. You got your ass beat."

"Laura." Mother's voice makes the Earth stop spinning for a second. I've never heard her sound like that. Sharp and callous, as emotionless as her face. Laura shrinks back into her corner, arms wrapped around herself.

"Laura has a point," I say. Even now, I revel in the way Mom's nostrils flare at my response. I hope that pissed you off.

Grandma's face falls, the disappointment rolling off her in waves. "Not now, girls, please. I'll go make you some tea, Hazel. Sarah, join me."

Surprisingly, Mom follows her out of the room and closes the door behind her.

I lean back and close my eyes against the headache that pounds under my eyelids. I must have a concussion; I hit that tree too many damn times to come out unscathed.

"What were you *thinking?*" Laura's voice holds a fresh disappointment that cuts through my heart like the daemon cut through my skin. She's hurt. She's scared.

And I did that. Not anyone else.

Me.

But I can't answer her question. I don't think she'd understand even if I tried.

"Who found me?" I ask instead, meeting her gaze.

Laura's eyebrows furrow. "Grandma. She has some sort of magical protection spell on us, apparently. She sensed you were in danger when he first hit you. The children helped her narrow down your location. She grabbed a few other people and stormed into the forest."

That'll do it.

"Ah."

"Ah?" She scoffs. "Ah, she says. Like you didn't give us all a fucking heart attack. Like you didn't give us all PTS-fucking-D from when Dad died. A fucking *demon,* Hazel. Are you an idiot?"

"I believe it's daemon, with an 'a'," I snap. The overwhelming guilt has my walls up. I don't want to face her, so I drop my eyes to my hands instead.

"No, Hazel, it's idiot with an 'i'."

My head pounds. The combination of the concussion, whatever spells Grandma put on me, and the bruises threatening to blur my vision.

That could also be the tears.

"You just don't understand," I whisper.

She throws her hands in the air. She has dried blood under her fingernails. Is that *my* blood? "What don't I understand? What is it that caused you to throw yourself at death like you're invincible?"

"I don't know!" I can't focus on the pain in her face. The floodgates have opened and I can't stop the rushing of words. "Did I have a moment where I could've turned around? Where I could've grabbed other people to help those kids? Maybe. But I didn't do it. I chose to do it myself. What does it matter anyway? I don't have a life."

Each word burns my lungs, but I can't stop. "You have *friends*, Laura, you're going to college, you have everyone wrapped around your finger—you have *me* wrapped around your finger. Have you ever wondered what it feels like to not have any of that? To not know what the hell you're doing at any given moment and never feeling like you belong anywhere? That nothing you do means anything?" My fingers dig into the heels of my hands. "The only things I have are anger and a desire to protect my family, and I saw . . . I saw children who needed to be protected the way we needed to be protected. I saw children and I saw us and . . . I don't know, Laura. I don't know what you want me to say."

Her eyes fill with tears, her hand coming up to hold her cheek as if she's been slapped. "Is that what we are to you? Nothing? Mom, Grandma, me, Noah? We're all nothing to you?"

Shit.

"Laura, that's not—"

"No, it's exactly what you meant. If I mean so little to you, you won't mind if I leave."

I try to lift myself out of bed to follow her, but it's as if my muscles are filled with lead. She's gone before I even get a finger to move.

And I know she's not coming back.

I don't deserve for her to come back.

I didn't mean that they meant nothing. I meant that they mean everything and I've never had anything for me. Not since Noah.

Shit. Noah.

How long have I been out? What day is it?

I turn toward the bedside table. Where's my phone? There's just a glass of water and a clock that doesn't work.

"Don't strain yourself," Grandma says softly as she opens the bedroom door. Despite everything, I smile at the two steaming mugs of tea bobbing along behind her.

"What day is it?" I croak. I hold my hands out for the mug and it settles calmly in my grip. The scent of peppermint dances in the steam wafting from the cup.

Grandma pulls a chair beside the bed and sits in it delicately. "Friday."

Ouch. Sitting up too quickly is a no-no. "I was out that long?"

"Unfortunately your wounds were extensive. We needed you sedated for the healer to work."

"Where's my phone? Noah must be worried sick."

Grandma hands me my phone from her pocket. "I texted him for you. I told him you weren't feeling well and were going to *crash* at your grandma's house. He has checked in a few times and I've kept him updated. He's quite the sweetheart."

"Thank you. I won't ask how you got past my password."

"Best not to." She pats my leg underneath the blanket. "When you're feeling up to it, we really should discuss what happened."

I blow out a dramatic breath. "Must we?"

"We must."

"If we must, can we do it later? The cold shoulder from Mom gave me freezer burn."

Grandma chuckles. "Of course. Rest up."

She leaves me alone with my phone, closing the door behind her. I want to text Noah but the combination of the peppermint tea, the concussion, and the warm bed is too tempting to resist.

THE NEXT TIME MY EYES FLUTTER OPEN, THE SUN SITS LOWER IN THE sky. Not exactly dusk, but it's long past noon. A few hours then. Rosie sleeps at the end of the bed like a little watch-cat, keeping me safe.

I'd be surprised if Laura were still here. The look in her eyes haunted my dreams during my brief nap. The way she reared back as if I had physically struck her with my words.

She doesn't understand. She doesn't get that I couldn't turn my back on those kids, even to get proper help. She doesn't get that it felt good—despite the fact I almost died—to have a purpose. Even for one moment.

To know that what I was doing was the right thing.

I sigh, shaking my head. There are some things we may never see eye to eye on.

It sucks that she doubts how much I love her. That she doubts how much she means to me. I would do anything for her. I'm *trying* to help her. I'm trying to get stronger so I can find this daemon who killed our chance at being a true, happy family. I'm doing this for her.

A nagging voice in the back of my head says I'm doing this for myself.

Maybe it's both.

Noah: I miss you.

Noah: How are you feeling? It's been almost a week and I'm not going to lie, I'm worried about you.

What up, soulmate? God, I haven't even seen him since that

revelation. But explaining my magic, my history, and our soulmate status to Noah is at the bottom of my list right now. He deserves to know, but I honestly don't even know where to begin with that.

It's a conversation that's just going to have to wait until I can actually sit up without wincing.

> Hazel: I miss you, too. This flu is a nasty one, but I'm on the up and up. Hopefully I can see you next weekend.

Granted, by next weekend I'll still have bruises, cuts, and whatever else is under these sheets that I'm too scared to look at. Lord knows Noah will have an opinion on that.

Hi honey. Oh, these bruises? Cuts? Slashes? Scars? They're nothing. Just remnants of the flu.

That'll go over well.

> Noah: Whenever you're ready. I just appreciate you keeping me updated. Let me know if there's anything I can do. Nonna Ricci makes a badass chicken noodle soup.

I have the best soulmate. Truly.

"How are you feeling?" The door to the bedroom opens, revealing Grandma holding a tray. She's loaded it with her own chicken noodle soup and a steaming mug of tea.

I shrug, the movement making me wince. "I think that's answer enough."

She smiles, placing the tray on my lap. She assists me until I'm sitting up against the pillows resting against the wood headboard.

"Grandma, can witches do glamours?"

Grandma arches an eyebrow in reply. Despite being the target of it most of the time, I truly do respect the woman's sass.

"I was watching this one episode of *Charmed*—"

"If you are about to compare our ancient magic to a television show . . ." Her gaze sharpens. "Don't."

Okay then. Message received.

"I'd like to see Noah soon, but I have some wounds that would be difficult to describe. And I'm not necessarily ready to have the 'I'm a witch' conversation. Is there a way to magically hide them?"

"Ahh, I understand. Yes, there is. I can assist you once you're feeling up to it." She picks up the spoon and hands it to me.

Each reach forward is excruciating, but I know I need to get moving. I've watched enough medical dramas to know that moving around after a serious injury is important. Thanks, *Grey's Anatomy*.

She clears her throat after I take a few slurps of soup. "I'd like to know what happened, Hazel."

I swallow a little too quickly and end up coughing up soup. Note to self, coughing while injured? Not a good thing. My entire body aches by the time my lungs stop seizing up.

"I have a question first."

"If you must," she says.

"I must." I take a deep breath. Ouch. "What happened to Botis?"

"He's gone. The intention was to question him, but . . ." Fear haunts her eyes as she stares at my soup. "He was destroyed before we could get our hands on him. Something did not want him talking."

The name Botis said. What was it?

"Draven," I whisper.

The candle on the dresser in the corner extinguishes in a flash of water, and all sound along with it. I half expect the house to start rumbling and explode.

"Where did you hear that name?" my mother hisses from the doorway.

Ah, so she's still here.

If looks could kill, I would be an eviscerated pile of dust right now. Her face is thunder, darkness threatening to swallow anything good forever.

"He sent Botis. I was supposed to be a message to the family."

Lightning strikes right outside my window and my body jumps involuntarily.

Grandma stands, approaching Mom like a baby gazelle might

approach a hungry lion. "Sarah, she doesn't know. She's just telling us the truth."

The death stare moves from me to Grandma, but Grandma stands tall. Confident. Unflinching as she continues moving toward Mom.

"Who is Draven?" I ask. I realize I'm pushing my luck, but I already almost died. And I'm feeling feisty after being stuck unconscious in this bed for a week.

Grandma's shoulders visibly tense, her mouth opening and closing as if she wants to speak but physically can't. "I cannot . . . tell you."

"Why? Mom, who is Draven?" I have a tingling in my gut, not just from my injury. A feeling like I know exactly who Draven is. But I want to hear her say it. "Who is he?"

"Sarah, if she's right then she deserves to know. They both do. It could be the difference between life and death." Grandma finally reaches Mom, putting a hand on her shoulder.

Mom shakes it off, the storm still brewing in her eyes and outside. Rain pounds against the windows. "Fine. But none of this would have happened if you would have just *stayed home.*"

Her words hit me like the killing blow. She's blaming me for the danger our family is in. Anger flares in my belly, causing my cheeks to heat and my hands to shake.

"Keep telling yourself that. But if you hadn't hidden magic from me for my entire life, I might not have almost died. I would have been able to defend myself, not just sit there like a harmless rabbit. My death would've been your fault and I'm guessing Dad's was, too!"

The storm turns to despair as Mom's eyes well up with tears.

Good. My anger wants her to hurt just as much as she's hurt me over the years. Just as much as I did when he died.

"Draven killed your father and now he's returned to kill the rest of us."

With that, she turns and leaves. The second family member to do the same to me in just a few hours.

Shit.

"That could've gone better," I whisper, trying to inject some sort of levity into all this.

Grandma shakes her head. "Not now, Hazel."

Now I really do have nothing, and it's all my fault.

CHAPTER 23

PEPPERMINT TEA

Everyone is acting as if I'm the villain. As if I'm not the only one trying to fix our family. We've been living in this toxic bubble of lies for years and I'm the only one trying to change that. Why is that so awful? Why is it so terrible that I want a *real* relationship with my family?

I guess I'll never understand them, just like they'll never understand me.

I just want Noah. I'm sick of being stuck in this house. In this bed. With these people.

Noah gets me. Noah understands.

Okay, Noah has no idea that this is even happening, but he *would* understand. He doesn't judge me or put pressure on me to be anything but me.

I whip my phone out before I consciously register what I'm doing and click on Noah's name. The phone is ringing, and wow I don't remember when I last spoke to someone on the phone.

"Hazel?" Noah's gentle rumble fills my entire body with a safety I've never felt with anyone.

"Hey," I breathe. I finally really breathe for the first time since I got slammed against that tree.

A gentle rustling filters through the phone, like pages of a book or manuscript. "How are you feeling?"

I have a giant gaping wound on my belly that I'm too scared to look at.

"Recovering. I miss you. How are you?" At least I'm not outright lying, I *am* recovering.

In finding myself, I'm also finding a lot of lies.

Shit. I need to figure out how to drop this witchy bomb.

"I miss you, too. I've been worried about you." His voice is soft, the kind of pure worry that doesn't carry guilt with it.

Despite the day—the week—I've had, he makes me smile. I imagine the world could be burning around us and I'd still be smiling if Noah were around. "I'll be back to normal eventually. I wish I could see you, but I don't want to get you sick."

I don't want you to see my battered pulp of a body.

He scoffs. "You know I don't give a fuck about that. If you want me, baby, I'll jump in the car right now."

This man and his words. If my run-in with Botis didn't kill me, Noah's sweetness just might.

"I'm at my Grandma's, she's been taking care of me . . ."

"If you want me, I will get in the car. I don't care where the destination is, so long as you're there."

How quickly could Grandma whip up a glamour? Because *yowza.* What I would give to see this man right now. "I'd have to ask her. And she's a really private person. I can't promise she'll say yes."

"Whatever you want. I can swing by Nonna Ricci's. Is there anything that sounds good to you?"

"You mean other than literally everything she makes?"

He laughs, a low noise almost like water trickling over rocks in the middle of the forest.

"I'll get you some good stuff if your Grandma says yes."

"I'll ask and text you?"

"Sounds good. I miss you, I'm glad you're feeling at least a little better."

As I hang up, Grandma materializes in the doorway.

Freakin' ears of a bat.

"Of course I want Noah to come over. Meeting your soulmate would be the perfect way to light up such a dark week. He will come over now. And I'll glamour you in the meantime."

There's really no point in me replying to her. She's decided it and I got what I want, so I'm going to keep my damn mouth shut.

I text Noah the address and relax back into the bed. Fatigue threatens to close my eyes once more despite my excitement for Noah to arrive.

"Rest. I'll let him in when he arrives," Grandma insists. A new cup of tea floats in and I raise a brow at her. Is she trying to get some alone time with Noah?

"Fine, but make sure to hide your witchy nonsense before he gets here. I haven't had that conversation with him yet and I plan to do it when I'm not covered in bruises."

She nods, waving her hand at me to drink the tea. At some point I'm going to ask her what's in this because there's no way it's just peppermint.

Drinking it in one not-as-scalding-as-fresh-tea-should-be gulp, I lie back against the pillows. Hopefully I can trust her to behave.

It's the sound of laughter that wakes me from my deliciously naked dream about Noah. If I had my way, he would always be naked.

It takes my brain a second to process why the heck there would be laughing until it clicks.

Noah is here.

Noah is here and laughing.

Noah is here, laughing, and alone with Grandma.

Oh no. Oh no no no.

I can't stand up to go in there and save him—and save myself from whatever embarrassing torture Grandma is putting me through.

They'll make their way in here eventually and until then I'm forced to listen to their laughter. Why are they getting along so well? It's unsettling.

Shit. My body.

I throw off the covers in a move that is both entirely too fast and entirely too painful to see that my cuts and bruises are covered. Grandma must have done the glamour in my sleep.

Thank God for small miracles.

The laughter approaches, bringing with it Noah's quiet, rumbling voice. Even just the sound of it drifting through the door brings me peace. I replace the blanket, much slower this time, and wait for them.

He's here. In all of his chin-dimple smile glory.

I barely resist the urge to make little grabby hands at him. I just want his touch, our electricity.

Us.

"Hey, you." The concern in his eyes.is accompanied by a kindness I can't begin to feel worthy of. He moves quickly across the room to my side.

My breath of relief is immediate and intense as he touches me and the electric buzz slides up my arm.

"Missed you," I whisper, practically yanking on him.

He tumbles a bit, but steadies himself and lowers onto the bed beside me. "Come here, baby."

I slowly nuzzle into his open arms, pressing my face into his chest and inhaling. His arms gently wrap around me, soothing my heart for the first time.

My eyes burn as the emotions from the last week threaten to overwhelm me. The safety I feel in his arms has allowed me to feel too safe. Feel too open. And I'm ready to crack. Ready to admit how genuinely terrified I was.

Am.

How hurt I am about Laura and Mom, how abandoned I feel. I almost died, and they're gone.

I would never leave them. Clearly the feeling isn't mutual.

"I'll give you two some time," Grandma says. She was here? The door closes behind her and I bury my face deeper into him.

"How do you smell so good after being sick for an entire week? Don't expect that from me." Noah kisses the top of my head.

I chuckle, my body protesting the movement. "Dork."

I pull away to grab the covers, insisting he get under them with me. I want proper cuddles, and that's not happening if he's not in my blanket nest with me. He gets the message and wraps himself around me within my cocoon.

"What were you and Grandma laughing about?" The curiosity is eating me alive.

He shakes his head. "That's between us. Ask something else."

"Fine. Then at least tell me what you've been doing this week. I need an update on you." I need to get my mind off me.

He sighs, kissing my forehead. "You mean other than worrying about you?"

"Definitely. Anything other than me."

"I went to work, went to the bookstore, went running every morning, went to see Nonna Ricci." He seems to search his mind. "Oh! We had a guys' night on Wednesday."

"Guys' night, huh? Tell me more." I wiggle a little, snuggling into his embrace.

"Don't get too excited. It was just Benji and Jason. We played some video games and ate a bunch of food."

My eyelids droop despite myself. "Benji is the one I saw at the bar? He hit on Laura?"

Noah chuckles. "That's the one. Never did handle breakups well. I hope he didn't bother her."

"Nahhh, she's used to it. She's the pretty one." Am I slurring?

"To me, Hazel, you are the most beautiful person in the entire world."

"You don't have a choice."

My response makes his body tense. Makes my body tense. I meant it as a joke, but he doesn't know the punchline.

Do I really believe that? Yes, he's my soulmate, but that doesn't mean he has no choice, does it? He has a choice. He could choose to leave me. He won't die if he's not with me or something dramatic like that. I still have to earn his love and respect by treating *him* with love and respect.

"Hazel . . ."

I meet his eyes. "I'm sorry. I'm exhausted. It was a self-deprecating joke, but it didn't land."

His expression softens, the tension sliding out of his limbs. "Would you like me to leave so you can get some rest? I just wanted to see you, but I don't want to get in the way of you getting better. I left your food from Nonna in the kitchen."

"Can—" Deep breath. "Can you stay? I sleep better when I'm with you."

"Whatever you need. I'm yours, Hazel."

He's mine. I never wanted something to be mine as much as him.

"I need you." The raw impact of the last week hits again in the second wave of the evening. My eyes burn as I allow him to wrap me up. What I wouldn't give to be able to hide in Noah for the rest of my life. But I can't.

The daemon who killed my father is coming after all of us now, and whatever hole I spent the last few years living in has officially closed over. I'm in this and there's no way to get out.

The lives of my family, of Noah potentially, and myself rest squarely on my shoulders.

No pressure.

CHAPTER 24

WARLOCKS

I don't hear anything from Laura or Mom again. Not when I can finally start walking, not when I move back to my apartment, not when I quit teaching art classes so I have more time to focus on magic and the store, not when I start training with Grandma again.

Nothing.

I bet Mom hasn't told Laura anything about Botis or Draven, so she's in the dark. My texts go unanswered.

So the fate of my family rests firmly on me. And Grandma.

At least Grandma is willing to help.

"Spells are for witches that don't have much power," she says as we sit cross-legged on the shop floor.

It's Sunday—training day. The fourth since I recovered from my accident. I can now levitate on demand, summon air to whip around me in a disorienting torrent, and use it to deflect most attacks. All defensive abilities.

"Then why are there so many spellbooks?" I ask.

"Because there aren't many families with our lineage." Her chest puffs with pride. "The Pruitt women are an ancient line, and we are well respected in our community. It is quite rare to be able to trace your powers all the way to Salem."

"Are we really so powerful?"

187

"Yes. We are. Why do you think Draven is so concerned about us? A line of women who grow stronger with each generation? I'm surprised he let us go for so long."

"And he's not a daemon? He's a warlock?"

She sighs. She's come up with excuses every time I've asked since Botis. She's always had an excuse, or some reason to flee to another room. "He's a warlock. A witch that turned."

"And how does that happen?"

"Slowly. Magic isn't inherently evil, but it is seductive. And it's very easy to feel invincible, like there's nothing you can't do. That line of thinking can turn you, turn the magic, and before you know it you can't recognize yourself anymore."

Gears turn in my head. "And what happens when you become a warlock?"

"The lust for power becomes insatiable." She rubs her temples. "Power becomes everything. And you are willing to do anything for that power. Hurt, maim, kill."

"Hence why Draven came after us. He wanted our power."

She nods. "I can't . . . I can't speak any more about it. My tongue is locked."

"Locked? Grandma, why does your face do that whenever I ask about Dad or Draven?"

Her lips purse together as if she sucked on a lemon. "My face doesn't do anything, and I would advise you not to suggest otherwise."

A shiver goes down my spine at her tone. Sometimes I let myself forget how much I absolutely don't want to mess with her.

She sighs. "I made a vow not to divulge the details of that evening. And I am unable to break that vow, no matter how much I regret making it."

"A vow? You promised Mom?" So much makes sense. Grandma has never seemed scared of Mom, so I could never piece together why she never answered my questions. But a vow? Maybe even a magical vow? That would ensure Grandma could never tell me anything.

Just another way Mom is controlling my life.

She nods. "Let us continue."

That conversation is done. If I ever want to really know what happened to Dad, I'm going to have to hear it from the horse's mouth.

And that horse has chosen silence.

"Today, we are learning offense. We have gone over defense enough and I believe you're ready for more offensive tactics."

I practically wiggle on my pillow. After facing—and promptly getting my ass kicked by—Botis, I'm ready to learn how to defend myself. And to kick ass in return.

Even if I can't kick Botis's ass because Draven beat me to the punch.

"Stop that. You must center yourself, Hazel. And part of that is knowing when to calm down."

She's pissy about Mom and taking it out on me. Has been ever since Mom stormed out of her house.

"Yes, Grandma."

"It's all about connecting to your element, then manifesting what you want to happen." She closes her eyes and opens her palms toward the floor. "For me, I am connecting to the earth. In situations where I must be offensive toward an attacker, I imagine the roots of trees coming up and tying them to the ground. How can the air, the wind, assist you in debilitating your attacker?"

I close my eyes. How can I offensively use the air? I snort. God, this is so weird. Normal people worry about things like *work*, and I'm over here trying to figure out how to debilitate an attacker using my little witchy magic.

"*Hazel*," Grandma snaps.

Right, right. Focusing.

I could trap someone in a vortex, like a little mini-tornado. I call the wind, the air, as I've learned to do from our lessons. I open my eyes and manifest. Direct my power toward the training dummy on the other side of the room. Trap that dummy!

The wind whooshes through my hair, whipping the auburn

strands around my face, and swirls around the dummy. It's not a full vortex, but it's something.

"Do you think I could defeat Draven?"

So much for letting that conversation go. She has to know that Draven won't rest until he kills all of us, and that I won't rest until he's gone instead. There's only two ways this all pans out and she's smart enough to know that. Despite Mom's denial, I would expect even *she* knows that.

"On your own?" She snorts. "No."

"But I thought you said I was powerful!" Am I pouting?

Her eyes narrow. "You are powerful. But no one is all-powerful. You would need help even just to banish him, let alone defeat him."

"There's a difference?"

"Sometimes I forget how little you know." It's not unkind, the way she says it, but it still pokes at the little place inside me that hates that I know nothing. I was useless against Botis, and I may be just as useless against Draven even after a month of training. "You can banish a warlock or daemon from Earth. They are returned to their world. To Hell. And it takes power and time to return to Earth. Although some don't return at all." She rubs at that same spot on her temple again as if she's trying to force away a migraine. "It's not a permanent solution, but it can be an advantageous one when fighting something more powerful than you. Time is not to be taken for granted. Time can mean the difference between success and defeat."

I know the importance of time. I've lost so much precious time and I'm like a hamster on a wheel trying to catch up—to make up for it.

"Do you plan to help me?" Maybe it's an aggressive question, but at this point she's my only potential ally. Laura probably doesn't even know what's going on, and is at the same disadvantage as I am. She knows even less about her magic than I do. Mom? Ha! As if she'd help me. She's proven time and time again that I mean nothing to her anymore.

Grandma looks at me. Her face is an impartial, unfeeling mask as she just *looks* at me. Seconds turn to a full minute and I'm squirming where I sit.

"Our family is at risk," she finally says. "I would not allow you to go up against Draven on your own. It is obvious he will continue trying to pick us off one by one if nothing is done about him."

I resist the urge to do a victory fist pump. While I may be trying to catch up, Grandma has had all the time in the world to refine her powers. I know she and I can do this together.

"But—"

Oh, shit.

"We will need your sister and your mother. You and I can't do this on our own."

I was afraid she'd say that. Way to harsh my mood, Grandma.

"Do you still talk to either of them?" Part of me wants her to still be talking to Laura at least, but the other part knows it would hurt if it's just me that's been iced out. Laura was my life for so long, and being left on 'read' is hurtful.

A sad smile breaks on her face. "Laura texts me from time to time. Your mother less so, but she's responsive."

"That's more than I have. If you want them to help us, I think it's up to you." My hands ball into fists. "Neither of them seem to care what I have to say."

"There is so much hurt here, on both sides. I can try to be the bridge as I have always done, but even I am limited. Someone will need to take the first step and be vulnerable and allow the others back in." Her hand lands on mine in what I assume is meant to be reassuring.

It's not. It's just infuriating.

"Why is it always me? Why am I always the one to take the first step and do something? What about Mom? What about Laura? I almost died and neither one of them has bothered to check on me and see if I'm okay. We've been threatened by the warlock that killed our father and neither one of them is trying to come up with a plan. You are the only one willing to help me and I can tell it's reluctantly." I ignore the flash of pain my words cause her and press on. "Why is everyone in this family so content to sit back and do nothing while we're being hunted? If I died, would you all clam up and pretend nothing happened, just like Dad? It's disgusting how his memory has been treated. His death was in vain, and at this rate mine will be, too."

My chest heaves.

Her mouth gapes open like a fish, but no words come out. Only silence.

That's just like this family. Everything is silence.

If it's up to me, then it's up to me. I'll figure out how to defeat Draven on my own, I'll figure out how to avenge Dad on my own, and I'll figure out how to keep all of us alive in the meantime.

On. My. Own.

"I'm done with this." I stand, wiping invisible dust off my pants. "I'll see you later, Grandma. Hopefully I haven't been murdered by then."

CHAPTER 25

FOR NOAH

Loneliness is a crushing thing. A boulder that sits heavily on your chest as a constant reminder that no one cares about you.

The only thing cracking at that boulder is Noah. Noah and his caring touches, his soothing laughter, his electric current. The way he truly cares about me and my well-being. Even if he has literally no idea what I am and what's hunting me.

It's awful that I haven't told him. It's just another weight on my chest, but every time he looks at me with those big, trusting brown-black eyes with his bushy eyebrows furrowed in concern, I just can't do it.

"What's going on, baby? You've barely touched your cheese-cake," he says, brushing a hair off my forehead and tucking it behind my ear.

We're snuggled up on the hand-me-down couch at his apartment. It's my second time here and I'm still getting used to it. It's very . . . man? I don't know. He lives with Benji and Jason, and it's obvious. Where a dining table should sit there's a giant pool table, and the kitchen is covered in takeout boxes and red cups. The place is clean—which I suspect is purely Noah's doing—but has that bachelor feel that has me searching for hand sanitizer.

I shake my head. "I'm just distracted. Family drama."

"You don't talk much about your family. A little about Laura and a little about your Grandma, but nothing else. You know I'm here for you, right?"

Twist the knife a little deeper there, Noah. I think there's still some depths you haven't reached.

"I don't even know how to explain it all." I sigh, burying my face into the soft skin of his neck. "I just like escaping with you to a place where I can forget all about it for a while."

"Whatever you need." His voice is muffled by my hair.

"What about your family? Do your mom and dad still live around here?"

His shoulders droop. "After Sam they couldn't really handle being here anymore. They packed up and moved south. They come up and visit during the holidays, or I'll go there, but it was just too tough for them."

"But not for you?" I press a kiss to his cheek, reassuring him that I'm here.

"No." He shakes his head. "I like seeing little pieces of him in the world around me."

The door bangs open as Benji and Jason stumble in with arms full of groceries. And by groceries, I mean energy drinks and pizza pockets. Typical bachelor food.

Benji is the taller of the two, lean but not lanky like Noah. His hair has the same tousled quality as Noah's, but is less curly. Just messy and brown. His eyes are a lighter brown than Noah's, more golden. Jason is the short king of the group. Not actually a short guy, but short in comparison and stocky as hell. His coarse hair is buzzed down so it's barely there. His bright brown eyes light up as he notices me wrapped around Noah.

"Look what we walked in on!" Jason says, slamming the bags on the kitchen counter. The sound reverberates through the apartment, and I instinctively try to make myself smaller. I can't stand loud noises since . . . Since Botis.

Noah, as if he can sense it, pulls me fully into his lap. His long fingers tangle in my hair and rub my scalp until I almost purr like a cat.

"Stop acting like you walked in on something dirty or she'll never come back, idiot." Benji slams into Jason's shoulder as he puts his own bags on the counter.

Jason laughs, a boisterous thing that's almost contagious. Almost. "You're just hoping Hazel will somehow convince her sister to call you."

"If she hasn't called yet, she's not going to." The words fall out of my mouth without any approval from me. Stupid scalp massage has me too relaxed.

Jason dissolves into giggles, hands on his sides. "I like her."

"I didn't mean to." I gaze up at Noah and breathe a sigh of relief at the chin-dimple grin on his face.

"Don't worry." He chuckles. "Benji needs the tough love. He's a little hung up."

"Can everyone stop talking about me like I'm not standing right here? Jesus fuck." He sighs dramatically, but winks at me all the same.

They act like brothers, the three of them. And it doesn't make me miss Laura at all.

Nope.

Doesn't make me long for a family dynamic like this one, either. Absolutely not at all.

"If you weren't standing right there, I'd be able to put this shit in the fridge. Can you fucking move?" This time Jason bumps into Benji. Personal space doesn't seem to be a concern in this group. It's oddly endearing.

Noah's lips tickle at the sensitive skin of my ear. "Do you want to head to my room?"

I nod. He stands and leads me toward his bedroom. The hallway is lined with photos of the three of them and their families. For a bachelor pad, it's a breath of sentimental fresh air. And probably all Noah.

Noah's room itself is practically a different universe. Where the rest of the house is bachelor city, Noah's room is calm and practical. A bed, a desk for writing, a closet, a bathroom, a bookshelf full of books, and a separate bookshelf full of *Warhammer* minis. Nothing fancy or frilly, just practical pieces that nod to his put-together personality. I can see how easy it would be to live with him. He would be in charge of the practical and sentimental side, while I would add the homey touches like fuzzy blankets.

I love my fuzzy blankets.

Without a word we lie together on his bed, staring at the ceiling, wrapped in each other's arms.

"Noah?"

"Mm?"

"Do you believe in soulmates?" I blame the scalp massage for my candor.

He turns to appraise me, his eyes trailing my face and searching for something. "Why do you ask?"

"Curiosity?"

His gaze goes back to the ceiling, his fingers trailing along my arm where it's wrapped around me. "I don't know. Sometimes I do. I like believing that there's someone out there for everyone, someone who could really understand you like no other. But other times I think about how sad that could be."

"Sad?" My hand falls on his stubbly cheek, turning him back to me. "How is that sad?"

"What about the people who never find their soulmate? Whether that be because of distance, bad luck, or death. I think about my brother. About Sam's soulmate." His voice wavers. "What do they do now that he's gone? Are they doomed to have a love that's less because my brother couldn't see a future in which he was happy or loved?"

This man. This beautiful, kind, heartbreaking man. If it were up to me, he'd never feel this kind of pain again. I'd take it from him if I could.

I drag his hand to my chest, pressing it right over my beating heart. "I'm here. And I'm never leaving you."

His smile is tearful as he rolls so we're facing each other. He presses his forehead against mine and closes his eyes.

He keeps his hand on my chest, feeling my heartbeat.

I have to do everything I can to keep it beating for him. He can't lose me, not after losing his brother. If for no other reason than this, I have to stay alive.

For Noah.

CHAPTER 26

FAMILY BONDING

I t's with Noah's heartbreaking gaze looping in my head that I stomp into the shop on Sunday morning once again, despite my dramatic exit last week. I ditched Tuesday's and Thursday's lessons to wander through the bookshop with Noah, so I'm honestly half surprised to see Grandma walking around the room lighting candles.

I figured she'd give up on me just like everyone else.

"You were right," Grandma says as I enter the room.

I almost stumble back. "Me? *Right?* Do you have a fever?"

"Sometimes your sarcasm is not as endearing as you believe it to be." Her eyes are hard. "The fate of our family shouldn't rest solely on your shoulders. Despite the self-righteous martyr act you've adopted, you are right about that. So, I spoke with your mother and sister."

"You did what now?" This time I do stumble back. Thank God for the bookshelf that catches me.

She nods. "They'll be here in half an hour. We will discuss this as a family even if we claw each other's eyes out first."

The memory of Noah's anguished face roots me to the ground despite my urge to run upstairs and hide under the fuzzy blankets. The only way I'm getting out of this alive and back to Noah is by working with them. "I'll stay. But that doesn't mean I'm going to enjoy it."

"Luckily for you, I don't think you'll be alone in that sentiment."

Instead of continuing to get my metaphorical ass kicked by a woman who has been out-sarcasming every person she meets since before I was born, I sit in the circle of candles she's created. I watch her hippie, witchy-chic skirts billow as she perfects her shop. Every herb, every crystal has a perfect space. She's creating shapes and flitting around, and it takes my eyes a few moments to adjust to the patterns.

It's like a giant altar.

Maybe she truly means to rip our cooperation out of us. It may be necessary at this point.

The jingling bell above the door sends a shiver down my spine. The skin on my hands is rosy from wringing them.

"Sarah, Laura." Grandma gestures warmly toward them. "Come sit down."

My eyes finally lift, and *damn*. Mom looks like she's been through war. Usually the woman is a drop-dead knockout, but today she's a shell of herself. Her normally liquid-gold eyes are sunken and dull, her brown hair is stringy and frazzled.

Laura at least seems put together, but her eyes dart around like those of an abused puppy.

She hasn't set foot in this shop since she was a child. I bet she's getting hit with the same memories I had when I came here for the first time. Her eyes are shiny as she sits beside me, leaving space so we aren't touching.

My hand itches to close the distance despite everything. She's my sister after all—when she hurts, I hurt.

As if sensing the sisterly love, she shifts uncomfortably, tucking her knees up to her chin. So much for that.

Mom, in all her messy glory, sits across from me. She refuses to look at me, only looking at Grandma—with a glare I bet she wishes could kill.

Grandma sits and claps her hands. "We all know why we're here. Our family is at risk."

Laura snorts. Fully indoctrinated by Mom, then. Awesome.

"I'm handling it." Even Mom's voice is broken. It's as if she hasn't slept in weeks.

"While I appreciate your strength, Sarah, you and I both know you can't do this on your own," Grandma says. While her voice is kind, her eyes are firm.

I'm lucky that Grandma has never had a problem calling Mom out on her shit.

"We wouldn't even be in this situation if Hazel didn't have a savior complex!" Laura spits from across the circle.

When did I become the center of all her vitriol?

I snap my head to her. "So has Mom just been poisoning you against me all this time? Or are you really so stupid that you don't understand what the actual situation is?"

The words escape me before I can stop them. Laura rears back, shock stopping her response.

Grandma raises her hands. "Girls, please."

"We'd be in this situation no matter what." I say. "Draven sent Botis as a message. He wants all of us dead. Whether I had been in that forest or not, Botis would've come. And Draven will, too."

"Draven will be handled. The girls won't be put in harm's way again, and neither will you, Mother." Mom stands. "That is the end of this discussion."

Grandma stands as well. Smaller, but formidable. "Sarah, don't do this."

Mom turns on her heel and exits the shop, leaving Laura behind. Good job, Mom.

"Laura . . ." I reach for her and she snatches her hand back as if she's been burned.

"Don't. Just don't."

And Laura is gone, too.

Great family meeting. Family bonding at its best.

A cold chill turns the room into a freezer, causing goosebumps to raise on my skin. It takes a second for me to realize it's from me, from my fear at the look in Grandma's eyes.

"Grandma?"

Her eyes are like pure blue liquid wrath, like blue fire. The earth trembles beneath my feet, threatening to send me toppling over.

Against my better judgment, I take a step closer. "Grandma?"

"Never. Never in all my days have I seen a group of more stubborn, bull-headed women. And to see it is my own kin acting in this shameful way." The ground settles beneath our feet as the fire leaves her. She deflates, shoulders sagging. "I have failed. I've failed all of you. You've failed me, and the price will be our lives."

Shit. I've seen a lot of things in my life, but I've never seen Grandma give up. She's supposed to be the most stubborn of us all.

And we broke her.

The guilt is like a slap in the face. I can't let her feel like this.

"I'll call them back."

She shakes her head. "I believe it may be far too late for that. And it wasn't all you, Hazel. Rest, dear. Talk to me when my heart isn't so far into my throat."

The shaking in my bones isn't because of the cold anymore. It's an overwhelming helplessness that not even Grandma can overcome. Where do I go from here? Where do any of us go from here?

My feet take me to the back door, to the stairs, to my apartment, and I'm whipping out my phone before I know what's happening.

CHAPTER 27

ROUGH

"Baby?" Noah's voice is accompanied by a knock on my apartment door not twenty minutes later.

I don't remember what I told him over the phone, but his electric current is more of a pulsing zap than a pleasant hum as I open the door and he pulls me into his arms.

For the first time since I heard my mother and sister were coming over, my whole body relaxes. Every muscle that had been taut is now liquid. I sag into his embrace and allow his scent, his electricity, his entire being to wash over me, a balm to my soul.

"Hazel, what happened?" He tries to get my attention.

I pull back to meet his gaze. Bushy eyebrows are drawn in concern over dark brown-black eyes, eyes that I loved before I even met him.

My hand comes up to his stubbly cheek, caressing his soft skin. Reminding me that he's here and he's mine. With that hand, I bring him into a kiss.

It's almost harsh as I nip at his lower lip and tangle my fingers in his hair, demanding that he make me forget. That he allow me to lose myself in us. In what we have, if only for a moment.

He's too sweet, however. He pulls back, searching my face for something. His arms remain wound around me, holding me tight.

I shake my head, refusing to loosen my grip on his curls. "Please, Noah."

His nose slides against mine, a slow drag that puts our lips within touching distance—just a breath away. "Is it bad that I love it when you beg?"

"Then give me a reason," I murmur, looking up at him from under my lashes.

His lips lift in a crooked grin at my challenge, brushing against mine just for a moment. "You know I can."

My heart flutters and I'm no longer content with the teasing. My lips crash against his, pulling his hair just a touch too hard. I want him to pull too hard, grab too hard—make me feel something. Anything other than this pit of hopelessness.

Clothes. There are too many clothes in the way of what I want.

I tear at whatever fabric I can reach, tangling my fingers in it and pulling as hard as I can.

"Got it," he chuckles, yanking his shirt up from the back and throwing it God knows where. His skin is warm underneath my fingers, and I soak it in, pressing in against him as close as possible.

His hand cups my cheek, tilting my head and deepening the kiss. It's still not rough enough. I need to be broken down and put back together in the way only he possibly can. I want to feel him on my skin, in my muscles, for days. I want to burn with the reminder with every step I take.

"What do you want, Hazel?" His voice is that gravelly, low timbre that melts me into a puddle.

I whimper. "You. And I want it rough."

Brown-black eyes fully dilate; his breathing picks up. "Yeah? You sure?"

I nod. It's the only thing I can do. The way he's gazing at me . . . My voice has been stolen.

His fingers dig into my skin and I gasp at the sensation, at the knowledge that he's leaving marks on my hips. I lean further into him, allowing him to take control. My head tips in submission, bearing my neck to him.

Teeth drag along the tender skin there, light enough not to mark but enough to let me know his intention.

"Take your fucking clothes off." The words rumble against my skin in tune with the current making the hairs on my arms stand on end.

I hurry to obey. My fingers tangle in the buttons on my shirt as I lay myself bare before him.

He steps toward me, the back of his hand brushing against the very tip of my nipple. It hardens under his touch and I arch, asking —begging—for more.

"You're the most divine woman I've ever seen. I could drink you in every day for the rest of my life and still be thirsty for more of you."

My eyes flutter shut as he presses me back against the wall. The coarse texture of the paint scratches my bare skin and I push up against Noah. A still partially clothed Noah. I lift my hand to help divest him of the barriers between us but he stops me. He takes my hands in one of his and presses them against the wall above my head.

"Did I tell you that you could do that?" Despite the harshness of the words, his tone is soft. Loving, but confident.

I open my eyes. "No. No, you didn't."

His other hand trails down and grasps my ass. "I'll spank you if you do it again."

"Oh, yeah?" A giggle escapes me. He's never spanked me before, and I mean . . . It's Noah.

The crack sounds before the pain blossoms on my skin. I suck in a breathy moan as the warmth travels up my spine.

An almost evil grin spreads on Noah's face at my reaction. "That's interesting."

I squirm, pushing myself into his hand and his chest simultaneously.

Fuck, why does he still have his pants on? This is almost offensive at this point.

"Noah." The word is breathless, almost too quiet, yet jarring in the silence of the room. "Please."

"I got you, Hazel. Let go."

A weight lifts off my chest at his words. I can trust Noah, I know Noah would never leave me. I love him.

I stop the struggle. My body relaxes against the wall, my hands go limp in his grasp, and I allow him to do whatever he wants.

His hand travels up my spine and rests on my cheek. "Come here."

The kiss is deep, as if he's trying to pull my very soul from me. Not breaking the kiss, he releases me from his grip to—finally— remove his pants. I keep my hands where they are on the wall despite the itch to help him, to rip him free from his confines.

He unzips his jeans, pushing them off to the ground with his socks and shoes. Warm skin presses me back against the wall, his large palm holding my jaw exactly where he wants.

"You're so good, baby," he murmurs against my lips. "Look at you. So good."

He lifts me from the wall and walks us to the bedroom, nose buried in my throat. It's all I can do to hang on. In a moment, we're tangled together on the flowered bedspread.

"I want you to ride me," he says, pulling me on top of him. "I want to watch you take exactly what you need."

He could tell me to do anything at this point. I'd do it, no question.

I steady myself on his chest as he lines us up and I finally sink down.

The stretch is *exquisite*, and then it happens again. My mind expands and it's not just me—it's us.

"Oh!" I gasp as our hips meet.

"Fuck, I can't help it." He sits up. I'm still in his lap, but his hands are all over me, crushing us together as he steals the breath from my lungs with his kiss. He slides to the edge of the bed, planting his feet on the ground.

We move.

Our kissing becomes more like panting in each other's mouths as we rock in a steady rhythm. My nails dig into his shoulders, leaving crescent moons on his skin.

"Baby," he breathes. "Hazel. I love you."

Our movement stutters for a second as my heart stops. But I can feel him, I can feel what he feels, and he means it. He's not caught up in the moment.

He loves me.

"I love you, Noah. I've loved you forever."

His smile is blinding, until it turns feral and I'm lifted by the hips. He holds me there, just barely inside me as I squirm.

"Beg."

"Please, please, please—shit, Noah, ple—"

He flips me and fucks into me in a movement so fluid I swear it's magic. There will be bruises on every inch of my skin in perfectly shaped fingerprints, and I'll press them tomorrow as a reminder of how he left his love on my skin.

His rhythm is punishing for the rest of the night.

∿

"I MEANT WHAT I SAID EARLIER, HAZEL. I LOVE YOU." HE squeezes me tighter from behind, erasing any distance between our bodies.

I smile to myself, running my fingers along the hair on his arm. "I love you, too."

"I need to ask something of you." He huffs a breath in my ear. "I need something from you."

"Of course. Anything."

"When Sam killed himself, it took me a long time to stop blaming myself. To stop thinking that I should've known something was wrong. To stop thinking I should've asked him more questions or been more involved."

"Noah . . ." My heart breaks for him. I try to turn, but he holds me steady.

"Let me get this out." Another deep breath. "I need you to talk to me. It isn't fair to demand it like this, but I need you to tell me the important things. Not everything, but honesty means everything to me. I need honesty."

Shit. It's not a ridiculous request—especially knowing how he wishes Sam would've told him what he was feeling—but it's one I haven't been honoring. I've been putting this conversation off for too long.

Tomorrow. I'll tell him tomorrow.

"Okay. I promise."

His relief is palpable. The tension melts out of his hold, his grip becomes less desperate and more caring. "I promise the same."

Despite my fear of this conversation, I can't help but soak up the moment. This is the happiest I've ever been in my life.

CHAPTER 28

LEVITATING

I feel safer in this moment than I ever have. With Noah and the morning light streaming in.

"I'm going to get you some coffee and breakfast. Be back in a few," Noah whispers, with a kiss to my forehead.

I fall back into the sweet comfort of sleep.

What could be minutes or hours later, I roll to the side, searching for him and only finding cold blankets.

My eyes crack open and confirm that he's not there. In the kitchen, maybe? I stretch lazily, shaking off the last of the morning and reveling in the ache. He wasn't gentle last night and I loved every second of it.

My feet land on the floor and I walk into the kitchen.

No Noah.

"Noah?" I call. My voice echoes against the brick walls, the only answer.

Coffee and breakfast couldn't have taken this long. My eyes dart across the apartment searching for him, for any sign of him.

My abandonment issues are practically jumping out of my eyes at this point.

I throw on a robe and almost trip in my haste as I jog down the steps to the street. I don't even know where I'm going but something in my very bones tells me something is wrong.

There's a scrap of paper stuck to the door with tape and magic. The magic is thick and oily and *wrong.*

I slowly approach the paper, dread filling my every step. Am I shaking? I wring my hands, causing them to burn just as much as my heart does.

It's a single sheet, folded in half.

"Hazel," I read aloud. "You will come to the address below at eight p.m. tonight if you wish to spare Noah the same fate as your father. It would be a shame. I don't play games. Tonight or he's dead. Draven."

My body vibrates. My ears burn as if they will catch on fire, as if my whole body will catch on fire.

I'll kill him. If he lays even a single hand on Noah, I will kill him. Or I'll die trying.

The door window cracks as wind gusts around me in a violent torrent. Leaves whip fast enough to cut my skin.

No more bullshit. No more family drama. I'm done with it. Those stubborn women are going to help me or I will tear that house to the damn ground. Sentient or not.

My feet don't touch the ground as I power walk—power levitate?—to my mother's house. I don't care if anyone can see me, they can just deal with it. Or follow me and burn me at the stake.

Screw it.

The door slams open before me as I blow in with a burst of wind.

"Come down here *now*!" I yell. It's the same as it has always been, except messier. I can't tell if that's because of my wind tornado or because they've let things go.

Laura is the first to pop her sleep-rumpled head round the corner. "Are you PMS-ing?"

My glare must be fierce because instead of continuing on whatever tirade she had planned, she hangs her head and comes the rest of the way down the stairs.

"*Mom*!" I demand, using the full force of the wind to carry my voice to every inch of this house. "Get down here now!"

Laura makes a show of covering her ears but remains silent. A smart move on her part. I'd probably tear her head off just like I want to tear off Draven's.

Mom leisurely waltzes in from the living room at the most turtle pace I have ever seen. She's almost reveling in being as annoying as possible. The clack of her heels slows as she rounds the stairs and stops at the bottom of them, next to Laura.

"Yes?" she asks, raising an eyebrow.

The *nerve*. "Draven took Noah."

Laura's eyebrows shoot into her hair but Mom's face remains passive.

"Who's Noah?"

"My. Soulmate."

Laura scoffs. "That's a little dramatic, Hazel. I know you like him, but soulmate?"

I ignore her, keeping eye contact with Mom. I watch as her face falls, as some of the carefully constructed mask cracks. As she realizes just exactly how fucked this entire situation is. And as she builds that wall right back up, the neutral expression slips into place as quickly as it left.

"I'm taking care of it, Hazel."

"How could you say that to me? You're *taking care of it*? I will be damned if that piece of shit takes another soulmate away from this family."

Her face hardens further, years of whatever the hell she's been repressing climbing up her skin, covering her like a suit of armor. "And I will be damned if he kills another member of this family."

"So no one cares that I have no idea what's going on?" Laura sighs. "Cool."

"Draven will kill all of us if you keep doing this lone wolf bullshit, Mom. We have to do this together," I say.

"Pot meet kettle," Laura mutters.

"*Laura*!" Mom snaps. "I refuse to risk you girls. I will not lose you."

It's like a little crack is finally showing me exactly why the crazy woman is acting this way. She's so scared that we'll die just like Dad. So scared that she isn't realizing she's getting in her own damn way.

"You've already almost lost me, Mom. You've pushed me so far away we can't even talk to each other anymore. And I want a chance to fix it. That's all I've wanted—to fix this family."

Laura's eyes roll so far back in her head I swear they're going to get stuck. "You're both morons. You're the same fucking person and neither of you can see it."

Maybe she's right, but I refuse to lose Noah like Mom lost Dad. Her fate can't be mine. I turn from Laura to my mother. The woman who promised to protect me, who kicked me out of the house. The woman who lost everything.

"Please, Mom."

A single tear falls down my mother's cheek. Just one. "What do you want me to do?"

"Just." My voice breaks. "Just help me."

"I'll call Grandma. She'll want to know that hell is freezing over." Laura walks toward the living room, but my eyes are locked with Mom's.

I'm too scared to do anything but stare at her, as if she'll change her mind if I make any sudden movements. As if the spell will be broken.

"Did Draven leave any instructions? What do you know?" Mom continues, not moving a muscle either.

I think we're both just scared shitless of each other.

I try to breathe, to regulate my heart that's been beating like a drum ever since I realized Noah wasn't in bed with me. "He left a note. With an address. I . . . may have destroyed it, but I memorized it."

"Where?" she asks. The pulse point in her neck bounces.

"Some warehouse in the middle of nowhere."

She sucks her teeth.

The memories of my dreams—my nightmares—flood my mind.

I've been so stupid.

"We were there once before, weren't we? All of us?"

She nods, a shaky hand coming up to cover her mouth. She sways as if she might collapse to the floor at any moment.

"Mom." I wait until she meets my gaze once more. "I've been dreaming of that night ever since it happened. I was convinced my mind was trying to make sense of the loss of my dad. But that's not true, is it? You took those memories from us, just like you made the ones of the shop disappear. Didn't you?"

Another nod.

The lengths this woman went to are astounding. But for the first time in my life, part of me understands her reasoning. Part of me gets that I will lose a crucial part of who I am as a person if I lose Noah. That I would never be the same. My worst-case scenario is my mother's everyday life.

The fact that she's still standing is a testament to her determination. I don't know if I'd have the same strength.

Despite it all, though. It's wrong.

"You took parts of my father from me. Parts of myself from me. I don't know how long it's going to take for me to forgive you, Mom, despite understanding you better than I ever have. For now, we need to save this family."

"I understand. Your Grandma should be here soon, and we can come up with a plan." She pauses. "As a family."

As we should have done from the beginning. But we're making progress, so I'll keep that to myself.

"We were there?" Laura's voice is small, meek, as she stands in the corner.

It is with pure selfishness that I find myself continually forgetting Laura's lack of knowledge in all of this. For the first time in my life, I'm utterly consumed by my own journey and my own reactions. It's as if I have no concern for her needs at all.

And I don't like it.

The exhaustion in Mom's shoulders weighs heavily on her as she turns to Laura. "I owe both of you a lifetime of apologies."

At least she can admit it now, but I don't know if a lifetime will be enough. It doesn't feel like enough. I understand her, but I still look at her and feel almost nothing but anger. Rage. It has my hands shaking.

"*That* . . ." Grandma enters the house with a sweep of her hand and a slammed door. ". . . is a phrase I never thought I'd live to hear you say."

THE HOUSE WARMS INSTANTLY WITH GRANDMA'S ARRIVAL. Magical or not, she adds a layer of life that is palpable. Or maybe the house just likes her.

Mom's shoulders tense, her wall threatening to creep back up. "Welcome, mother."

"Laura told me about Noah." Grandma turns to me, grasping my hands in hers. "We will return him to you, Hazel. I will not allow history to repeat itself."

My eyes burn with tears I've refused to let myself shed. I can't imagine a reality where I lose him. "We have to."

In a gasping breath, I'm pulled into Grandma's arms. Her hug is tight, almost too tight, but I need it tighter. To feel safe.

"Can someone get out of their own ass for five seconds and tell me what the fuck is going on?" Laura practically hisses.

Grandma sighs, releasing me. "Sarah, would you like to or am I allowed to speak?"

My gaze darts between the two of them.

"I release you from your vow. Say whatever you wish."

"Thank you." Grandma ushers us into the living room.

"Thirteen years ago, the warlock Draven began targeting witches and stealing their power. It got so bad that a few families came together and had a meeting about how to deal with him. It was decided that your mother and I would handle it." Grandma takes a deep breath. "We were the strongest. It just made sense. What we didn't know was that Draven had a family of his own. And we thought we had found him, but we had found his younger brother instead. We banished him, and Draven swore revenge. While we were celebrating our victory, Draven was planning. He took your father."

Laura's eyes are swimming with tears and I'm not doing much better. A simple mistake is what took my father from me? What destroyed my entire family? Will a simple mistake take Noah from me, too?

Grandma reaches for Laura's hand, holding her dearly. "We received a note indicating your father's location. Your mother left immediately, and I stayed to watch you both. We were supposed to watch movies and eat popcorn, but there was a feeling in the pit of my belly that told me to follow. Even if I had to bring you both. By the time I arrived, your father was . . . Your mother had wounded a few of them, but she was wildly outnumbered. I cast a cloaking spell, and she took the two of you to hide. I drew their attention elsewhere and eventually they got tired of looking and left. It appears Draven doesn't believe the debt has been paid, and he has returned for the rest of us."

I turn to Mom, her face as hard as stone. "What happened before Grandma got there?"

"No." She shakes her head violently. "I refuse to . . . No. We will plan for now, but I can't."

"But it could help Noah!"

"I said no. I will help you, we will do this together, but I refuse to relive that night more than I am forced to. And that's final."

It's more than I had before. But still not enough.

"And in your grief, you ripped us from our magic, from our grandmother, and from our memories. Then swore Grandma to secrecy," I finish.

She nods. Barely a hint of remorse in her gaze.

"So that's why Hazel's been a massive bitch," Laura says, voice trembling. "What is all this nonsense about soulmates?"

"The Pruitt women are blessed." Grandma straightens her back. "We all have a soulmate. It has been recorded since the beginning of our line in Salem."

Laura's face screws up as if she bit into a lemon. "Ugh. How do you even know if you've met your soulmate?"

Grandma looks to me, a soft smile on her face.

"The first time you touch . . . it's like you put your finger into an outlet. It's a spark, an electric shock that doesn't make any sense. But it changes as you spend more time together. It becomes more of a soothing buzz." My fingers twist together. "We're wasting time. What's the plan?"

The room is silent except for the groaning and moaning of the house. I think it would help if it could.

"Draven knows how many of us there are. There's no point in trying to use our numbers to our advantage," Mom says. "It may behoove us to simply walk in the front door."

"Draven. Can we stop him, kill him, whatever it is you do to warlocks?" Laura asks.

Grandma and Mom share a look. A look that says everything without saying anything at all.

"No." Grandma turns to Laura. "Not without any prep time. Our best option is a banishment."

"And that's different how?" Laura blinks twice.

Mom sighs. "It doesn't kill him. Banishing to Hell is a Band-Aid, a temporary fix to buy us some time. Crawling his way out of Hell will take him at least a few months while we figure out how to stop him permanently."

"It's much easier. Your mother and I can do it and draw from your power. Your presence is all that is needed."

"Good, considering I know literally nothing about magic." I don't imagine the bitterness in Laura's tone. As far behind as I am, she's even farther.

Because I didn't take her with me. I left her here.

"We should do a focusing session. Call unto our magic so we're ready for Draven. We will have a small window of time to perform the banishment and we should be as ready as possible. Especially because he will probably be expecting it." Grandma stands. "To the shop?"

CHAPTER 29
DEAD BITCHES

"Do you have an element, Laura?" I ask as we walk to the shop. Mom and Grandma are in front of us, quietly murmuring to each other as their feet crunch fallen leaves.

The image of Noah strapped to a chair, or beaten on the floor, sticks in my head permanently. I can't scrub it from my brain no matter how hard I try. Maybe focusing on Laura, and how I've also failed her, will help distract me.

"A what now?" she asks, blonde hair whipping and tangling around her face in the breeze I can't quite control. Her arms are crossed and she keeps a few feet between us as we walk. Closed off as ever.

"Every witch has an element we're connected to. You know, water, fire, earth, and air. Grandma is earth and I'm air. Mom is water."

"Hmph." She glances at their backs. "I didn't know that."

There's so much you don't know. There's so much we both don't know.

"I'm sorry they took Noah," she continues, her eyebrows drawing together in concern.

The breeze ruffles my hair, sending a shiver down my spine. "He was taken while he was getting coffee. I was only a few feet away and I had no idea. He's gone and I didn't even try to protect him."

Our next few steps are in silence. The early fall morning swirls around us in a wash of reds, oranges, yellows, and greens.

"Do you feel like it's your fault? Like he would've been better off if he weren't your soulmate? Because I think sometimes Mom regrets falling in love with Dad . . ."

I kick a pebble down the sidewalk. "He'd be better off without me for sure. At the very least he'd be safer. But I can't regret a single moment spent with him. I love him."

Her eyebrows raise up into her hair as those liquid-gold eyes burn a hole in my side. "You *love* him? I didn't think you could love anyone."

"Thanks." I try to hide the physical pain that comment causes. Doesn't she know how much I love her? How I'd do anything for her? She was my entire life, I practically raised her. I wouldn't do that if I didn't love her.

"That's not what I—" she blows out a heavy breath. "Never mind."

The shop comes into view, as do the residents of Chagrin Falls enjoying their mornings. Completely oblivious to the pain enveloping four random women.

"How do you know what your element is?" Laura asks, arms still wrapped around herself like a shield.

I shrug. "You just know. Something happens that's out of your control and it's like a little clue. I controlled a breeze and Grandma said it was because I was connected to the air. Then I levitated."

Her forehead creases in thought.

"You haven't allowed your magic to run rampant. Mom has suppressed it in us for years. I wouldn't be surprised if you've never really had any accidental magic."

She nods, but her expression hasn't cleared. I don't know if there's anything I can truly say to help her feel better, so I say nothing at all.

Grandma opens the shop door and ushers us all inside. She flutters around, lighting candles and collecting items as the rest of us stand in the doorway allowing her to do as she pleases. I think we're all too scared to get in her way.

"Come, come!" Grandma directs us to the middle of the circle she's created. She positions us in a little square. "North, south, east, and west. Yes."

"One guess as to who's the Wicked Witch of the West," Laura mumbles under her breath.

I don't think I want to know if it's me or Mom.

"Unhelpful, Laura." Grandma's gaze is sharp, brokering no argument. "Join hands and open your mind. Allow magic to flow through you freely."

It starts as a gentle breeze, flowing over us in a warm wave. It slowly morphs into the scent of seawater, salt heavy in the air, then the smell of earth. Trees and flowers so potent that I would swear we were in a forest.

It burns away in a crackling fire that heats me from the tips of my toes to the top of my head.

It's comforting and strange, natural and unexpected. Each element, each part of us morphing together to wrap us in the thing that makes us special and binds us.

Pure magic.

"We ask the women of our line to protect and strengthen us this evening as we defend our own. Noah is one of ours, and we refuse to lose him. Stand with us," Grandma says, the words muted as the room has gotten smoky and hazy in the candlelight.

The scent of approval is sweet and heady. It's like hundreds of hands are helping keep me standing. Generations of witches that came before are with me.

"Thank you," Grandma says, a gentle smile on her face. It's the first smile I've seen from her in a while. "Sisters, we thank you for your blessing. And we close our circle."

"Let's eat some lunch and rest. We'll leave at sundown," Mom says.

Laura scoffs. "Don't know what a bunch of dead bitches are going to do for us, but whatever."

"*Laura.*" Grandma's voice booms across the room, bouncing off the bookshelves. "I will not have you disrespecting your ancestors in my presence."

"Grandma, she doesn't know. We haven't taught her," I quietly interject. Despite where our relationship is right now, I can't help the protective sisterly nature.

Grandma's stormy face mellows as Laura's darkens.

"I don't need your help," Laura hisses.

For the first time, it feels like Grandma, Mom, and I are on one side and Laura is on the other. And I can't understand how it has happened.

TIME MOVES AT A SNAIL'S PACE. I BARELY TASTE MY LUNCH DESPITE it coming from the literal best sandwich shop in the country. The chatter of my family—Mom and Grandma, mostly—hangs above my head like the candles Grandma has bewitched to float around us.

I'm glued to the corner of the room in one of the poofy armchairs next to the bookshelves. It's situated in front of the window overlooking the town.

People walk around as if it's just another normal day. As if my person wasn't kidnapped by a literal crazy warlock with a horde of daemons.

"I know how you feel." Mom's voice startles me out of my daydreams.

I sigh, stretching out my sore legs. They've been underneath me for who knows how long now. "That doesn't help. But you probably are the only person who actually gets it, aren't you?"

"I never wanted this for you. I wouldn't wish it on anyone, but my own daughter? It's my worst nightmare."

I hold my tongue. It would be so easy to attack her, to blame her. To tell her that if she had just *talked* to me, there's a high chance we wouldn't be in this situation. That Noah wouldn't be in this situation.

But there's an ache in her voice, a pain in her eyes, that I know is reflected in my own. I can't kick her when she's down.

I gesture to the opposite armchair instead. "How do you breathe each day?"

"At first, by force." She collapses in the chair as if all the energy escaped her body at once. "Because I knew if I left you girls, Peter would never forgive me. I believe I will see him again, and I want to be worthy of that moment."

It's honest. Too honest, if the painful thumping of my heart is any indication. Part of me understands—couldn't imagine putting one foot in front of the other without Noah. But part of me, the daughter, can't rationalize why my own mother has to force herself to keep going for me.

She heaves a heavy breath. "It was awful in those first few years. But breathing has gotten easier as I've gone on. I haven't done anything right since Peter died, but I'm in a better place than I was."

"You didn't leave. That was right, at the very least."

"At the very least." A weak chuckle leaves her.

"It's sundown," I say, watching the sun dip below the buildings. "We should get going."

"Hazel."

I turn to my mother as I stand.

She stands as well, taking my hands in hers. "I will not let anything happen to Noah. It doesn't matter the price, I promise you he won't be harmed."

My brows furrow. "Mom?"

"Let's go, girls!" Grandma calls.

Mom squeezes my hands and drops them, going to Grandma.

It seems that any time I think I get a handle on my mother, she always pulls a twist. Why do I feel like she knows more than she lets on?

"Hazel!" Grandma snaps. "Come!"

"I'm not a schnauzer," I grumble, following her out of the back door regardless.

We walk to Grandma's car, the air crackling with magic burning under the surface.

Laura scoffs as we sit together in the back seat. "What? No broomsticks?"

"Would you prefer to ride one? It can be arranged." Grandma's eyebrow raises in the rearview mirror.

"You'd have to pull it out of your ass."

"You first, dear."

My forehead falls against the cool glass of the window.

I just want Noah. I hope he's safe, I hope Draven hasn't . . . Shit. Images of Noah beaten, bruised, strung up, and worse flit across my mind. Draven only said he wouldn't kill him, but he said nothing about hurting him in the meantime.

"Hurry, please," I whisper.

CHAPTER 30
PEANUT

The world blurs as the car passes through suburbs, city streets, and finally rows of warehouses and alleyways. Somewhere in this maze is Noah and as we approach, the buzz prickles across my skin. Calling me to him.

"Faster," I almost whimper as a shock rushes through me. He's not okay. He needs me.

The car slows instead. "We're here." Grandma nods at Mom, grasping her shoulder tightly for just a second.

It's rare to see a moment of intimacy between them. So rare that sometimes I even forget they're mother and daughter.

No more words are spoken as we exit the car in front of the warehouse. It's set off from the rest; a pang of familiarity causes my heart to clench. Memories threaten to fully break through the block Mom placed on me, just like when I first entered the shop. Memories of how I lost my father, in the same place I may lose Noah.

My knees wobble. I can't lose Noah.

Out of the corner of my eye, I watch as Laura's hand stretches toward me as if in comfort before retreating.

I've lost everyone, haven't I?

Laura and I walk behind Mom and Grandma through the double

doors of the large building. It's almost entirely bare inside, just some boxes, pipes, and *them*.

There's three of them—daemons, I presume—waiting for us. Same as Botis, they each wear long black cloaks, only this time they have them over their heads. No horns to be seen, but claws still stick out from their sleeves.

My eyes flit past them to a small door on the back wall.

Noah.

"He's alive," a human-sounding voice says. A figure steps from the shadows. A tall, imposing man in a black button up-shirt and black jeans. "Although why take my word for it? After introductions, I'll bring him out myself."

The hairs on the back of my neck prickle as he approaches, and I resist the urge to hide behind my mother's back as I did all those years ago.

"Always one for the theatrics, Draven. You know you've gone too far this time," Mom says, stepping forward.

The monster chuckles, moonlight lighting up his face for just a moment. He's more man than warlock, with a strong, straight nose and Superman-esque chin. His white teeth glint in a smile. "Nice to see you again, Peanut."

Peanut? *Peanut*?

My mother has never been called Peanut in her life.

"This is between us," she continues, as if all three of us aren't gaping at her. "Release Noah. He's innocent."

"Is anyone? Was my brother innocent when you banished him to Hell?"

Grandma scoffs. "All we did was banish him, you act as if we killed him."

Draven only smiles, black hair shining. With a snap of his fingers, two of the three daemons open the door. It cracks against the wall with inhuman force as they haul an unconscious Noah out of the room.

He doesn't have any scary angles indicating broken bones, but there is a heavy bruise blooming under his eye. Rage boils my blood, making a torrent of wind whip at our backs.

"No." Grandma's hand stops me as I instinctively step toward him. "You must wait."

"But he's—"

Her head turns sharply to me and I'm frozen in place by her icy glare. I'm forced to wait as he's carried to us and placed on the floor.

His breathing is labored. Something's wrong.

"I haven't injured him, he's merely in a coma," Draven says, waving a bored hand toward Noah. "One quite easy to reverse. Even for a witch."

What does he want? That's the piece that's missing. What is it that has made Draven care so damn much about our family? What started this vendetta? Is it really just the power our line possesses?

Draven chuckles, a low, dangerous growl that ripples down my spine. "Smart questions, Hazel. Why don't you ask your mother?"

My eyes bug out of my head. He can read *thoughts*?

"Give us the boy, Draven." Mom's back straightens, face hard as if she knew exactly how this was going to go. "You have me here, you have what you want. Let him and my family go."

"That may have worked before, but you and I both know it's not enough anymore."

Laura leans in close. "Do you know what they're talking about?"

I shake my head; Draven turns to us, a sickeningly sweet smile on his face. He may seem like a man, but that smile is all warlock. An evil twist of a thing.

"Would you like me to tell the story, Peanut, or would you like to tell your family how your husband's death was your own fault?" he asks, drawing out each word and playing with it like a cat with a mouse.

The daemons shift beside Noah's limp body. Their cloaks cover their features, but the one closest stretches his claws.

"Do *not* touch him," I say, unable to stop the possessive growl. "Unless you wish to know a fate worse than death."

Mom takes Grandma's hand without warning, closing her eyes. "Away with you, daemons."

A rumble jostles my footing, knocking Laura and I together, as a crack in the earth opens beneath the three daemons. A wave of water springs forth from the hole in a giant crescent, enveloping them and pulling them down. It happens in an instant, just a second. We're alone with Draven. No longer outnumbered. They didn't even have a chance to scream.

Draven simply blinks at the display. "And you claim I'm dramatic."

It's as if he expected it, as if he knew exactly what she was capable of. Which is more than I can say. My mouth may be permanently stuck to the floor.

"Did you know she could do that?" Laura whispers, jaw in a similar state as mine.

I simply shake my head in response. Even Grandma looks slightly impressed, and I'm pretty sure Grandma has never been impressed by anything. Least of all by Mom.

Mom takes a single step forward. "Give him to me, Draven."

It's as if her proximity flicks a switch in his head. His face twists in pain, as if he was punched in the gut. As if that single step forward was the most painful thing he's ever endured. As if *she* is the most painful thing he has ever endured.

His hands ball into fists, shoulders squaring. His chest visibly heaves with each deep breath, as if he has to physically control himself.

"Not until you tell them. That is my price. Tell them what you've done, and I'll hand him over willingly."

"Tell us what?" I scream. They've been dancing around it for the entire time, whatever *it* is. And I won't lose Noah to it.

Mom's head drops, arms wrapping around herself protectively.

"I'll start at the beginning."

"It began when I was a young woman. I'd moved out of your grandmother's house and had my first real taste of freedom," Mom says, turning to face the three of us. Her usually liquid-gold brown eyes are dull, muddy as she speaks.

"I played with magic in new ways, tested boundaries and learned so much about myself and about my craft. I explored the magical world, met magical people . . ." She hesitates, glancing toward Draven. "Met Draven."

Grandma's hand flies to her décolletage. "Oh, Sarah."

Mom shrugs. "Draven was interesting and intelligent, dangerous but I never felt unsafe. I felt powerful as he showed me magic I had only imagined. A part of me always knew that it wasn't sustainable. That we were too different. That eventually it would drive us apart."

The words hit like an expected punch. Some part of me knew it was coming, and yet I didn't block it. Couldn't.

"Liar," Draven snarls. He's still here? "We are two sides of the same coin, and you never thought we were different until you met him."

"Dad," Laura and I say at the same time.

My gaze settles on Noah, where he lies unconscious on the ground. What would I have done if I were already in a relationship when I met Noah? The soulmate bond is too strong. I wouldn't have been able to fight it.

"I met Peter by happenstance." Despite the mood, despite the circumstance, the corners of her mouth lift at the mere mention of Dad. "I was at the grocery store, and we reached for the same avocado. I instantly knew who he was, what he was. What Draven wasn't and never would be. Meeting Peter changed me. I wanted to do better, be better, for him. Stop dabbling in magic I had no business touching. And Draven . . . Well, I knew that it was time to put that friendship away."

He scoffs. "Trying to downplay what we were as *friendship*."

Mom stands taller, as if his rebuttal strengthened her resolve. "Friendship. Don't make it out to be more than it was."

He snarls, smoke streaming from his nose.

"As you can see by this display, Draven didn't take it well," she says. "But there was nothing he could do. And I thought we could go our separate ways relatively peacefully, but I was wrong. It took a few years—years of him doing God knows what, years in which I stupidly got comfortable. Built my family, had you girls. Then the attacks started. I knew it was Draven, before Mother volunteered us to take care of this issue. I knew it was him."

Grandma shakes her head. "You knew the warlock we banished wasn't Draven."

"Yes. I figured Draven would see the act of mercy as an olive branch, as a warning from an old friend. I was very, very wrong."

"Banishing my brother as an act of mercy? If you only knew . . ."

"You act as if I killed him, when he's probably back and has been for years," Mom spits. "But I'm not a murderer. Not like you."

The way he focuses on her, the way his eyes track her every movement, it's as if no one else is in the room. After all this time, after everything, some part of him loves her still.

"You knew how close I was to Drinek. You *knew* how he looked up to me, and yet you still cast him away like some sort of object. Like he meant nothing. And then he died in the pits of Hell you banished him to." The flame flicks up his arm, an uncontrollable burning that flashes with each word he speaks.

Mom visibly deflates, any strength she'd pulled together drifting away on the whistling wind through the rafters of the warehouse. "That was not my intention."

"And so I took what was owed to me. A life for a life. But you, Peanut, you took it further, didn't you? Tell them how you couldn't let sleeping dogs lie. Tell them what you've been doing for the last thirteen years. What you did after I left."

For the first time tonight, the space is silent. The wind stops whipping, the leaky pipe in the corner stops dripping, and all eyes are on Mom. Even the moon is drawn to her, shining its light down on her alone.

"I've hunted down every goddamn daemon or warlock I could find, and I destroyed them, and that is why Draven has returned. To stop me."

There is no remorse in her tone, despite Noah lying on the floor because of her actions. Because of Draven's action.

Because of both of their actions. Despite Dad dying because of them.

She took my magic away and has been out here daemon hunting. Putting all of us at risk for what? Her own hypocritical vendetta?

"You two are disgusting." I'm unable to hold my tongue. "You are twisted together in a vile tangle that has dragged everything and everyone good down into the depths. Your obsession with each other has killed multiple people, and while many of them have been daemons, one of them was our father. And I refuse to be part of it any longer. I refuse to let Noah be more collateral damage in your obsession."

For once, Grandma seems to be speechless. Her mouth opens a few times as if she's finally formed the words and then closes again. Laura stands still at my side.

Finally, Mom turns to me. Any light that ever lived in her eyes is gone. "I have no intention of letting anything happen to Noah. I promised that before we came, and I plan to uphold that."

Draven's right eyebrow raises, flame calmly receding to his fingertips. As if he's amused by her attempt.

Calmly, Mom walks over to the three of us. "I apologize for my actions. I can't ever atone for what I've done, for the choices I've made. But I will attempt to do so today."

She hugs Grandma, looking for the first time like a daughter seeking comfort from her mother. "Mom, I pushed you away because I knew if I kept you too close you'd know exactly what I was up to. And my pride, my self-righteousness, couldn't handle the mirror you'd hold. You'd force me to see my hypocrisies. Thank you for not letting me disappear completely."

She releases Grandma and takes Laura's hands, tears welling in her eyes. "Laura, you are beautiful and far more intelligent than anyone gives you credit for. I know I created a hostile home for you, and my only hope for you is that you learn to trust someone again. Anyone. Even just yourself."

She touches my shoulder, and I feel her drawing on my magic. Feel it filling her up alongside Grandma and Laura's. "Hazel. Thank you for challenging me, thank you for finding yourself and being the strength that I couldn't provide for you. Protect Noah with everything you have, which is more than you could ever imagine. You are powerful, you are strong, and you can do anything you set your mind to."

Without waiting for any of us to reply, Mom turns and effortlessly glides toward Draven—who, despite his insistence that he wants us all to suffer, hasn't taken his eyes off her this entire time. He doesn't stop her; he welcomes her as she approaches. She takes his hand.

"Forgive me."

In a moment too quick for us—or Draven—to do anything, they're encased in a globe of water.

And the water collapses.

And they're gone.

CHAPTER 31

NO SHIT I'M NOT FOCUSING

There is no time to mourn, to question, or to make sense of anything that's happened in the last few minutes. Not for me.

"Noah!" I race to his side, falling to my knees next to him. He hasn't woken up. His breathing remains labored as he lies on the cold concrete.

Finally Grandma shakes her head and moves, placing a trembling hand on my shoulder. "We need to leave. Immediately."

"You expect the three of us to carry a full-grown man out of here? A man well over six feet?" Laura scoffs. "That's not happening, and definitely not quickly."

I hate to agree with Laura, but Noah's lankiness may work against us in this instance.

"Hazel. Lift him with your element." The demand is non-negotiable. "We don't have time to find out if Draven has more of his 'family' here."

Right. No problem.

"Does she even know how to do that?" Laura says, a bite in her tone that speaks only of fear. Fear of what's coming. Fear of what's happening. Fear of everything.

I shake my head, but I have no choice. I have to figure it out and get us out of here in case Draven has a backup plan. He seems the type.

"Center yourself by focusing on your breathing, block out everything else but what you need to do. You can hold my hand." Grandma holds out her hand. I take it. "Draw from my power, from our bond, to help you."

Thanks, Mom, for not letting me train growing up. I'd actually know what the hell I'm doing right now.

Fuck, okay, don't think about Mom. That's a situation I do not need to unpack while I'm trying to levitate an entire human. My human.

Laura bumps into me. "I don't think you're focusing."

"No shit I'm not focusing."

"Girls." Grandma's voice booms in the empty warehouse.

I close my eyes against all distractions—against the wind, the leaky pipe that is dripping once more, my sister's judgmental gaze burning a hole in my side. Deep breath in, longer exhale. I lengthen the exhale with each breath until my heartbeat slows and all I can feel is Noah. Noah's staggered breaths, Noah's heartbeat.

"Well, I guess we may just get out of here. And speaking of, can we finally *get out of here*?" Laura's voice forces me to open my eyes.

Noah is hovering before me, still unconscious, at approximately waist level. Waist level is workable.

A window breaks. Our heads snap in the direction of the sound.

"Move," Grandma says.

We hasten through the warehouse, Noah gliding in front of us as we make for the car. I don't feel anything following us, but that doesn't mean I have any intention of slowing down. We maneuver Noah into the car, Grandma fires the engine, and we speed off in a trail of smoke.

"How are we going to wake him up? Can we? Draven said we could, but . . ."

Grandma doesn't meet my eyes in the mirror. I'm in the back seat with Noah resting on my lap. "He'll be fine."

"Are you going to call that weirdo healer lady with all the beads and feathers you got when Hazel was injured? Because she was a lot, Grandma," Laura snorts from the passenger seat.

Grandma sniffles, and I catch her wiping a tear from her cheek. "Her name is Clementine and she is the best healer on this side of the Mississippi. You will respect her as your elder."

Noah's brown curls brush my arm with a bump in the road, turning his face closer to me. His eyebrows seem less bushy than usual. "She was gone before I woke up. Will we be calling her?"

Grandma nods.

We'll be home soon and then we'll wake up Noah. And then . . . Well, shit, I have no idea. I have no goddamn idea.

"Is he gone?" It's Laura who breaks the silence, voice shaking just a touch. There's no question who she's referring to. "Is *she* gone?"

My fingers tangle in Noah's curls. I hope to God Grandma has some sort of answer because I've got nothing. It's as if I'm a hollowed husk of a person.

The car rumbles on as we leave the city behind us. The moon-light filters through trees instead of buildings as we get closer to the safety of home.

"We'll be fine," is all Grandma says.

CHAPTER 32

CLEMENTINE

I'm not going to lie, Clementine the healer is just as strange as Laura implied. But considering that I was able to heal as quickly as I did, I have no problem moving aside to let her do what she must.

Beaded bracelets trail up her arms all the way to her elbows, jangling as she waves her hands over Noah's still form. Her glasses are too big for her face and so cloudy I'm unable to see her eyes behind them. She's chanting something as herbs and candles burn on the bedside table.

Laura sits in a plushy armchair in the corner of the same bedroom I was in a month ago. Grandma observes from the doorway. Neither speak, they just watch as Clementine tries her best to wake up my soulmate.

Clementine lets loose a heavy breath and turns to me. I still can't see her eyes. "He will wake."

With that, she stands and walks toward the door. Away from Noah. Who is still very much unconscious.

"Um." I stand as well. "When?"

A grimy, toothy grin breaks on her face, and I have the sudden urge to brush my teeth. "When he is ready. Soon."

"Thank you, Clementine," Grandma says sharply, cutting a glare in my direction.

Yes, thank you, oh vague one.

Laura snorts as Grandma walks Clementine out of the room, and presumably the cottage. We came back here instead of Mom's house. I guess I'm thankful for that. How do I tell the potentially sentient house that she's gone? Can someone else have that job?

"Told you she was weird," Laura says, curling in on herself.

I scooch my chair closer to Noah's side. "You were definitely right about that."

"Why is there a bunch of garnet in here?" Laura nods toward the bedside table. Along with an assortment of herbs and candles, little polished garnet crystals sit.

"They're supposed to be helpful in healing. This one here is unakite, which also helps with healing the body, and some quartz to amplify both."

"Guess there's a lot more to this witchy stuff than I initially thought."

I nod. "More than I ever imagined. I don't even know a small fraction."

"You know more than I do," she says. "And you did it all without me."

This conversation has been overdue for a while. More than a while, if I'm honest. I can't let it go sideways like last time. I can't lose her after losing Mom.

Shit.

"And that was selfish of me," I reply, meeting her gaze.

She sucks in a breath, the finger twisting her hair slowing to a stop.

"It's hard for me to truly explain, Laura, but something in me snapped. I couldn't see past my own needs, and what I needed was to get out of that house. I was so stuck, rudderless, and I needed to figure out what the fuck I was doing with my life. It didn't need to be without you, it shouldn't have been without you."

She lets loose a heavy breath. "It wasn't just you. You did what you needed to do, and Mom . . . I couldn't leave her, too. She broke when you left, and I didn't know what she'd do if I went with you. I didn't know what it would come to if she knew I was exploring magic with you."

"I didn't realize things were that bad." The guilt is a wave. Disappointment, anger, all broiling in a big pot of guilt. How could I not know? How could Mom put all that on Laura, on me? How could she be such a hypocrite—banning magic for Laura and I and then turning around to hunt daemons? How can I still be angry with her after she saved Noah's life?

She shrugs. "Why would you? You were off starting a new life, why look back at what you'd left behind?"

I struggle for a response. There's a wall between us that never existed before I left, and I hope it doesn't last forever. I hope I get my sister back, but I can tell by the hurt in her eyes that it won't be today. Probably not tomorrow either. Or the next day.

"I understand more than you probably think I do. But that doesn't mean it's okay," she says, eyes hard.

"For what it's worth, I am sorry for how everything has happened. I would do things differently if I could."

She stands with a shallow nod, heading for the door.

"Laura." I stand as well, taking a step toward her. "Would you like to stay with me? Or at least with Grandma? I can't imagine you in that big house by yourself. I don't think it's good for you."

"I'll think about it. But for now, I just want to go home," she says. With a smile that doesn't reach her eyes, she turns and leaves.

I've never been more worried about her in my life. Where is my funny, over the top, Pink Puke Mobile Laura? This sad, broken person who doesn't trust me barely resembles her.

My gaze drops to Noah. His breathing is finally even, his face a peaceful calm. At least someone is resting.

～

Despite how comfortable Grandma's chairs are, sleeping all squished up is a young woman's game. My aches have aches.

But I will not leave his side.

I stretch my arms above my head, several pops and cracks rippling up my back, and readjust. I'm so tired I can't open my eyes, but I refuse to move. I was so close to losing him forever and I don't know if I'll ever be able to leave him again.

"Hazel?" Noah's voice is as rough as sandpaper.

My eyes snap open with force and I turn to him. He's barely awake, eyes bleary and eyelids drooping. But he's awake.

A full body sob shakes me as I fling myself forward to grab his hand. He's awake.

He's awake.

"I'm here," I finally manage to reply. "I'm here, Noah." I grab the full glass of water on the bedside table and lift it to his lips. He drinks it greedily, spilling some on his chin and shirt in his enthusiasm.

He drains the cup and I place it back, reaching for his hand once more. "You're safe now."

His hand slips away from mine.

"Hazel, I need an explanation, because what I remember . . ." He shakes his head. "It doesn't make sense."

Shit. It's not like this is surprising. I knew I'd have to explain all of this to him. But how do I explain something I barely understand myself? Explain something that I haven't even begun to fully process?

Years of therapy are a prerequisite to this conversation, and I have had none. I have to attempt it, though. I really have no other choice.

Today is the day for hard conversations, that's for damn sure.

I breathe in. "I wanted us to talk when we woke up. I wanted to explain everything to you myself when we were relaxed and safe, after you told me you loved me. I'm sorry that this happened this way, that I wasn't able to tell you myself."

He stares at me, brown-black eyes hard under those goddamn bushy eyebrows I love so much.

"I'm a witch."

Apparently we're going for blunt today.

"I figured it was something like that, considering the giant monsters that picked me up from your place. I don't remember anything after that, was I unconscious?" Anger flares in his eyes. He hasn't tried to touch me.

I nod. "They knocked you out. You've only been out for about twenty-four hours."

Craziest twenty-four hours of my goddamn life, that's for sure. A breeze whips the candles to flicker on the table with the erratic beating of my heart.

With a wince he lifts his hand and rubs the back of his neck, curls bouncing in front of his face. Even now, even with him as frustrated and upset as he visibly is, the simple motion causes my heart to swoop up into my throat. I love this man so much.

Even if he refuses to ever speak to me again, I'll never not love him.

"It's not even that you are what you are."

Jesus, okay. Ouch.

He clears his raspy throat. "It's that you lied. And it's not even a small lie, a lie about what your favorite food is or if you hate my hair or the way I laugh. You lied about your very being, about what makes you who you are. You hid something vital to your entire person from me."

Panic thrums in my bones, my stomach rolling in a way that almost makes me nauseous. "I—"

"I told you about Sam." His voice breaks over his brother's name. "I told you about all the cracked and broken places inside me, and I'm finally realizing that you never reciprocated. At all. I know barely anything about your family, about your life. What you are. You've kept me at a distance and *lied*, Hazel."

My eyes burn with tears, my vision blurs. He's not wrong, and he's going to leave me. The person who makes me feel happy, feel whole, is going to leave because I wasn't ready to share my whole self with him.

I've never shared my whole self with anyone.

He shakes his head again, hair tickling the edge of the bruise under his eye. "You gave me the safety of knowing you would never judge me. You made me feel heard and seen in a way no one ever has before. You are beautiful, intelligent, and kind. I loved you so goddamn much and all I asked was for you not to lie. And you chose to lie about the biggest thing in your life."

"I do love you, Noah." I'm wobbling, stumbling over my words. "I just didn't know how. I wasn't ready."

He drops his head into his hand. "I can't think right now. Every single part of my body aches like I've been slammed into a wall. Which I probably fucking was. I'm exhausted and I can't. I can't."

"Noah—"

"I can't." Finally he meets my gaze and it's broken. Anguished. But final. He won't be discussing this. Not now. Maybe not ever.

I nod, tears escaping to make little trails down my cheeks. "I'll let you rest."

Despite it being physically painful—like a knife cutting through my abdomen—I stand and walk toward the door. I may never want to leave his side, but I can't force him to want me there.

"I'd like to leave tomorrow," he murmurs.

I turn as his eyes close.

"Okay," I whisper.

Closing the door behind me is the hardest thing I've had to do. And tomorrow will be worse.

What if he never comes back? What if my soulmate rejects me? I know I won't die or anything dramatic, but I know I won't love anyone else. Ever.

What if he gets married? Has babies? Moves on with his life as if I never existed and I'm just stuck here in a soulmate bond by myself?

Alone forever.

"Hazel, come. Stand up," Grandma's voice calls to me.

Am I on the floor?

I'm wheezing, I'm barely breathing. I'm apparently in the middle of a goddamn panic attack and I'm so wrapped up in my own thoughts that I had no idea.

"I don't have the energy to help you up, dear, you have to stand on your own," she continues, her voice weary and small.

She lost her daughter today.

How the hell have I not even processed that fact until this moment? I'm wrapped up in Laura, in Noah, and myself, completely ignoring the shit Grandma must be going through.

It's been a hell of a twenty-four hours.

With a strength I barely knew I possessed, I manage to stand. To address the woman who has been nothing but a pillar of strength to me for my entire life. "What do we do?"

She shakes her head, leaning heavily against the floral wallpaper in the hallway of her cottage. "I have no idea."

My thoughts are on Noah. On Mom. On Laura. On all the people I've let down, who have let me down. On all I've lost today. I run my fingers along the warm wood door separating me from the person I love most.

"He'll forgive you," she says.

A pained chuckle that hurts my chest escapes me. "No, Grandma. I don't think he will."

CHAPTER 33

DIRT AND HONEY

He leaves in the morning, just like he said he would, in a quiet retreat. I only know he's gone because I can't sleep. So I get the honor of witnessing the door closing behind him.

He didn't even say goodbye.

Tears splash from my eyes on the knotted wood floor below. Will I ever not ache like this? Will I ever not hurt in that small spot in my rib cage reserved for him? He's carved out a space there and I know no one else will ever fill it.

"I'll make us some tea," Grandma says instead of good morning. Her yellow floral slippers pad along to the iron kettle on the stove.

I sigh, wiping my cheeks. "The strongest stuff you've got, please."

She murmurs a spell under her breath and the stove comes to life instantly. Flames lick at the bottom of the kettle, steam already rising. I sit in a creaky wooden chair, at the matching table in her perfectly sunny breakfast nook, as she opens a particularly witchy cabinet full of herbs, crystals, and things I've never seen before.

Is that a small animal skull?

I don't think I want to know, honestly.

"Why do you have a skull in your cabinet?" Good to know my mouth still functions without my brain as per usual.

A smile breaks on Grandma's face for the first time since Mom disappeared into a water bubble with a psychotic warlock. "Do you not, Hazel?"

"Was that a joke?" I smile back, the ache still there. It'll always be there.

She takes a few herbs and grinds them with a mortar and pestle. "An attempt. It's part of a protection ward I purchased at the market a few years back. I assume it's nothing more than decoration, but it amuses me."

It matches her decor well enough. If ever there were a witchy woman, it would be my grandmother. Her and her little cottage in the woods.

She finishes preparing the tea and, bringing two surprisingly bland brown mugs to the table, sits beside me. The scent wafts up and I wrinkle my nose involuntarily.

"What the hell is in this, Grandma?"

"A mixture of amaranth, eucalyptus, marjoram, and valerian root." She gestures to the raw honey sitting on the table. "You may want that."

"I realize I asked for your strongest stuff, but why did you pick this mixture exactly?" I lift the steaming cup to my lips and take another whiff. *Yeesh*.

She sips hers delicately, not even making a face. "Amaranth for repairing a broken heart, eucalyptus for health, marjoram for easing grief, and valerian root for helping couples reunite. The honey is purely for taste."

Have to give Grandma her credit, she nailed that mixture. Despite it tasting like literal dirt. I pour more honey in, more than is probably appropriate. But I intend to drink this entire damn mug and I can't do that as is.

The silence is a heavy blanket on top of what is actually a beautiful autumn morning. The sunlight streams through the red and orange leaves of the woods and into the kitchen by way of a large bay window. Even the air smells of crunched leaves and soft ground despite us being indoors. It's my favorite time of year.

At least it used to be.

I sigh, the sound escaping from the most wounded part of my heart. "What are we going to do?"

It's the same question I asked last night, and I'm not sure why I expect to hear a different answer. I don't really, but it would be nice.

She simply shakes her head, two tears slipping down her cheeks, sipping her tea.

Fuck this.

"Well if no one else is going to figure out what the hell we're supposed to do next, then I'm going to. Because this sucks, and I refuse to let us all wallow."

Grandma's eyes raise into her silver hair, but she remains quiet. Allowing me the space to do whatever it is I'm doing.

I swallow more tea and clear my throat. "For one, this whole family rift thing is shit. I don't like whatever is going on between me and Laura, and I can't fix that from the apartment."

"I would agree with that statement," Grandma says, nodding for me to continue.

Let's go. "I'm going to move back into the house, and I think you should, too, for a while. We need to heal as a family. I won't let this be like Dad again. This isn't going to further separate us. And we're going to train, teach Laura and myself more about magic so we can be prepared for whatever Draven has planned. Because he will be back, and we need to have something in place for when that happens."

She nods, a prideful smile replacing the tears on her face. "And Noah? What about him?"

Right as I was getting into the groove, Grandma? Et tu, Brute? The imaginary knife embedded in my chest twists a little deeper at the mention of his name. The crack in my armor.

"I can't force Noah to talk to me." My voice cracks over the words, as true as they are. "I can't force him to be ready. I will always be here, but there's not much more I can do. He knows where I stand."

At the very least, I know that to be true. He knows I'm here and I'll be here for the rest of my life.

"I do hope he comes back, but if he does not . . ." She places her hand on mine. "I'm on your side."

My Grandma. In her fuzzy white robe, her thick floral slippers, and with her silver hair piled on top of her head. The most constant person in my life.

"And," she continues, "I think moving back into the house is a very good idea and I'm happy to accompany you. A woman needs her space, so I won't stay every night, but I will stay a majority of the time."

A snort-like sound bubbles from my throat. It's not a real laugh, I don't think I'm capable of that right now, but it's something.

The slight smile on her face falls. "You're also right about Draven. We haven't seen the last of him, or the band of daemons he calls brothers. We suffered a major loss yesterday and I will not accept another."

I merely nod. For some reason, I just can't wrap my head around Mom. When Dad died, I cried immediately and for days. But this feels different. Maybe it's because I'm older, maybe it's because Mom and I were in such a troubled place. It's different.

I forcefully clear my throat. "I guess I'm on my way back to the house. Think Laura changed the locks on me?"

"Probably." Grandma stands, taking our empty mugs to the sink. She's not wrong. Laura would absolutely do something like that, despite the slightest progress we made last night. If anything, it'd be more like her than the woman I spoke to.

"Can you send my stuff back to the house? Someone promised to teach me how but then never did." I stand as well, shooting her a look.

She at least has the decency to look vaguely guilty. "I'm happy to."

I guess I should probably brush my rat's nest of an auburn mess and head over. Right as I reach the bathroom, a thought strikes me.

"Grandma?"

"Yes?"

"Is the house sentient?"

A slight chuckle is my only answer.

CHAPTER 34

THE HOUSE IS SAD

Grief rolls off my old home in waves. The day may be sunny, but the house is gray and clouded. Makes sense though, considering how much Mom loved this place.

I walk up the stone pathway to the tiny porch, the dark wood double-door entrance. I try my key in the fancy, old-as-hell lock and it opens.

Huh. Guess she didn't change the locks. Maybe it was too much effort.

I step lightly into the foyer and my heart sinks into my toes. Laura is in mourning, but the ache in the walls comes from the home itself.

I lay a hand on the faded wallpaper. "I'm sorry."

"You're talking to yourself now?" Laura asks from where she was apparently watching me at the top of the stairs. She's in one of the retro sleeping gowns she adores. It's a lacy, long-sleeved, floor-length thing—absolutely Scarlett O'Hara worthy.

I attempt to smile at her. "The house is sad. Don't you feel it?"

She wrinkles her perfect nose at me, blonde waves tumbling over her face in effortless Hollywood glamour.

"Anyway." I drop my purse on the floor. "You have a new roommate."

Her gaze drops to my purse, liquid-gold eyes squinting. "Please tell me you're trying to buy my affection with a puppy."

Shit, that would've been a good idea. I could've at least brought that animal skull.

"Nope." I shrug. "Just me. If you'll have me."

I'd leave if she insisted. I'd put up a damn good fight first, but in the end, this was always more her home than mine. And I've learned from Noah that I can't force anything. If she lets me stay, it's proof that she's at least semi-willing to repair this rift between us. If not? I'll cross that bridge if I come to it.

She stares at me. Gaze flicking between my purse and my face. Despite the urge to yell "come on, sis," I keep my mouth shut and wait.

Still, though. Come on, sis.

Her mouth opens. Shuts. Opens. "Fine."

I sigh with relief. It's not the open arms I would've loved, but it's an inch. And you can bet your ass I'm gonna run a mile with it.

"Good, because I already told Grandma to send my stuff back."

She scowls. "What if I'd said no?"

I smile, piling my auburn hair on top of my head with a big, black scrunchie off my wrist. "We would've had a very awkward encounter."

"Yeah, because this is such a lovely encounter we're having already." She huffs, brushing an invisible piece of lint off her gown. "I'll be going back to bed now."

"Sounds good, sis. I'll have lunch ready in a little bit!" Am I being obnoxious on purpose? Yep. But that's how we get back to normal. Maybe. Hopefully.

With a roll of her eyes, she disappears back upstairs and it's just me and the house. Me and the sentient house. Totally normal.

The house itself is as chaotic as my thoughts. Magazines, mail, blankets, shoes, and all manner of other things are strewn about in a ridiculous mess. Serious work needs to be done here and I know exactly how to do it.

Purgomundus Purus. My first spell—and the only reason my

apartment didn't look like hell itself. Should I ask Laura if she wants to participate? Yes, she did sweep off to her room with a dramatic flourish and Lord knows she'd hate me for ruining a perfect exit, but I need to involve her in my magic. She wants to learn, she needs to learn, and that's only going to happen if I start actively reminding myself to bring her in. Even with a simple household cleaning spell.

Do I really view this spell as simple now? It wasn't long ago that I found pride in moving a single speck of dust, let alone cleaning an entire house. Now I can levitate myself and others. I've come further than I give myself credit for.

I'm going to be subtle. I can be subtle.

"Oh, look at all this mess! Luckily for me I know a cleaning spell! Guess I should start using magic now!"

Nailed it. The painting next to me totally didn't rattle with the volume of my voice. I am the picture of subtle.

Laura's gown is practically silent as she glides down the stairs after a few painstakingly long seconds. She stands there, watching me with her big eyes. She's like a woodland creature, all innocent and wide-eyed.

"Purgomundus Purus," I say, over-enunciating each syllable. I want her to hear me. With an airy wave, the dirt and dust disappears. We're still going to have to organize the items themselves, but a big chunk of the work has been lifted.

A slight gasp turns my gaze. Laura stands in awe at the literal magic performed in front of her.

"I was the same way the first time I saw that done." I don't mention that I did it myself the first time. Maybe I should bring her to the shop soon and give her *Household Spells for Beginners*.

Her bottom lip trembles slightly in a completely un-Laura way. Laura doesn't cry, Laura is sunshine, rainbows, and sass. Never sad. And in the same instant, she's giving me a blinding smile. It's a mask, a fake. Even after this rift, I know the difference between her real and fake smiles. "Cool! Look at you go, Hazel."

Oof. "I learned it from a beginner's spellbook in the shop, would you like a copy?"

"Maybe later." She flips her curls over her shoulder. "I'm going out tonight, by the way, if you want to have Noah over and bang his brains out."

Whatever joy I had clung to empties out of me. My face falls, and it takes everything in me not to collapse on the floor. The ache in my chest is that all-encompassing. The next breath is gasping, a desperate plea for air.

"Wait—what's wrong?" Her bitchy mask slips for a moment. "Is he okay?"

Yeah, he's fine. He just hates me. All good. "I'm not sure he'll ever forgive me."

"Oh," she giggles. "Is that all?"

I huff in reply, wrapping my arms around myself protectively.

She smiles—a real, genuine Laura smile—and steps closer. "He'll forgive you, Hazel. You forget, but I was there when you two first locked eyes on each other. He was in love with you the moment he saw you. He may be hurt—hell, his pride may be wounded. But he'll come back. Plus, he's a guy. If he takes too long, go over to his place in sexy lingerie and he won't even remember why he's upset."

I chuckle despite the ache. "I think it may be beyond lingerie."

"Well, then you're on your own." She strides into the kitchen with a whip of her hair.

CHAPTER 35

CUCUMBER SANDWICHES

A weight presses on all of us—Grandma, Laura, and I—as we sit together in the living room two days after I move in. We're silent and have been for the past thirty minutes. It's the first time we've all been together since the night Mom . . .

Since Mom.

And it's obvious. The little cucumber sandwiches I made go untouched on the antique coffee table. The tea has long since gone cold. Laura and I sit on opposite ends of the large couch. Despite our distance, we're both underneath the same hand-woven cream blanket while Grandma sits on the regal armchair next to us. Rosie snores in her lap like the grumpy old princess she is. I wring my hands, eyes bouncing between my sister, my grandmother, the blanket, and the wall.

We need to talk. We have to decide how the hell to move forward. Make sense of what happened, but it's still so fresh.

The grief is too raw for anyone to want to begin.

"Should we be planning Mom's funeral?" Sometimes, I swear my brain and my mouth aren't attached. I can always count on my blabbering to happen at the most inopportune moments. But it's something I wanted to know.

Laura jerks as if she's been slapped, Grandma's hand flies to her heart as she trembles.

"No." Laura speaks confidently, despite how my words obviously affected her.

I regard her. She's so young, and she's lost both of her parents in catastrophic ways. "No?" I try to be kind, to clarify what she wants.

"No," she repeats. "It's not time."

I resettle on the couch, trying not to fidget. "I know you aren't ready yet. I don't want to do this either, but . . ."

I trail off as my eyes meet Grandma's. She has unshed tears building. She hasn't been the same since Mom.

"This isn't some overwhelming grief moment!" Laura exclaims, her own tears betraying her. "While I realize you two still see me as a child, I'm not one. It isn't time."

Grandma sits straighter at that, scrutinizing Laura's face. "How do you know?"

"What do you mean 'how does she know?'" I practically stumble over the words. How can it not be time? What are they even talking about?

"I know." Laura takes a deep breath, false confidence pouring off her. "Because I do."

Maybe I'm pushing her too hard. Maybe I'm just thinking about myself again and she needs more time before we face the finality of Mom being gone.

I try to smile at her. "We can put off discussing it for another week or two."

She rolls her eyes and stands. "Thanks, sis."

Laura's chest heaves for two beats—three beats— then she turns on her heel and leaves.

The front door slams behind her.

Even the house is too scared to make a noise. It ceases its normal moans and groans in her wake.

"Can you blame her?" I quietly ask.

Grandma exhales a heavy breath, finally meeting my gaze. "No.

No, I don't blame her. We are all confused, hurt, and we're going to deal with our grief in our own ways."

"I guess we'll talk about the funeral in a few weeks. But what about Draven? What should we do about him, or whoever we've potentially pissed off by banishing him?"

Grandma's eyes slip to the cucumber sandwiches. "One problem at a time, dear."

"Grandma, we can't just ignore this. There's going to be retaliation and we can't be unprepared like we were this time. We almost lost Noah—" my voice breaks at just the thought of him. Of the person I wish were here, who hasn't spoken to me since he walked out. "—that way."

I understand her hesitation, her need for a break. God, if I could lie in bed crying for the next year, I would. But I won't risk losing any more of my family. If it's up to me to lead the charge, then that's what it is.

"I understand. Can we please just have a moment, wait until we can discuss the funeral with Laura? And then we will address Draven. Please?"

Her voice cracks in such an un-Grandma way over the word 'please' that the refusal dies on my tongue. "Okay. We'll wait a little bit longer."

She nods. "I'll go make some lunch." With that, she's up.

I haven't been in the living room for what feels like ages—I've been purposely avoiding it since I moved back in—but has really only been two months, and the family portrait still hangs.

I haven't thought about it since I left. I don't know why I would expect a painting to change, but it's the same. Grandma sits in her high-backed, royal-purple armchair, with Mom and I standing behind her. Laura sits on the floor with her playful, youthful gaze.

It's Mom I can't look away from. The joke was always that Laura was Mom's clone—Mom looks like just an older, brunette Laura—and that I was Dad's. It's not until this moment that I truly notice just how similar they appear. Same gentle waves, despite the difference in hair color itself, same golden honey-brown eyes. Even their noses are the same.

"I miss her, too," Grandma says, quietly coming up behind me.

I wipe my face—and the tears I didn't realize were even falling —before facing her. "Our relationship was complicated."

"When people leave us with much left unsaid, it can feel as if we will never get closure. So, we must create that closure for ourselves, whatever that looks like for you. When your mother's father left . . ." She pauses for a breath. "I wrote him a letter. I never sent it, but I said what I needed to say. That, and time, has helped."

I smile, the only response I can give. I'm terrified that if I open my mouth, I'll sob, and I won't be able to stop. I've kept a lid on whatever shit I've been feeling, and I have to keep it up.

For Laura.

She needs me to be the strong one—hell, so does Grandma. I don't have time to break down, and I won't.

Maybe if I say it enough times, I'll convince myself.

CHAPTER 36

BLINKING

Later that evening, I'm staring at my desk. Grandma left a small, brown leather notebook there for me to write a letter to my mother. Writing has never been my outlet though—it's art. I wouldn't even know how to write anything.

Noah would. Noah would have the perfect words. Maybe that's why it was so weird that he wouldn't even speak to me. Noah wants to talk about everything and anything, and I would listen for hours if he let me.

Stop it, Hazel. You're just torturing yourself.

I need to sketch, paint, do something. Grandma's spell placed all my things from the apartment back perfectly, without me having to touch anything. Too perfectly, since my desk was still messy. Could've used some organization in that spell. I rummage through the drawers and find a dusty sketchbook. It's halfway filled with little creatures and cartoons I drew in high school.

Just going to flip on past that embarrassment.

I reach an empty page, grab my stupidly expensive colored pencils, and lie against the pillows.

I'm past the point of no return before I even realize what I'm drawing. Noah's eyes. Brown-black, with the little star of green in the right eye. His bushy eyebrows hang above like furry curtains.

Before I even knew him, I knew exactly what his eyes looked like. I knew every little detail of them. Every fleck of color. I spent hours of my life drawing them and I know somewhere deep in my broken-ass heart that I'll continue no matter what he decides.

"I miss you," I whisper to the eyes.

They blink.

Wait, what?

I'm going crazy, obviously. Paintings and sketches don't move. They don't. That's not a thing. Right?

"Are you, um, blinking at me?" My voice trembles.

This is totally normal. I'm just asking a sketch if it's sentient. Shit, the house is sentient, why not anything else?

It blinks. Just once, but in the exact same way as before. I wait a few more seconds. Another blink. Almost like it's a timed action.

"Grandma?!" I call, not moving a single muscle other than my face.

Grandma opens the door with far too much nonchalance for my liking. This is a family that has been through some shit in the last few days. I would appreciate a little hastiness. Maybe a door slam.

"My sketch is blinking at me."

She smiles. *Smiles*. "Yes, and?"

"What do you mean 'yes, and?' The sketch. Is blinking. At me."

She pads softly over and sits on my floral bedspread, smoothing the fabric with her hand. "Witches who have artistic abilities have been known to imbue their work with some of their magic. It's not uncommon for witches to sell paintings that move, or for books to allow you to smell the foods described inside. It's part of our gift."

"And you didn't think to mention this to your granddaughter obsessed with painting?" I barely suppress the most epic eye roll in history. May have been record breaking. We'll never know now.

Her smile tilts downward, guilt weighing heavily in her eyes. "I figured you would have seen it at the market. I suppose there is much I forgot to tell you over the past few weeks."

I sigh. "I'm behind in a lot of ways, but especially when it comes to magic. It's not your responsibility to get me completely up to speed."

"While I appreciate your uncharacteristic understanding, you and your sister have both been failed. And I have played a part in that. Would you like me to take you to the market? Show you the artists and their pieces?"

I consider her offer. Going there would be good for all of us—her and Laura included.

"If we can convince Laura to join us, I think it would be good for us to get out of the house as a family."

Always the eavesdropper, Laura pops her head round the corner in the way she used to when she was younger. "I need new shoes. What the fuck are we waiting for?"

IT'S NOW THAT I REALIZE I'D COMPLETELY FORGOTTEN ABOUT THE existence of Ash Cedar, and that Laura has decidedly *not,* if the way she's tugging me in the complete opposite direction of his smirk is any indication. Those green eyes follow us until he's out of sight.

"Have you seen him since the last time we were here?" I ask, my feet tumbling underneath me, threatening to send me headfirst into the dirt path.

The market is exactly the same. Herbs and smoke cloud the air, witchy gowns flow around the ankles of ancient women and cats weave between their legs. The market comforts me, despite the attack last time I was here. It has a homey warmth that relaxes all my limbs.

Laura scoffs, squeezing my hand tighter. "I don't know whom you're referring to, but the answer is no."

"How can the answer be no if you don't know whom I'm referring to?"

"Because it's no!"

"Girls!"

Laura abruptly stops, causing me to run smack into her back. It's the only time I'm grateful she's taller than me, because her hair cushions my impact. We turn back and wait as Grandma catches up with us.

She huffs as she approaches. "You walk as if the devil himself is behind you."

"I mean." Laura smiles in the way that makes me want to curl into myself. She inherited it from Mom. It's the I'm-about-to-say-something-bitchy smile. "Have you seen yourself lately, Grandma? When was the last time you combed your hair?"

Grandma blinks once and a giant piece of dirt flies from the ground and right into Laura's perfect blonde hair. "I don't know, dear, but it looks like you have something in yours."

Goddamn that's savage.

Instead of the bitch fit I expect, Laura giggles. A delicate thing, but the first real laugh I've heard from her in a very long time. "Touché."

Before anyone can ruin this moment, I link elbows with both women and continue our walk through the stalls. Maybe the Pruitt-slash-Hollis women can get through this. Maybe we're strong enough to suffer through multiple deaths and lies and daemons and warlocks and losses of soulmates. Maybe.

"So, to whom are we not referring?" Grandma says as she takes control, leading us toward a white tent-encased booth with multiple paintings set up.

An ear-splitting screech erupts from Laura. "I can't believe you heard that!"

"At this point I'm pretty sure everyone heard *that*," I mutter. Instead of indulging in what will surely be Spar Part Two between them, I break free and step under the white tent.

Inside is my wildest dream. At least twenty paintings line the sides of the tent and stand on easels in little rows. They're all different sizes, ranging from above-the-mantel to little-postcards-by-the-register.

And they're moving.

One of the larger paintings shows a roiling sea with a stormy sky above it. A lighthouse sits in the distance, blinking so subtly I almost don't catch it. My eyes feast on this painting as if I haven't eaten in years.

This is what I want.

This is what I'm meant to do.

I've struggled so long with who I am, what I am, what I want. Who I want to be. And for once, I know. I know what I want, and it is *this*.

I want to create paintings, drawings, sketches that do this. And I want to sell them in my own little booth. Have my own register, my own business cards, my own witchy muumuu.

Okay, no, I don't want a muumuu. If I ever wear one, I expect Laura to curse me. I'd welcome it.

"I was overcome when I first saw the shop," Grandma says softly, her hand landing on my shoulder. "It is a beautiful thing, to discover your purpose in life."

I rub the back of my hand against my cheek, and then the other, clearing the tears. Oh, I'm crying in the middle of a stranger's business. Yep. Very cool.

"I want to do this, Grandma." My voice is steady, confident.

Of course I want to do this. I'm having some sort of emotional breakthrough in the middle of a random woman's stall. But it needed to be said aloud. There's something powerful in words.

She nods. "Then that is what you'll do. You will practice and create, and once you are ready, we'll get you a booth of your own."

Laura watches the paintings, avoiding looking at either of us. It's obvious she doesn't know what to say, and I don't know what she's thinking. I used to always know what she was thinking.

Before I can open my mouth, as if summoned by her magic itself, Ash Cedar strolls by. He's still quite lumberjack-esque, taller than a man ever should be and wide enough that I wouldn't be surprised if he could lift a car.

He doesn't say a word, but he brushes Laura's shoulder ever so slightly as he walks past and she . . . shudders. Rears back as if she's been burned.

Interesting.

I'll be poking that bear later, but for now I stand in awe of what will hopefully soon be mine. A booth where I can sell my paintings. Where I can be happy.

And maybe I'll be forever alone, but some part of my heart still hopes that Noah will be by my side.

Actually.

"Ash!" I call, running after the hulking figure. I can feel Laura's displeasure from here, but he's the only one who can help me.

He slows, turning to face me as I catch my breath. "Yes?"

"I need your help with something."

CHAPTER 37

SPECIAL DELIVERY

My hands shake as I walk up the steps to Noah's apartment, clutching the parcel. It took Ash one week to craft the special minis I made of us. I can just see them on his shelf with his *Warhammer* minis.

But these would be different. Ours.

I also found a woman who makes custom paint at the market and bought some, to include in case he wants to paint them. I tried not to go overboard and buy him every color she offered, but the box is relatively heavy.

The scent of bergamot and old books tickles my nose as I approach his door. Noah.

Tears spring to my eyes, the heat of despair threatening to pull me under and I haven't even seen him.

I don't plan to.

Noah said he needed time, and I refuse to push him before he's ready. He deserves his boundaries, and he deserves his space.

If I've learned anything in these past few months on my own, it's that boundaries are important. I need them with Laura—I can't be her surrogate mother anymore—and I need to respect when someone puts them up with me. Even if the weight of anxiety pulls on me so hard at night I cry myself to sleep.

Despite that, he also deserves to know that he's loved and that I'm still here. It's a gesture, a small thing to let him know that the door is open when he's ready to walk through it.

I deposit the box—which includes the first drawing I ever made of his eyes before I knew him—on the welcome mat and turn.

I love you, Noah.

"He'll come around."

I jump at the distinctly male voice. I turn to see Benji standing there with a grocery bag and a sheepish smile.

I put a hand on my galloping heart. "Benji, I'm sorry I didn't see you there."

He shrugs, the paper bag rustling in his hand. "I have that effect. Noah calls me Spider-Man."

"He never mentioned that." A small chuckle escapes me. "It sounds like him, though."

"He will come around, Hazel. I'm not sure exactly what happened between you—he's being uncharacteristically vague about the whole thing—but I know he loves you. I've never seen him like this, and I don't think he's stupid enough to give it up."

The tears that never really went away drip down my cheeks. "It was my fault."

"Regardless." His smile is genuine. "From how he talks about you, I'd be surprised if whatever you did was malicious. People make mistakes. Part of loving someone is knowing that they will inevitably hurt you by accident. No one is perfect, and he never expected perfection from you. That doesn't mean we don't need a moment alone to process our emotions, but it also means we don't give up."

Love has never been explained that way to me. A small flicker of hope ignites in my chest.

"Tell him I love him? And—" I turn and pick up the box "—make sure he gets this."

Benji nods and takes the box in his other hand. "It'll be fine. And we'll spend more time together, too. We're family now."

THE DAYS MELD TOGETHER UNTIL A FULL WEEK HAS PASSED. I SPEND my time working in the shop, painting, and trying to be more of a sister to Laura than the parent I was forced into being.

She refuses to discuss a funeral, just keeps saying that it's not time. Grandma insists on not pushing her, but I worry that she's sitting in her grief or hasn't accepted what happened.

Mom is gone, and there's nothing that can be done to change that.

It's two against one though, and I won't bulldoze everyone with how I think things should be. I won't be Mom.

Two knocks rap on the door and Laura pokes her head in. "Drawing?"

I nod, looking up from my sketch. "Trying something new."

"You should come downstairs. Something came for you." She slips back out just as quickly as she appeared. Laura hasn't lingered lately.

I put everything away and exit my room. I take a deep breath, and with it—electricity.

I practically fall down the stairs in my haste, my eyes searching. Standing in the foyer with his hands in the front pockets of his jeans is Noah.

Noah.

He's beautiful. Handsome. Lovely. Comforting. And all I want is to run into his arms and forget everything that's happened. But I can't. The uncertainty of our situation keeps my feet rooted to the floor.

For a moment, we just stare at each other. My eyes rake his body, taking in all the small details that I remembered but know my memory didn't do justice. All the pieces and parts of him that make him exactly who he is.

His lips turn up in a small smile, chin dimple deepening. "Hey, Hazel."

A sob wrenches itself from deep in my chest at the sound of his voice. "Hey."

"I have something I need to ask you." His footfalls are solid, sure, as he walks toward me. Until we're so close I can count his eyelashes if I wanted to.

"Yes?" I whisper into the inch of space between us.

He lifts the mini of him. "Do you think I'd look better with a red shirt or blue?"

I laugh. It's a sobbing, relief-filled exhalation that takes so much weight off my shoulders I practically collapse into Noah's sweater.

He's here.

He wraps his long arms around my trembling body, pressing his nose into my hair.

I repress the urge to just word-vomit all over him. He'll speak when he's ready and for now, I'm just happy to be near him again. I ache with the way I missed him, with how I still miss him.

"Would you like to take a walk with me?" he asks, pulling back just a hair to make eye contact.

I nod. I glance down at the hand I've wished I could hold so many times since I last saw him and slide my palm into his. Our electric pulse skitters against my skin in a reassuring hum.

AUTUMN LEAVES CRUNCH UNDERFOOT AS WE WALK THROUGH THE residential area of Chagrin Falls. The air is nippy, and snow is coming, I can feel it. Maybe not today, not tomorrow, but in the next few weeks. Each old Victorian home has pumpkins outside, left-overs from Halloween. I was so wrapped up in everything going on that I completely forgot the holiday existed. I guess that happens when your mother sacrifices her life for the man you love.

"I need to apologize to you, Hazel," he says, brown curls so tangled with his bushy eyebrows that I can't tell where one begins and the other ends.

I do a double take, unsure if I heard him correctly. "You need to apologize to *me*? Noah, I can't think of anything you'd need to apologize to me for."

"Hazel, baby, your mother died protecting me." He shakes his head. "And I had no fucking idea. I was so wrapped up in my own feelings about the whole situation that I didn't even let you tell me. Laura had to tell me."

"Laura?"

"She told me she took my number from your phone while you were showering and called me this morning. Told me I'm an absolute moron and explained what happened that night in full. She read me the fucking riot act, if I'm honest, and I deserved every single second of it."

I'm shaking my head before he even finishes talking. "No, I lied to you. I lied about everything, and you didn't deserve that."

"Laura kind of explained that, too. Told me how you had been taught to repress your magic for so long and went against your mom to finally discover that part of yourself. I can't imagine how tough that must have been for you." His fingers slide against mine at our sides. "I do wish you would've told me, but I believe that you would have."

"Noah." I stop walking, forcing him to turn and face me. "Why are you letting me off the hook? You were so upset, and I know what I did triggered something deep for you."

His hand comes up to cradle my cheek. "Hazel, I love you. I've loved you since the first fucking second I saw you and I've loved you every day since. The lies hurt me, on top of the fucked up situation of being kidnapped, and I needed to retreat. Lick my wounds. But I never stopped loving you. If I had known your mother died, I would have been here sooner. I would have never left. I love you, and I'm here for you during the easy shit and the hard shit."

"I thought . . ." I don't want to tell him what I thought. That I so easily believed that when he walked out that door he was gone forever. That I believed I deserved it.

"I am so sorry. I know what you thought, and I never should have made you think that. I should have communicated better."

My eyes burn, my vision swimming until all I can make out are the black-brown eyes that have haunted me for months. Years. "I shouldn't have lied. I won't lie to you anymore. I won't hide any pieces of myself from you."

"You didn't know who you were, Hazel. I finally understand that you were still discovering. How could you be honest when you didn't know what the truth was?" He pulls me into his chest, and I bury myself in the warmth of him. "I'm sorry. I promise to communicate. I won't ever leave like that again."

No more lies.

"Did Laura tell you what you are to me?"

"I don't think so? What are you talking about?"

Now or never. I steel myself, pulling myself out of his chest to meet his gaze. "The Pruitt women are blessed by an ancestor from Salem. She gave us the power to recognize our soulmates. And you are mine."

"Soulmates? Like in romance novels?"

He wasn't kidding when he said he read romance. "I guess. It's the buzz. The electric shock I used to give you when we first met? That's the sign I've found my person."

"I asked if you shuffled your feet on the ground and zapped me," he chuckles. "Did you know then?"

"No, I had no idea until we had been dating for a little bit. I just thought it was a weird witchy thing, which it kind of was, but . . ." I trail off with a shrug of my shoulders.

"Hmm." His mouth quirks in a little half smile. "I'm your soulmate, huh?"

"Yep. I'm never going to love anyone else for the rest of my life." I smile to soften the seriousness behind those words. Because it's true. Noah Rogers is it for me.

He's quiet for a moment, thumb trailing along my cheek before it slips to trace my bottom lip. "I can think of no better fate."

He presses the gentlest kiss to my lips, a sweet caress. My hand lifts to his stubbly cheek as we press against each other. His hands hold my hips just a little too tight, as if to reassure him that yes, I'm here. I'm real.

I nip his lower lip and the kiss deepens. I inhale his scent and feel his body underneath my fingertips and lose myself in the love we share.

With panting breaths, we part.

"I love you, Noah. I will love you until this world stops spinning and beyond. You are mine, and I am yours."

"I love you, Hazel. You are mine, and I am yours."

"Sexiest octopus I know."

He blinks. "Wait. What?"

This is going to be fun.

CHAPTER 38
EPILOGUE
LAURA

A *few weeks earlier . . .*

THE FIRE WHISPERS TO ME.

It has for as long I can remember, but I've never been able to make out what it is saying. Only soft murmurs and unintelligible sounds. But I knew it was communicating with me. Somewhere inside, I knew.

And I got damn good at ignoring it.

Unit now.

Until Hazel—my own fucking sister—suggested we have a funeral for our mother and the fire said no.

The candles sitting on the coffee table flicker and snap and I've never been more sure of anything in my life.

"No."

Hazel's emerald green eyes regard me. The pity there is new. She never pitied me before. Not before she left and started a whole life without me. "No?"

"No," I repeat. "It's not time."

"I know you aren't ready yet." She resettles on the plushy New

England style couch in the living room of the house we grew up in. The house that is currently agreeing with me—if the groans and creaks are anything to go by. "I don't want to do this either, but . . ."

Hazel and Grandma look at each other. They're on the same team now, ever since Hazel started training with Grandma. They're on the magical side and I'm over here. By myself.

"This isn't some overwhelming grief moment. While I realize you two still see me as a child, I'm not one. It isn't time," I say, before either of them can bulldoze over me. Despite the tears falling down my cheeks.

Grandma's eyes narrow. "How do you know?"

"What do you mean, 'how does she know?'" Hazel splutters.

"I know." I sit up straighter, ignoring Hazel. "Because I do."

I don't want to tell them about the fire yet. The fire has always been mine, and not even Mom was able to take it from me. It has been my secret for as long as Dad has been gone.

Hazel visibly deflates, a warm, comforting breeze ruffling my hair. Pity again. "We can put off discussing it for another week or two."

I roll my eyes and stand. "Thanks, sis."

I don't know her anymore. I don't know this person she's become. Part of me enjoys seeing Hazel actually have a spine for once in her life, and of course I love that she's found her person. Even if he's not speaking to her currently. But the other part of me misses when she cared more about me.

The sister I knew would never leave me alone with our mother, and then barely see me for months. The sister I knew would never risk her own life to fight some daemon and then blame me for not having a life worth protecting.

The sister I knew loved me.

But this Hazel? I'm not so sure.

ABOUT THE AUTHOR

Zoe Shae has always been fascinated by stories. Whether she was creating them with her father, or reading them, they have always been a constant. Creating them now is a dream come true.

Zoe spends her time writing, reading, singing, and chasing around her rambunctious toddler. She hopes to show her daughter how to follow her dreams.

You can follow Zoe on social media everywhere at @AuthorZoeShae